D1553521

THE AMATEUR AMERICAN

THE
AMATEUR
AMERICAN

J. SAUNDERS ELMORE

THREE RIVERS PRESS · NEW YORK

This is a work of fiction. Names, characters, places, and incidents either are the product of the author's imagination or are used fictitiously. Any resemblance to actual persons, living or dead, events, or locales is entirely coincidental.

Copyright © 2009 by J. Saunders Elmore

All rights reserved.
Published in the United States by Three Rivers Press, an imprint of the Crown Publishing Group, a division of Random House, Inc., New York.
www.crownpublishing.com

Three Rivers Press and the Tugboat design are registered trademarks of Random House, Inc.

Library of Congress Cataloging-in-Publication Data

Elmore, Joel Saunders.
   The amateur American / Joel Saunders Elmore.—1st ed.
   1. Americans—France—Fiction.   2. Translators—Fiction.   3. Arabs—
France—Fiction.   I. Title.
PS3605.L478A8 2009
813'.6—dc22

2008051147

ISBN-978-0-307-45287-0

Printed in the United States of America

Design by Level C

10 9 8 7 6 5 4 3 2 1

First Edition

To Pamela Sue Elmore

Sometimes he was like a man in flight, but running toward the enemy, desperate to feel upon his vanishing body the blows that would prove his being.
    —John le Carré, *The Looking Glass War*

THE AMATEUR AMERICAN

Article from *Le Parisien*, 23 March 2003:

AMERICAN SOUGHT IN LOIRE BLOODBATH

Gendarmes responded to an anonymous tip yesterday and found Roland LeMercier, a senior agent with the French National Police, shot dead in his Lourange home. LeMercier had been working on a classified assignment in nearby Ste-Térèse at Lycée Corbières, where former school *proviseur* Georges Brule was poisoned two days ago, police said. At the scene of LeMercier's death, gendarmes found photos and correspondence linking LeMercier to the slaying of another federal agent who had been conducting classified investigations into an Algerian jihadist cell in the Loire region.

When asked to comment on the three deaths, Inspector Guillaum of the Lourange Police Department stated that a nationwide search for a recently disappeared American and Lycée Corbières employee, Jeffrey Delanne, has been issued. The inspector noted that Delanne had previously been arrested in the company of illegal aliens suspected of jihadist ties, and that Delanne is believed to have played a hand in all three killings. Delanne was last seen in Tours.

THREE WEEKS
PRIOR . . .

MUCH BETTER THAN
YOU ARE HERE

Even the cold was treacherous that day at Lycée Corbières, but it was too early in the morning, and I was too bleary to know any better. I'd beaten the stampede to the Xerox in the profs' room, but before I could squeeze out a single copy, the machine decided to jam up. It stood there blinking at me like a cow. I kept my cool—all I had on deck were a dozen copies of John Lee Hooker's "Hobo Blues" lyrics, for my advanced students—though I had half a mind to take a swing at that Xerox's bulky headpiece, out of good old-fashioned payback.

That was when I saw Dreyfus making his way around the big oak table in the center of the room. He had on a wrinkled blue button-down, baggy brown slacks, and a rich, sideways grin. And as so many of his countrymen tended to do, he came over and stood unnaturally close—close enough to give away his breakfast: sausage, onions, and something unnamable laced with garlic. Then for a moment he stood there staring, tilting that overgrown frizzy hairdo of his, those little eyes inspecting me as you would an abstract painting, as if, even after six months of my working at the school, the only way he could make sense of me was at an angle.

"You are working too much here, Jeffrey?" he asked.

My mind scrambled between English and French. "Sorry?"

"You have no time for extra work? You are overworked?"

I hardly knew Dreyfus, but I knew what was on his mind: he wanted to ask me if I'd visit one of his classes, as every other English prof at the lycée had done already. Would I mind playing classroom specimen, *Homo americanus, l'assistant americain,* for the sake of his students?

Sure I'd mind. That didn't free me up to say no. As a foreign assistant on a temporary work visa, I couldn't exactly dodge requests from permanent faculty. In fact, I was supposed to bend over backwards and appreciate my job while it lasted.

I sprawled for a clever excuse anyway, but came up blank. Out came the truth: "Not really."

Dreyfus and I had exchanged words exactly twice. Once in December when we'd wound up across from each other at the profs' lunch table, he asked me in English how I was "holding down" and then gave me an unsettling wink before devouring a cheese-smothered something or other. The other time had been in the third-floor hallway, when he told me in English that he himself had been a teaching assistant, but Stateside, in the French Department at the U. of Minnesota. He'd said something, too, about being a fanatical Woody Allen scholar, and I remembered thinking *what bullshit* but keeping my mouth shut.

When our eyes met this third time, I could tell that Dreyfus had something more straightforward in mind. He raised an eyebrow and smiled nonchalantly.

"I ask this because when I was an assistant, I knew many who took additional jobs. For a little extra, *tu vois?*"

He rubbed his thumb and forefinger together in a slow circle. Truth was, I'd been hurting for a little extra—I was two weeks behind on rent, and worse off than that on my credit cards.

"There is a man I know," Dreyfus went on. "A private businessman type—he needs an English speaker, you see, someone discreet, someone living here in Ste-Térèse. Just an interpreter. For a few hours a week. Of course, you would be paid much better than you are here."

Beside us the Xerox grumbled and jumped into gear, and my copies started spilling into the tray. I muttered an apology to the profs waiting behind me, and then my eyes landed back in Dreyfus's narrow gaze.

"I should give this businessman your name for an interview?" he asked.

I thought about how carefully I'd avoided crossing paths with the director of the international *foyer* where I lived, about the exact amount that I owed him, and the exact difference between that and what was in my bank account. Dreyfus was acting chill about the matter—as if he'd just as soon offer the job to one of his older students. I was willing to bet that I needed the money more.

I told Dreyfus to count me in, and we broke to go teach.

AFTER THAT, FOR the better part of a week, Dreyfus disappeared. I got caught up thinking about all that potential *extra* anyway, and started asking around at Corbières for him. But nobody knew what rock Dreyfus had crawled under. Gradually I came to grips with the fact that I was sinking; I had three more months left on my work contract and not enough money to cover the bills. I'd have to move back into the cheap apartment I'd rented during September and October, a desolate squat in a boardinghouse on the edge of the city, where I'd spent the fall season either alone or waiting for buses into Ste-Térèse proper.

By Wednesday night of the next week I'd stopped hoping altogether and decided to carry my remaining euros up the street and around the corner to the Rougerie, a low-key dive where over the winter I might have spent too much time. Françoise, who when she wasn't drinking wine taught English at Corbières, was hunched over a full glass and a full ashtray at the end of the bar.

She bought me a rum punch and I asked her point-blank about Dreyfus.

"*Him* . . . he's supposed to be one of those visiting profs," she said spitefully. "Here one year, one or two honors courses . . . but what a dandy of a hairdo. Bloody awkward, if you ask me."

Françoise was old enough to be my mother but had introduced me to the Rougerie crowd, a group in their late twenties like me, back in October. That was five months before, back in '02, just before the invasion of Iraq, when not everyone in France automatically thought *war* when they thought about the U.S.

I told Françoise about the potential interview. She held back a chuckle.

"Never wait on an interview, Jeffrey. It's an old expression we have."

Then she carried on for a solid hour about the rising unemployment rate in France, and about how her daughter—a slender young knockout named Marine who'd befriended me over the long winter months—had been looking for a job in her field for the past seven years.

I'd heard it all before but hadn't come to the bar to refuse any drinks. I also valued Françoise's advice, anywhere along the drunken spectrum, and anyway I knew Dreyfus's offer had been too good to be true: *a few hours a week, as an interpreter, paid much better than you are here.* And so with each drink I learned to digest the hard truth: I wasn't making enough money, and debt was closing in on me, which meant my days living in *centre ville*, walking to work, and working out my French at the local bar with friends were numbered.

I said good-bye to Françoise early that night and went to bed fully clothed and angry.

• • •

THE NEXT MORNING I found Dreyfus sitting alone in the profs' smoking room, a congested little cave adjacent to the profs' room, equipped with a coffee machine, a flimsy wooden table with chairs, and a few lockers for the foreign assistants. He had on the same wrinkled blue shirt he'd been wearing the last time I saw him, sleeves rolled up to his elbows, a leaning tower of papers in front of him, and a burned-out look in his eyes.

"It is tomorrow that he wishes to meet with you," he said in English.

My thoughts seemed to crawl from one dark corner of my brain to the other; I had a foot-long rum hangover wedged into the inch or so between my eyes.

"An interview with the businessman?" I managed.

"Sure." Dreyfus's eyes moved to the papers in front of him. "You could call it that, yes."

My mind stuttered. "What should I show interest in? What's his business?"

Dreyfus said, "Show interest in working for him. In being his interpreter. In being *loyal.*"

He enunciated the last word in a way that confused the hell out of me. I went over and fed the coffee machine thirty centimes. When the machine started blinking malfunctions at me, I let a god-awful French expression spill out of my mouth.

Dreyfus chuckled. "You are quickly on your way to becoming French, Jeffrey Delanne."

Before I could object, the coffee machine grumbled, ejected a little plastic cup into the slot, and squirted out two fingers' worth of sugary espresso. I took the cup and held the rim of it to my nose like a potion. Dreyfus stood and handed me a piece of paper. On it was scribbled a time, a few directions, and the word *Lourange,* a city about half an hour northeast by train toward Paris.

Before I could ask anything more about particulars, the five-till-nine bell rang. Dreyfus picked up his mountain of papers and made for the door.

"Oh yes," he said, stopping in the doorway. "There is one more thing, I almost forgot. This will perhaps be difficult for you to understand."

"Try me."

"This job, if you are offered it, would be none of my business," he said. "The businessman's name is Nabec, and I am sending you as a type of . . . a favor, *tu vois?* This Nabec, he does not often come into contact with young men like you. He is a very old . . . well, he is a very old Arab, Jeffrey. Do not think that I condescend by saying that. Go and talk with him, and if he wishes you to work for him, it will be between you and him, *tu vois?* While I know him, I myself cannot be concerned."

Dreyfus left me in the smoking room with my aching doubts. And sure, it would have been wisest for me to carry on with Françoise's advice and keep my hopes down. But deep down I knew what I would do. I hadn't come halfway around the world to snub a clean shot at a new life.

NO LONGER EXPERIENCE THESE NEEDS

The next afternoon I rode the two-o'clock TGV to Lourange, drinking in the Loire valley countryside from a window seat and trying to remember why I hadn't left Ste-Térèse more often. Outside the city to the south lay miles of low hills covered with vineyards as valuable as oil wells. To the north, where the earth wasn't nearly as blessed, patches of smallish, knotty evergreens lived. I'd heard that there were more strange tales about what had once dwelt in those abandoned little forests than there were people who could claim to have spent any time in them. Just beyond those forests lay Lourange.

Outside the Lourange train station I grabbed a bus that ran north across the Loire to the university campus. Deciphering Dreyfus's sloppy directions as best I could, I wound up joining some college students on their way down a cobbled sidewalk toward a cluster of classroom buildings. For the first time in weeks the sunshine was splintering through the clouds, a rare delicacy in that part of the country. You could actually feel a little warmth on your face, and everyone was excited over it, as if the sun's guest appearance meant a permanent end to the region's chronic fog.

Dreyfus's instructions ended at a huge university cafeteria. I was ten minutes ahead of time, so I snooped around the wide semicircular vestibule of the building, where droves of students were gathering in lines up to a few cashier booths, then slipped past the food stations and entered a massive eating area. There were no old men hanging around anywhere, and no one who looked particularly Arabic.

I looped around to the other end of the cafeteria and stepped out the back doors onto a patio that overlooked a network of sidewalks. There was a wide green that connected several more red brick classroom buildings, a few newer buildings beyond that, rolling fields in the distance. I walked down the steps to the nearest sidewalk, calculating my next move, then shot a glance back at the café doors.

Two thickset men in dark suits were standing against the wall beside the doors. Both wore dark sunglasses and had identical buzz cuts. A younger guy was sitting at an outside café table beside the men. He was swarthy and slick-haired, dressed in a tan lightweight suit and dark black shades. And he was staring directly at me.

Before I could turn away, the young man smiled and motioned to the empty seat across from him. I pointed to myself. When he nodded, a team of sirens went off in my head: this Arab didn't look any older than I was, and I was uneasy about the kind of businessmen who ran around with bodyguards.

I started to walk away, but a thread of guilt broke loose inside me. What did I know about people like that, outside of movies and detective novels? I glanced back and caught the young guy still watching me. And when he smiled this time, my curiosity took hold. I calculated what I had to lose: fifteen minutes, maybe half an hour. A coffee or a beer, on him.

I went over as casually as I could and took the free seat, letting my eyes dart from the young Arab to his bodyguards, then to the glass of red wine in front of him. He had a long, oval skull, a faint, jagged scar above his left eyebrow, and a slightly crooked nose. The knuckles on his right hand looked ink-stained, and there was a bright V-shaped cut on the middle finger of his left. After greeting me in French, he muttered something to his men that sounded Arabic, and one of them ducked inside.

The young Arab faced me. "Apparently they don't serve Porto here."

His French was quick, short, and clean as a whistle. My mind sprawled anyway: I'd missed something.

"Le Monsieur suggests Porto with business," he explained. "You would not work for me, you see, but for le Monsieur. If it pleases him. This is what he wants me to say: forget that these men are here with us, and tell me about yourself."

I went hunting for verbs, unsure how candid I should be—I was only sitting here to see what this business was really about.

"Okay, I was educated in the States," I said. "My mother was a French teacher, so I started speaking French when I—"

"Then you enjoy France?"

"Sure. I enjoy it."

"You enjoy what?"

"Well . . . certainly the people," I said, feeling generous. "And the mentality here, and the food, certainly. The countryside, too, is magnificent, completely different. Even the smell."

Rafa scratched the scar above his eyebrow. "Did you say the *smell*? Different from what?"

"Other places," I said. It was trivial, but I wanted to make clear my point. "The smell is different in Canada, see. The air is different in Arizona than it is in other places."

"*Arizona* is what?" he asked.

"A state in the south of America."

"Ah, yes, South America," he said. "I've always dreamed of going to South America. The French have a *départemente* there, you know. You have been?"

"No, no. Not at all." I doubted now whether it was worth explaining, and let it drop.

Rafa lit a cigarette and offered one to me. I took it, but when one of the bodyguards stepped up with a light I flinched without meaning to. After that, Rafa started tapping his middle finger on the table, keeping time to a beat I couldn't hear. I looked across the green at the scattering groups of students, then back at our table, where there was now a demi-pint of beer sitting in front of me.

I glanced at the bodyguards and gave them both a casual nod of appreciation. Then my eyes rose to meet Rafa's dark sunglass lenses. He blew a thick stream of smoke out of one nostril without plugging the other, a feat I'd never even heard of, and his mouth curled into a grin. He was waiting for me to speak, I realized, reveling in the awkwardness that I was only making worse with silence.

Finally he said, "Why did you come here, Delanne?"

"To this interview?"

"No. When you left the States."

"French is the only other language I speak," I said. "Though I know a little Spanish—"

"Why not the south of France, where the weather is better? Why not in La Dordogne, where the food is better? Why here in the northwest, where they use the short pronunciation and give the double-cheek kisses, one-two-one-two?"

He rattled this off much faster than anything he'd said before. I took a long drink of beer and paired up a few pertinent nouns with adjectives.

"This region has a rich history," I said, thinking suddenly about one of the regional wines. "And then there's the Muscadet *sur lie*."

Rafa gave me a pleased smile this time, though I could still feel his shaded eyes scrutinizing, deciding whether or not his monsieur would approve.

"You are wondering what his business is," Rafa said then. "But there is no appropriate name, no correct word for that. He has, you might say, his fingers in many cakes. What concerns you is that my English is worthless, and your French is not, well, horrible."

I drank my beer and held my tongue. What kind of half-cocked interview was this? The guy didn't even know what questions to ask, couldn't even be polite about it.

"This is also what he wants me to say," Rafa continued. "Last month he was in Geneva, in a meeting with some men from Scotland. Scotsmen. He was buying goods from them, you see, and they were men with whom he had never done business. So, of course, we had no idea what to expect. And who would guess that these Scots didn't speak French, in Geneva? It was unthinkable. Nor could they speak German, incidentally. So what the hell were they doing in Switzerland? Le Monsieur and I had taken with us the usual case of Chinon. I don't remember the chateau names as well as le Monsieur, hard as I try. He has a remarkable memory, le Monsieur—just one of his extraordinary talents. There are too many minuscule duties assigned to me . . . but I should add that these Scots had been polite enough to bring a fine bottle of very mature Armagnac. Which is to say that they'd dealt with the French before. Still, we couldn't do business together, because they didn't speak French any more than most Americans. No offense."

"None taken," I said. "And I see your point."

"No, Delanne, you don't. It was an expensive waste of an evening. I speak of grown men—civilized, cultured gentlemen—sitting in silence with important business on the table. We were reduced to pointing, mimicking, making ridiculous charades—grunting at one another like cavemen. Animals, Delanne. This is what he wants me to say. What le Monsieur realized that night was that in the future, if he kept pursuing his business without an English-speaking assistant, he would lose money. And what you must understand, Delanne, is that le Monsieur does not lose money—never, even if he makes a bad deal. Which has never happened. This is what he wants me to say."

"I see," I said. But now I was both confused and irritated. He'd torn through the story at such an unnatural speed. Why was he trying to throw me off?

I watched him kill his drink in one wide-mouthed swill. I finished mine likewise.

"Then—" said Rafa after a moment. "Where was I?"

"Geneva. Last month. Having to grunt like cavemen didn't even lose your boss money."

Rafa smiled, genuinely this time, and sat back, uncrossing and recrossing his legs.

"You understand French very well. Permit me to ask you something, Delanne. Between us only. Me, I am French. I am content to be French. You, you are American. Then. All this business between our countries—who refuses support, who refuses to acknowledge UN decisions, etcetera. What do you think of it all?"

Determined not to be misunderstood this time, I chose my words carefully.

"Our leader and your leader," I said, "they don't speak the same language. I think of it this way: I grew up speaking one language, and I love that language. But I'm trying to learn another."

Rafa's expression didn't budge. He lit another cigarette and nodded slowly. "Good answer, Delanne. Then you are not angry that many French have recently come to dislike your people?"

"Haven't the French *always* disliked my people?"

Rafa chuckled, but I could tell he'd spotted the irritation on my face. "True, very true. It is not French, this name Delanne?"

"No," I said, feeling pretty proud of myself. "Though my great-grandfather—"

"Interesting. I will recommend to le Monsieur that he *use* you. Then. The decision has been made. What you must learn to do now, Delanne, is keep silent. This is the language le Monsieur would have you learn. He is an exceptional, extraordinary man. It is not easy to put into words . . ."

Rafa stood without finishing, and right away I lost track of the
questions I had on deck. Truth was, the thought of attending posh
business dinners in Switzerland had already seized my imagination. And if all I was being asked to do was translate . . . Still, I had
a bad feeling—I didn't like the way Rafa rolled his cigarette nervously between his fingers, the way he kept crossing and uncrossing
his legs, the way he hadn't really conducted an interview at all.

I stood. "M. Rafa, I'm still not sure what you're trying to say."

"There is no end to the story of Geneva," he interrupted. "Those
men were the ones to lose money, and le Monsieur made certain
decisions. With so many foreign clients, and so many who speak
only English, he needs a young man just like you. Experience and
education do not matter in this. Discretion, dedication, loyalty—
these are what matter. You are a young American, but such trifles
do not concern le Monsieur as much as they do others. Though he
would like to know your age."

"Almost thirty." It almost hurt to say it. "A few more weeks and
I'll be thirty."

"Perfect," Rafa said. He looked down at my coat, then at my
shoes. "And you are clearly in need of money, and with le Monsieur, believe me, you will no longer experience these needs."

Rafa took an envelope from his jacket pocket and placed it on
the table without looking at it.

"This will get you home, Delanne."

At that point I didn't hesitate. "If that's money, I can't accept—"

"This is what he wants," he said. "He will come for you when
he needs you."

Rafa nodded and started to turn away. I said, "Of course, I
haven't agreed to any . . ."

But Rafa was finished listening. He and his men walked up the
sidewalk to the parking lot. One of the men broke off separately,
and a minute later a sleek black luxury car pulled around—a classic Mercedes, by the looks of it.

I waited until they'd pulled away to open the envelope. Inside were a return train ticket and two crisp one-hundred-euro bills. I glanced around before shoving the envelope into my coat pocket. Because it was money that I needed—money I would later come to curse, though of course I couldn't know that then.

It wasn't until my train was pulling out of Lourange and heading west toward Ste-Térèse that I understood the extent of my fix: an unspoken deal had been struck, and there was no way to back out.

And this, in one way or another, was the story of my life.

RICH FRENCHMEN AND ALL THEIR MONEY

The next morning I woke to the sound of amplified voices out in the street. I scrambled to the window and saw a white minivan with cabinet speakers roped to its roof, surrounded by a flock of townspeople with signs and banners, all moving past Place Théâtre toward *centre ville*.

I'd overheard plenty of rumors at the Rougerie about the march. Apparently the French National Assembly was in a controversial state of transition and planned to replace *surveillants*, or university student aides in lycées, with government personnel. And everybody in Ste-Térèse was locked and loaded over it, prepared to protest the decision, which would be a big win for the right-wing, pro-nationalist factions of the National Assembly. The problem was that Ste-Térèse and its region were predominantly left-wing, and there was a high percentage of college students working as *surveillants* for its five major lycées, which meant that truckloads of students would be forced to drop out of college in order to find outside work for room and board.

I'd had a hot night of flopping from dream to dream. While part of me wanted to get dressed and join the march—a couple of

the Rougerie guys had pressed me about protesting with them—
another part of me felt ready to betray any noble cause for a few
hours of steady sleep.

I crawled back into bed.

THAT AFTERNOON, AFTER paying my rent with Rafa's cash, I found a
warm café and got revved up on espresso, which of course sent my
mind whirling toward all Rafa had said before leaving me in the
lurch. They could send for me if they wanted. And I could tell
them to go straight back to hell. Anyway, I hadn't given them any
contact info—I'd signed nothing, agreed to nothing, and had still
made out like a bandit. Open and shut.

That didn't keep me from wondering how much Rafa's boss
might have paid me. Rafa had acted pretty confident when he'd said
that I wouldn't have "these needs." I found myself chuckling at that.
I'd always had these needs: I owed big for student loans, my credit
card was in a constant state of being frozen and thawed, and there
was no point in moaning about it. This was life. And Rafa's two
hundred euros would help me buy another month of it.

THAT NIGHT I went to dinner *chez* Paul, another prof at Corbières
who'd befriended me back in the fall. He'd also invited a few teachers from our lycée and the nearby Lycée Dubois, among them
Amelia, an Italian assistant at Dubois who everyone seemed to
think was my girlfriend. I drank a little too much bourbon and
told Paul and one of his colleagues that Amelia lived in the same
foyer as I did, in the building next to mine, which was just too
damn close for romance. They laughed, though I was pretty sure
I'd flubbed something crucial in the French. I tried to fill my
mouth with hors d'oeuvres, and not just to keep from talking—the
food was excellent, thanks to Paul's wife. But outside of the usual
alienation, it was the company that ran me off early. Everyone was
less interested in pleasant conversation than they were in my ex-

planations for the ultimatums the U.S. was giving Iraq—why was my country threatening to drop bombs without UN consent?

I was more interested passing on a simple truth: How the hell should I know?

After I'd made my escape with Amelia and resisted her fluttering eyelashes outside her building, I wound up back at the Rougerie with a glass of Bruno's rum punch and a handful of darts.

Patrick and Joël—two members of the Rougerie crowd I'd met through Françoise—had wrangled me into a game, but my attention kept drifting off to Rafa's world, which for some reason no longer seemed half as ominous as it had before. I threw darts for an hour and after my third rum punch told Patrick about the job offer.

"Back in the States?" Patrick asked.

"No, man—right here, for this rich Frenchman. I'm skeptical about taking it."

Patrick placed a sweaty hand on my shoulder. "Watch out for those rich Frenchmen and all their money. Christ knows you don't owe us any drinks."

I tried to cough up a good-sport laugh, but the blow stung.

"You know I'm just kidding," Patrick said. "Nobody holds a drink or two against you."

We finished that game, but I'd grown agitated. I said my good-byes and handed my MasterCard to Bruno and watched with even more irritation while his machine kept denying it.

"No dice," Bruno said finally, handing my card back. "You're going to tell me that you're out of cash."

"Look, Bruno. That card is supposed to be working. They told me on the phone just last—"

"Jeff, my man. You're an honest guy, you don't have to explain. But I got a business to run here." Another long uncomfortable stare. He wasn't happy about this part of his business, and I couldn't blame him for sticking to his own rules. "This has got to be the last time, Jeff. You can cover this when you get paid again—in cash. But it's the last time."

"Agreed."

Bruno glanced out the front window and squinted, mumbling something about some idiot's car being parked illegally across the street.

My breath caught when I saw it for myself: it was a black luxury sedan—a Mercedes, exactly like the one Rafa had climbed into. At each end of the car stood a thickset man in a black suit, just like the men at the university café. In the darkness I couldn't see their faces very well. But I could feel them gazing in at me.

My stomach took a plunge: so Rafa's boss knew where I could be found.

I stepped away from the window, moved past Bruno into the back room. There was a faint ringing noise coming from some-where nearby. Patrick was laughing. Joël was throwing against a slim stranger with long hands. I could see their mouths moving, but I couldn't hear any words. In a wild flurry my mind ripped through all Rafa had said about his boss, Geneva, the Scots, never a bad deal. I imagined myself sitting down to a sumptuous private dinner with a crew of European high-rollers. Riding in that gorgeous Mercedes to some spacious villa on the edge of town. Playing some crucial translating role, a glass of choice Chinon in one hand and a Cuban cigar in the other.

But that wasn't it. That wasn't what drew me—those were just distractions. All I needed, all I was really hoping for, was some cash; I needed to get through another few months without sinking.

A moment later I was walking back through the bar, nodding good-bye to Bruno, and snatching my coat off the rack beside the front door.

Outside, a fine, cold mist was slanting down. I crossed the street to the Mercedes, trying to remember how to breathe. The sedan sat there purring. It was the kind you only see in movies and magazines, never within arm's reach. One of the suited men came around, slung open the front door, and slid into the driver's seat. The other opened the back door on my side and stood next to it. I gave him a hard look, studying his eyes for some kind of guarantee. But he seemed to be gazing through me.

"Good evening," I said. "Do you know who I am?"

No answer—just a nod. I hesitated. Of all the risks to take, I thought, this couldn't be more than a pinprick, a drop in the Atlantic. I'd left the States on sketchy terms—some bad checks and a few unsettled misdemeanors—and scoring the job at Corbières had been, in part, one last-ditch effort to bail myself out. On my own terms.

Now here I was again, almost sunk, no better off than I'd been back home, and standing penniless in the rain.

I climbed into that swanky car and let a stranger shut the door beside me.

YOU WILL FIND HIM
GAGGED

In the plush backseat of that Mercedes my mind ran down one distraction after another, sidestepping its own warnings. But the ride was intoxicating, more powerful than an army of drinks.

I closed my eyes and felt myself being shuttled through space. When I opened them, we were leaving the city, drifting past a pocket of suburbs, then pulling off the highway into the sparse, rolling countryside. I let my window down an inch, took deep breaths. We drove in and out of a few forests, into that sparsely populated, haunted stretch of territory between Ste-Térèse and Lourange. Then we slowed to a crawl and turned onto a gravel driveway, where behind a thin grove of knotty evergreens stood an unkempt stone cottage.

We pulled in beside a long black Bentley, another classic model whose windows were tinted so black that they looked like mirrors, and stopped. The door beside me swung open, and when the cold night air flooded in, it took all the will I possessed to get out.

One of the men led me around the front of the cottage along a stone pathway that smelled like smoke and pinecones. When he opened the front door, I took a good look at his face. He had the same buzz cut as the others, no facial hair, thin eyebrows, and faint wrinkles around his eyes.

I moved past him into an empty front room that reeked of tobacco. There were stone tiles in the floor, exposed timber in the ceiling, zero furniture, and minimal fixtures: only a slender lamp near the opposite wall, and an end table with an overflowing ashtray on it. To the left were a closed door and a hallway leading into darkness. To the right, down a shorter hallway, another door stood half open.

The man came in behind me and indicated the room to the right. I nodded to the bodyguard, crossed the front room, and went in.

At once I knew that I was standing before Rafa's monsieur—Nabec, the old Arab Dreyfus had spoken of. His presence announced it, even if his bare surroundings didn't. He was sitting at a short foldaway table with a fat cigar in his mouth and a squat bottle of Porto in front of him. Behind him stood a powerfully built bodyguard, shirtsleeves rolled over his elbows.

There was nothing else in there besides the empty seat across from the old businessman. When he gestured to the empty seat, I obeyed.

"I am content that you have come," he said in an elegant voice. "You were free not to."

I muttered something about being grateful, but my voice shook beneath the words. Mostly I was unnerved by his awkward comportment: one of his shoulders stood slightly higher than the other, and he had all ten of his fingers lined up on the table, as if he'd just been inspecting his fingernails and wasn't quite finished.

He was decked out like an aristocrat—swanky wool suit, sharp striped tie, immaculate shave, and manicured hands. He had a full head of gray hair peppered with black, a thick but flawlessly groomed mustache. His deep, dark eyes gazed into mine and stayed there for an excruciating minute.

Finally he took his fingers off the table. "You must not be afraid, Jeffrey Delanne. Fear will only distract you."

My name in his smooth dialect sounded strange, almost non-sensical, like a noise where a word belonged. He poured two glasses of Porto and pushed one across the table.

"You speak very good French," he said. "Where did you learn it?"

He glanced up, and when our eyes met, my stomach instantly calmed.

"My mother is a French teacher in the States," I said. "But I've learned a lot in France."

He smiled warmly. "I myself still have hopes of learning English. There are not many I know who would speak it with me, however. But please, drink."

The Porto went down like nectar. It was far and away one of the best things I'd ever tasted.

Nabec puffed his cigar and drew it carefully from his mouth. "In the other room, Jeffrey, is my client. You will find him gagged." He paused, watching me closely. "You are not to assume that he is reasonable—nor entirely truthful."

I felt all the blood drain from my face. My breathing quickened, and I tried my best to play it off. But he'd said the word *gagged* like he might have said *bathing:* you will find him *bathing.* I downed my drink, cornering the French words for *unwilling, unprepared, unfit for the task.*

Before I could say anything, Nabec raised one finger. "A location," he said. "Only this."

But I couldn't remember how to form a sentence. "Pardon?"

"A location. My client in the next room knows of a location, but he does not understand French. This is all I would like you to learn from him—a location."

"With all respect, monsieur," I managed. "I don't see how I can do what you're asking."

The old Arab leaned back. "You must take your time, of course. One of my men will accompany you. Remember that you are not being paid by the hour."

Now, this wasn't the first time I'd been faced with the option of doing something slightly askew for a little bit of cash—nor would it have been the first time I'd exercised the option. That didn't mean that I wanted to continue my old habits overseas.

When I stood, neither Nabec nor his bodyguard budged.

"I truly appreciate this opportunity," I said. "But there's been a mistake. I'm not—I'm just not prepared to do this—I'm not the right man for this kind of job. So if you'll excuse me."

Nabec fixed his eyes on my midriff. Then he filled our glasses with Porto, and as he raised his eyes to meet mine, a strangely benevolent look appeared on his face.

"Please, sit down and have another drink, M. Delanne. It puts you under no obligation."

But he wasn't asking—he was telling. I sat back down and drank the Porto in one gulp, closing my eyes as the exquisite ruby beverage rolled down the hatch. When I opened my eyes, they met Nabec's. His head was cocked, but he didn't seem to be scrutinizing—he seemed fascinated.

"You have misunderstood," he said. "I am offering to pay you to help someone. All you must do is *inform* him that he must tell us a location to be set free. Does *this* prepare you?"

I searched the old Arab's eyes. He seemed willing to understand, though I knew he wasn't so willing to let me go easily.

"It's not just—" I stopped and chose my words carefully. "Look, I'm an American on a temporary work visa. Yeah, I need money. But I can't get involved in this kind of thing. So if you'll forgive me for wasting your time—"

"With *what* kind of thing, Jeffrey?" Nabec was smiling now.

"It's simple." I lowered my voice. "You said the man's gagged. And if he's being held against his will . . . I just can't be involved in that. I wasn't told, in fact, that—"

"And what *were* you told, Jeffrey?" He poured another round of Porto. "Please, explain to me your thinking. I wish to understand it."

I studied his eyes again, wanting to disbelieve his sincerity, trying hard not to let the smooth, peaceful sound of his words obscure the meaning of his proposal.

"Please," he said. "You were referred to me, and approved of. Now you have been brought to me. So, please, explain to me your thinking."

I drank the Porto, but still didn't know where to begin. Nabec immediately refilled my glass. Our eyes locked.

"Do you know what my business is, Jeffrey?" Now he too had lowered his voice.

"No, and with all respect, monsieur . . ." I held back.

"Please, go ahead. Speak your mind, Jeffrey."

"I mean to say . . . it's just that I don't *want* to know your business."

Nabec's smile was huge now, full of gleaming white teeth. "You have been well chosen, Jeffrey Delanne."

"How's that?" I asked.

Nabec loosened his tie with three deft movements of his hand.

"We have an expression, Jeffrey, to the effect of what you have just said: 'What you do not know cannot hurt you.' If it's trouble you're afraid of, young man, I can give you my oath that you will meet with none for speaking with this man. And you shall only need to know that you have helped a fellow anglophone to his freedom."

I sipped my Porto, thinking how easily I could become addicted to such a drink. I realized that I was starting to believe the old man, even though I had no concrete reason to.

"It's a gray issue for me, is all I'm saying," I said. "You make it sound as if, as if—okay, can I speak hypothetically?"

"Please do."

"Okay, I came here because I thought I'd do some translating, as I was told, and I'd get paid, and that would be all. So I get here and there's a not-so-small matter of a gagged man. You're making it sound as if it's a minor detail, like it's as easy as going to the guy, walking in there and freeing him myself. But what if he won't talk? I just think this is more complicated than I'm ready to deal with. I'm just a schoolteacher, after all—"

"And I am assuring you, Jeffrey, that we are out here in the middle of nowhere, and that your only job would be to walk across to the next room and remove my client's gag. And if he did not tell you what I wish to know, your job would be finished. And you would still be paid handsomely. Yet—if you could be convincing—well, then you could help a man go free."

I pushed my empty glass toward him. He refilled it. I lit a cigarette and watched the flame of the lighter quiver with my hand.

"You must first relax, Jeffrey," said Nabec. "Let me distract with a question that also concerns translation, a simpler translating task . . ."

He puffed at his cigar, but it had gone out. In a blink his bodyguard was there to light it.

Nabec continued, "I have begun watching American films, you see, in hopes of learning English. I particularly enjoy the gangster genre, though I am fond of what you call artistic films, as well. Still, I find that I cannot enjoy these films as I wish, because I must always be reading the French subtitles, until viewing becomes an exercise in learning to read subtitles quickly, rather than a lesson in English comprehension."

I smiled, remembering my first several weeks in France. "I used to have the same trouble. You've got to block out the subtitles, or turn them off, or else you'll never make any progress."

Nabec leaned back, drawing the cigar from his lips and narrowing his eyes at the ceiling.

"When I contend with another language," he said, "I often suspect that I have been nothing but a fool, and that my understanding of the world, beyond my small corner of it, has been simpleminded and will not suffice. That in fact after all these years my life has been nothing more than an illusion."

My eyes latched onto the deep creases around the old man's eyes. He couldn't have explained my predicament any better had he stolen into my mind.

We drank. After another long moment our eyes locked again. His were penetrating, deeply in earnest.

"There is nothing for you to misinterpret here, Jeffrey Delanne," he whispered. "Will you not help my client do what he has come here to do?"

My head was swimming now, and not from the booze. "What did he come here to do?"

"To rid himself of his own treachery."

I tore my eyes from his, and found myself glaring at the bodyguard's huge forearms.

"I don't understand," I said. "Why his own treachery?"

Nabec's eyes were still locked onto mine. "Simple. My client believed falsely that I would pay him for something which he has no right to sell—information that I wish to have. He is a traitor to his people, and what he deserves is to be delivered to them for punishment. But you, Jeffrey—you can help relieve him of his burden. In English, he might be more easily convinced that his only payment will be his freedom."

The room was silent except for my own heavy breathing. For a minute there, I felt as if we'd been talking about something larger.

But I was too afraid to name what that was—too afraid that in fact we were talking about my own freedom as well.

My stomach tightened down hard. "And if I do this, I'm free to go?"

"Yes, Jeffrey. And with the remuneration you have come for."

"And your client? He'll go free? Absolutely?"

Nabec nodded. I closed my eyes and drank the last of my Porto. Voices stormed through my head, but only one rang true; it said to do whatever it takes—just do what the old man wants and get the hell out, forever.

NEVER TRULY BE FREE

In the center of the opposite room sat a thin man with a red gag lashed around his jaw and neck. He had short brown hair, a sunburned face, and bare feet. He wore dirty khakis and a sweat-soaked blue polo shirt. His hands and ankles were tied to the legs of his chair with thick gray cord. Another chair leaned against the wall, and a lantern hung from the ceiling at the front of the room. Otherwise the room was empty: an uncarpeted concrete floor, a forsaken brick fireplace, bare timber joists in the ceiling. Both windows were boarded up from the inside.

The man who'd escorted me inside from the Mercedes stepped in behind me, shut the door, and assumed a casual position in the corner.

The gagged man wouldn't look at me. My mind froze for a long moment. I couldn't let him see my fear—if he didn't take me seriously, we were stuck.

"I'm here to help," I said finally. "All he wants to know is a location. Then you'll go free."

He still wouldn't look at me. I waited a minute, then approached him carefully, reaching around his head and undoing the hard wet knot of the gag. It fell onto his lap. I moved away and racked my brain for what to say next.

"How long have they had you here?" I asked finally.

The man dropped his eyes and mumbled something I didn't catch.

"Sorry?"

Finally his eyes flashed to mine. "I said fock off, ya focking Arab."

I kept quiet for a minute, trying to imagine how hot I'd be if I was in his position.

"Now, you know I'm not any Arab," I said. "What's that accent of yours? Scottish? Welsh?"

He looked over at Nabec's man in the corner and cursed, stretching his jaw from side to side. I got out a cigarette, lit it, and held it to his lips. He wouldn't take it.

"Look," I said. "I'm just an interpreter. If it was up to me, I'd just untie you. But I can't do that. I'm just supposed to come in here and tell you that he'll let you go if you tell me the location."

The man glared at me and said nothing. I stood a few feet away and smoked, staring back at him until I couldn't resist the urge to ask.

"Come on, don't you *want* out of this shit?"

He shifted around in his seat. "Bloody right I want outta this shite."

I said, "So I'm not supposed to do anything but come in here and ask you about a location. And tell you that he means business."

"And I'm not s'posed to be toyed up, now am I?" he asked.

"How should I know?"

We exchanged narrow looks. I was ready to be finished, growing more irritated by the second—mostly with myself, for having walked into this mess.

I turned to Nabec's goon in the corner. He was cleaning his fingernails with a pocketknife.

"*Ça ne marche pas,*" I said to him: It wasn't working.

The goon shrugged. I ran my fingers through my hair, realizing it wasn't going to be as simple as in-and-out, like I'd been counting on.

"You're blowing your best chance here, you know that?" I asked the Brit after a minute.

He shook his head. "You know that focking Arab don't say what he means? Here I come wiff information he says he needs, and here's how he pays me."

"You're missing the point," I said. "Even if you're right, you're still—"

"You'll see, mate. It's you what's focked next—you're working for a focking double-crosser."

He glared at Nabec's man, then spat at my feet. His face and neck were all red—he looked willing to beat the hell out of the next living thing he could get his hands on, once he was free. My hands wouldn't stop shaking. But it wasn't just fear, I realized: I was angry.

"You're making this too complicated," I said. "Forget who *he* is. Let's get *you* out of this. All you've got to tell me is the place."

He narrowed his eyes. "And I'm s'posed to believe 'at?"

"Try me," I said. I moved closer, sensing a connection. "Help me help you. Just tell me the place, and watch me leave."

"Help you *what*?"

"Help you. I'm here to help you get free, man. You tell me the place, he lets us go."

Our eyes were still locked. "He already broke his deal once," he said. "He'll keep me in here an' work me for everything he finks I know. And you after me."

"Just tell me the place, man. I already know you know it—I can tell you know it."

He looked away. "Ahh . . . places are everywhere. Lots of *um*."

I found myself clutching a handful of my own hair. "But which is most important?"

"How the fock should I know?"

"Guess!" I snapped. "You're all out of choices, man. That's what you're refusing to see. Why don't you get that?"

"Ah, fock off, ya focking Arab Yankee."

My fists clenched. I took a deep breath and walked around behind him so he couldn't see my anger. I had a bad feeling now. It was beginning to dawn on me that getting the man's confession was not just his only chance out of here, but mine too.

From out of nowhere came a rush of adrenaline. I'd never felt so much of it surge through me, fear and frustration bound up with panic. It felt hottest in my neck and arms. My face and fingers tingled. I looked at the back of the man's head, fighting to detach myself. Because sympathy wasn't going to help him—he wasn't thinking right, he didn't understand the stakes. Then I raised my hand to run my fingers through my hair, and the man flinched, bracing himself.

At once another realization hit: the guy was scared of *me*—not just of Nabec and his goons. Maybe he thought that I'd be the one to rough him up, that he'd have to take a few blows from me anyway, before it was all said and done. Was that why he was hesitating? It didn't make any sense, unless he was ready to be smacked around. Maybe he even *wanted* to be smacked around, before he could feel right about coming clean.

I imagined hitting him—a harmless jab to the jaw, a light hook to the chin. I could make it hurt without going too far. No real damage. Then he'd be ready to tell. It would be over, and once it was over, he'd thank me for it—once he was out on the street, free as a bird, he'd be grateful that I'd pushed him to do what he'd come here to do.

That impulse lasted only a minute. I shook my mind free of it, then came around and faced the poor man, taking out another cigarette and offering it to him. When he refused again, I knew he was just too stubborn—I had to at least try to convince Nabec that it was an absolute no go.

I turned to Nabec's man. *"C'est impossible. Il veut pas le dire."*

The goon nodded and put away his pocketknife. But he didn't head for the door. Instead, he walked over, stood in front of the Brit, and without pause struck him six hard times with an open hand, back and forth across the face. I remember taking one step toward them, but stopping myself. I looked away, then slowly raised my eyes to witness the beating. Awful as it was, I was a part of this. It might as well have been me delivering those blows.

When Nabec's man was done, he wiped the blood off his hand with a handkerchief and stepped back. The Brit's head hung limp. His breath came loudly through his nose. Blood and gobs of drool fell from his mouth onto his pants.

Nabec's goon put away his handkerchief and glanced back at me. What was done was done. I had to say something.

I approached the Brit and spoke quietly. "It's only going to get worse, man."

He raised his head, and his slim muscles suddenly bulged against the ropes that held his arms and legs. Then he let out a half-silent sob.

"Come on," I said. "Let's put an end to this. There's only one way."

The Brit's eyes met mine. Nabec's goon had gotten his pocketknife back out. He pinched its blade with two fingers, running them along its sides to the tip.

The Brit turned away. "Focking Chroise . . . it's the ol' cathedral he wants. 'At must be it."

"The ol' cathedral where?" I asked.

His eyes were on Nabec's man. "In the Bouffay," he said.

I nodded to the goon. He went out the door.

"I'm sorry this is happening to you," I said, once the goon was gone. "I didn't know it was going to be like this."

I backed toward the door, and the Brit's expression turned suddenly frantic.

"Doan just leave me in here, mate. Tell 'im to let me go. Tell 'im I focked up . . ."

But all I could think about was putting a door between us. All I wanted was to get as far away from him as I could.

BACK BEFORE NABEC, I tried my best to act collected, but it was hard to think beyond emotion. He poured me another Porto. I downed it in one drink, still too shaken up to look him in the eyes.

"Not as painful as one might guess, no?" he asked.

I shook my head to keep from speaking.

"Jeffrey," he said. "Nothing worthwhile is straightforward. Absolutely nothing."

"I see," I said, but only because I didn't dare disagree with him. When he stood and put on his overcoat, a wave of relief washed through me.

"Come," he said.

Outside, the rain had picked up. Both the Mercedes and the long Bentley were running. In a daze I followed Nabec to the Bentley. A dim golden light came on in the ceiling after I got in and shut the door. The inside of the car was enormous, twice as large as the Mercedes, with another bench seat facing ours. The soft leather of the seats made a gasping sound when I sat. The car's heat almost instantly eased my nerves. But I still had a queasy feeling in my stomach.

I told Nabec the location, almost expecting him to say I'd been lied to—that there was still more work to do. But the slightest smile appeared on his face.

"He did it," I said. "You'll set him free?"

Nabec looked at me as if I'd asked him a question without an answer.

"Yes," he said. "But this man, you must understand, will never truly be free. He is a traitor—he betrayed his own to come to us, and his own, rest assured, will track him down. Men like this, Jeffrey, live their lives in constant slavery. Men like this would be better off dead."

Nabec reached inside his coat and took out a single bill, a note I'd seen only on posters in banks and post offices—a five-hundred-euro, tall and blue and more than half my month's salary at Corbières: payment for less than an hour of work, for a name that translated the same in either language.

I stared at the bill, but didn't take it—not right away. When I did put the thing in my pocket, I felt thoroughly rotten, like the worst kind of crook, even though I knew it was rightfully mine: my payment, or punishment, or some combination of both.

When I got out, I didn't look back at the old businessman. I didn't need to. He seemed intuitive enough to know that I never wanted to lay eyes on him again.

Two of his men drove me home in the Mercedes. I closed my eyes and focused on the hum and thump of the wheels against the road, fighting to believe that as long as I occupied that luxurious seat, I could avoid remembering.

We stopped in front of my building. I climbed out and watched the car pull slowly off. Then I marched up the empty stairs to my room and flopped into bed like a corpse. For a long time I couldn't turn off my mind. I wound up flipping on the lights and playing Robert Johnson's *King of the Blues* end to end twice, gazing up at the ceiling until the music shut off and its absence felt gradually like sleep.

DIFFICULT, WITH ALL
THE BOOZE

I hardly slept the next two nights. Monday morning I called in sick to work, and Tuesday after teaching two agonizing classes I fled back to my place, where I stayed till after dark, starting and abandoning letters to old friends back home, dialing long distance and hanging up. Guilt seemed to saturate my every thought and deed. More than once I put on my coat and stood at the door, prepared to hike across *centre ville* to the old cathedral in the Bouffay, as if there I might actually find absolution. I even thought about going to the police. But what could I tell them? What evidence did I have? And what if old Nabec found out that I'd squealed and then came for me again—this time with another sort of payment in mind?

FRIDAY WAS HANDS-DOWN my heaviest day of the week—four classes, beginning with a hopeless bunch of midlevel brats and ending with a clever group of high-level honors kids. I slogged through my morning classes, then at lunchtime couldn't find an appetite, so I opted for the computer lab, where I found a tricky article in English about American high schools. After going over the article with my three-o'clock class, my favorite group of the six I taught twice a week, I asked if any of the kids had part-time jobs. Not a single hand went up.

"Aren't there after-school jobs for students in France?"

Still no hands. My eyes fell on Solène, my strongest and most cooperative student.

"Yes and no," she said. "There are jobs for university students, but not for us, really."

"This is causing a problem right now in France, isn't it?" I asked. "Anyone willing to explain the *surveillant* problem in English?"

I knew well enough that across France *surveillants*, who were like a mix between teachers' aides and student life coordinators in lycées, were losing their jobs to government lackeys—I just wanted to get the kids talking. After another long silence, Léo, a charismatic eighteen-year-old with zero business in my advanced class, raised his hand.

"It is too much difficult in English," he announced. "We can not use za same words."

The class erupted, which I should have seen coming the minute I'd called on him. Léo could be a real smart-ass, but he was also a ringleader at Corbières, one of those kids you had to keep on your good side to maintain general favor with the masses. He had a serious side as well: he'd let on more than once that he was politically active with a few university groups that did fundraisers and helped organize local demonstrations and such. He'd also initiated a couple of quasi-aggressive e-mail discussions with me, going so far as to forward me anti-American junk mail. I'd had to remind him more than once that I wasn't to blame for my country's governmental decisions, and more than once he'd stared at me from his desk with a contempt that was hard to understand from a kid so green. As for his English, it needed to be put to death and resurrected, which seemed to him beside the point.

After Léo fumbled through an excruciating explanation of the *surveillant* problem, Solène stepped in for the save.

"It is a new problem," she said. "Our National Assembly is in a—how do you say?—transition, yes. Many fear that there will be a change of majority after the election next, and this law of replacing university students to be surveillants is a part of this change."

When the students took to disagreeing in English, I redirected the conversation back to the article I'd brought in, which somehow led them into the old "is it really true in America" question-and-answer routine. I fielded several ridiculous questions about fast-food consumption in the States, and at some point my eyes landed back on Solène, who was smiling at me as if I'd just asked her to the senior prom. After that my mind wormed its way out to Nabec's cottage, and I fought with a powerful wave of guilt, imagining what my students would think of me.

A minute before the bell rang, I called class to a close. Then came the inevitable line up to my desk. First was Lucien, Paul's son, with whom I'd traded CDs over the months. He handed over my Big Joe Williams along with a Georges Brassens disc I'd asked him to burn for me.

I said, "Tell your mom that she's a magician in the kitchen."

"Sure." An irritated expression came over Lucien's pimple-ridden face. "See you."

Léo stepped up next and presented me with a blue flyer. "It is propaganda only," he said. "To invite you wiss it, tomorrow. A *manif*."

Aside from hanging out with Paul's son Lucien, I'd been in the habit of turning down invitations from students. But it was a tough call with my high-levels, most of whom were eighteen and ran around with more decorum than your typical American college grad. When I'd talked to Paul about it, he'd laughed and told me that keeping what I was calling a teacherly distance, particularly since I was only a foreign assistant, was absurd.

"It is small *manif*," Léo was saying. "Peace-fool, *contre la guerre* in za Mideast."

I grinned. "What war in the Middle East?"

"*Mais contre . . .*" he started to say in French. "Against za threat of bombs to Iraq."

"Okay, okay. Where will the *manif* happen?"

"We hope to have everywhere," he said. "But—*je peux le dire en francais?*"

I nodded.

"You know Place Graslin?" he said in French. "The march will go down Rue Théâtre to Graslin, and the demonstration will begin around three."

I could think of only one reason to tell Léo that I'd join the antiwar march: to solidify in his mind, and in the minds of his followers, that I didn't fit neatly into his stereotypes. I told him I'd be there, and he saluted me before heading out.

Solène stepped up next and said hello. She'd taken her curly blond hair out of its bun and was playing nervously with the ends of her long bangs. A month or two ago, I'd noticed the T-shirt she was wearing now, and had gone so far as to point out in class that the image in the left corner, a melted blue clock, was out of a Dalí painting. The T-shirt was faded beige, one or two sizes too small, tight across the shoulders and very snug over the chest.

I made sure to look straight into Solène's large blue eyes.

"Do you know Elise?" she asked.

"Elise?"

"Elise from your Tuesday *terminal* class?"

"Elise, yes. Of course I know Elise."

"We are going to a football match tomorrow. You told her class that you never see these, and we would like to invite you, if you like, to come with us?"

It sounded rehearsed. I kept my eyes locked in her gaze, trying to plot a graceful excuse.

"I would," I said. "But I've just told Léo that I'd meet him at the *manif* tomorrow."

I came around the desk feeling like I'd just dodged a bullet.

"We are going to the *manif* also," Solène said. "The match will begin after. There will also be enough time for a beer, if you like."

She had me pinned now, and she knew it. My passion for beer was common knowledge among my older students, because I was always using beer as a stock noun in grammatical examples, and I made profuse references to drinking beer in stories. Anyway, beers and a soccer game seemed harmless. I'd always imagined a European game would be too pricey, like pro football games back in the States. Then, when I remembered Nabec's cash lying in my drawer, I suffered another wave of guilt—a milder one than before.

Solène was looking up at me with wide eyes. I couldn't think of another student I'd rather accommodate.

We agreed to meet at a café near the east-west tramline after the *manif,* and I made sure not to let my eyes linger on hers when we said good-bye.

IN MY MAILBOX in the main foyer building that evening, I found a note from Amelia, whom I'd successfully avoided since the dinner party at Paul's. It said: *Je pense á toi, Jeffrey, plus que je veux dire.* So the young Sicilian was thinking of me plenty, but was failing to see that I'd never asked for that.

I went to the Rougerie to mull it over, then decided it wasn't worth mulling over.

The bar was empty except for a few dart throwers in back. I took a half-pint over to the pinball machine and had played maybe a half-dozen balls when Françoise's beautiful daughter, Marine, showed up with a few girlfriends. Keeping my back to them, I tried to concentrate on the erratic moves of pinball, but Marine's image was burned into the reflection of the upright glass—her tall, narrow frame, the way her dark hair fell over her shoulders. Truth was, I would have traded the better part of my soul for a half hour alone with that woman. But Marine was in deep with another

Rougerie regular named Julien, a guy my age who'd returned to
Ste-Térèse in late December, after a three-month business trip—
after I'd already set my sights on his girlfriend.

This kind of thing was always happening to me. I let myself
feel burned by it every time.

At least happy hour was fast approaching: another debaucherous
Friday night loomed on the horizon, and soon the place would be
billowing with music and cigarette smoke, overflowing with the
chatter of voices. There'd be Patrick, of course, and Marine's chosen
one, Julien, who could be a pretty funny guy when he wasn't giving
me the hairy eyeball for conversing with his lady. There would also
be Joël, our barrel-chested dart companion, who always waited until
he was full of liquor to kiss me hard on either cheek, clap my shoulders, and invite me to his place for *grenouille* the likes of which I
could find nowhere else. Françoise, who had thirty-some years on
all of us but brought a ton of life to the place, usually stumbled in
too, for either an hour or a handful of drinks, whichever came first.

One drink invariably led to another, and by ten o'clock I was
absorbed in the scene, my thoughts firing off in French and my
tongue loose with cheap booze. We'd staked out the back table,
and I was sitting between Françoise and Marine, who was giving
me more attention than usual, looking my way every so often, as if
there were something she wanted to ask me but wasn't sure how.
At some point I let something slip about not sleeping much lately.

"That explains it," said Marine. "Your eyes look tired. They're
usually bright, full of energy—get more sleep, Jeff."

I was so dazzled by the full frontal attention from her that I
found myself sprawling for something funny to say, as camouflage.

"I'd do anything for sleep," I said. "Even to sleep four or five
hours a night, I bet I'd—"

"Spoken like a true American!" someone shouted from across
the table. "He'll do anything!"

I turned and saw Michel, the bar's most outspoken French

patriot, who also happened to be one of Julien's right-hand men. Red-nosed and full of political animosity, Michel drank strictly Calvados, never anything quieter. He also wore a clownish smile, and ribbed anybody and everybody about whatever he could.

Now Michel was grinning like a madman, holding his shot glass over the table and watching it with one eye closed, as if any minute the drink might come alive and scurry off.

"To bombs, eh! Here's to American bombs!"

I raised my beer and smiled back. "No, here's to leaving American expats out of it."

But Michel had only begun. "I was just talking with Patrick," he shouted over the noise. "It seems you guys are a bit ruffled— *ruffled!*—that our president won't be a puppet like the British prime minister. They're even planning to boycott French goods! You've read this?"

"Yeah," I said. "But I don't believe everything I read in France."

"Ruffled! That our government won't come to the aid of yours. That their so-called influence over here isn't holding up. Ha! Talking about Normandy, this business of saving us over and over, history, history, history. And ruffled because we won't send our bombs to Baghdad!"

I glanced at Françoise. She was looking at me as if to say, *say something*.

"Looks like you're the ruffled one," I shouted to Michel. "Who do you know in Baghdad?"

Michel laughed at that, but kept one eye closed. "Patrick, he's got the idea. He says: Remember old Lafayette? Old Lafayette in '76? He says: Remind them of the American War for Independence. The Big One, eh? There's history! Where would you guys be without old Lafayette?"

"That's a little hard to say," I called back, glancing at Marine. "Where would you guys be without old Henry the Fifth?"

"And you guys want us to go in like cowboys," Michel went on.

"Imagine an army of French cowboys! Patrick, he's got the idea. He says: You don't help the big bully kick a little guy around, just because the little guy won't surrender his slingshot. What you do is say *no!* You say, *Not me, my friend.* You say, *Quit bullying for oil, America!*"

Patrick had dropped this same logic on me the other day. It was a tidy analogy that left little room for cross-examination.

I glanced at Julien. He was leaning over the table and listening intently. But I was satisfied to have headed Michel off with a joke or two. I killed my drink and headed to the bar, where Patrick was bellied up. As usual his nose was running, his clean-shaven face sweaty with banter and booze. We drank several apiece—all on me—and sometime before closing, Julien joined us and invited me to an after-hours party at his place, an all-time first that I could hardly make sense of, outside of the fact that he was bombed.

The short walk to Julien's apartment was blistering cold and almost not worth it. Nights like these, I always wondered why it never snowed in this corner of France. Probably because that would take away from the gloom. There were a dozen or more of us, and along the way several paired off, holding each other to keep warm. As we waited at the foot of the stairs for Julien to work his building lock, I wound up next to Joël, who had his big arms around his sister Angelique. I could hear Patrick's voice, and Julien's, and a few others, and I could see the backs of several familiar heads. But I didn't see Marine anywhere, wasn't even sure now if she'd come with us. Then once the door came open and people started pushing in after Julien, I felt an arm go around my back. It was Marine, huddling against me, her coat collar turned up and her teeth chattering. I gave her a friendly squeeze, and the heat from her body burrowed through my clothes and under my skin. A moment later, as we pushed up the stairs behind the others, the feeling was gone.

Inside, everyone was chattering and handing around lukewarm beers. We crowded into the kitchen, which featured an undersized refrigerator and an oversized floor-model radio. A bottle of whiskey moved from hand to hand, and after one turn on it, my guts started to sizzle. I ducked into the living room to shed my coat. I wasn't gone a minute before I heard Julien call my name.

"Bring him here, then," someone said after that. "We'll hold a Caps Olympics."

When Patrick entered the living room smiling and holding the whiskey bottle, I leered at him.

"Your participation is requested," he said. "Humbly."

But I knew enough about the game of Caps to know that I wanted zero part of it.

"I'll watch you professionals play."

"It is, how you say?" Patrick announced in English. "Your Rite of *Passage*."

Next thing I knew, I was sitting on the kitchen floor with my legs spread in a V and a burning candle between them. On my right sat three shot glasses, one of them filled with high-octane rum. Maybe five yards away, facing me, sat my opponent, Joël's sister Angelique, her own legs spread with a burning candle between them. The rules were simple: if you could extinguish your opponent's candle flame with a toss of a bottle cap, the onlookers would set fire to one of your opponent's shots, and she had to throw it back with as much honor as she could muster. Three shots and you lose, loser stays and plays the next challenger.

The first two rum shots I'd had already were staging fiery protests down in my stomach, and I couldn't hit that flame between Angelique's legs to save my own liver. Everyone had crowded around us, cheering us on and alternating "The Marseillaise" with butchered snatches of "The Star-Spangled Banner." My vision was doing an unfamiliar kind of swagger. I kept aiming and missing, and after five more throws of the bottle cap, Angelique finally snuffed out my flame a third time for the win.

The crowd went wild, and I was hoisted to my feet for the third flaming rum.

Once I got the thing down, I endured several slaps on the back, followed by an assurance that I'd done my country proud anyway—that someone, after all, had to lose.

"Might as well have been the American!" Michel announced.

Even I laughed at that one, but I would have fielded it all with more grace had it not been for my desperation to find the bathroom and drain the excess beer. Patrick directed me down a dark hallway, the walls of which I had to grope along to keep from pitching sideways. When I could see a faint strip of light along the floor, I fumbled around for the doorknob. But the door was locked.

"Not as easy as it looks, is it?" a voice said.

I couldn't see her face, but I knew it was Marine. Now that she'd spoken, her presence was like an invisible fire. She moved closer, close enough for me to reach out and pull her against me— though I didn't dare. My stomach knotted up. *She's Julien's,* I reminded myself. But I was too drunk, too vulnerable. I had the urge to confess everything to her, then and there.

"It's difficult," I said. "Much too difficult, with all the booze."

Marine laughed. "That's the idea. But they'll let you quit soon."

"I quit now," I said. "Officially. Enough competition for one night."

"It's not competition until you've played me," Marine said playfully.

My eyesight had adjusted, and I could see her face now. She was gazing into my eyes. When she moved close, I kissed her, though she was the one who pulled our bodies together.

When the toilet on the other side of the door flushed, we jerked apart. She didn't look afraid or even coy now. She shook her head and held a finger to her lips.

The bathroom door opened, and out stumbled Julien. He slapped my shoulder, unleashed an enormous belch, then squeezed past us without even acknowledging Marine.

While Marine was in the bathroom, I leaned against the opposite wall and tasted her lips on mine, wondering whether it would have been as exciting had it not been taboo, kissing a woman in her boyfriend's hallway, while he pissed in the bathroom, just feet away.

Back in the kitchen I struggled through two more games of Caps, the first of which, against Joël, I almost won. During the next game, against Marine, I had to fight hard to focus on the candle flame between her legs. She beat me three to one, and wore a cocky smile from start to finish.

After the games came plenty of backslapping and mock praise for heroism, and when Julien approached me afterward, I was moony from all the rum.

"Ah, partner in crime," he said. "Thanks for coming. Marine wants to give you a ride home."

"No, no," I said. "She shouldn't drive. I'll just walk."

"But she insists, she insists. And anyway, she didn't drink as much as you, partner—nobody did. You know, I think she likes you."

An uncomfortable drunken stare. We had a comparable look, Julien and I—same height, same build, similar facial structure—even though his hair was much lighter than mine, and he dressed much better than I could afford to.

"Don't get your hopes up," he said sarcastically. "She won't come on to you or anything."

I found Marine in the living room with Joël and Angelique, guzzling water from mason jars. We argued briefly about driving.

"I've driven from here to there blindfolded," Marine kept saying.

I'd known her long enough to figure out that she was a hyper-possessive car owner, ready to go with her heap to the grave, just to keep the thing from getting towed. That, and the thought of being alone with her again, kept me from carrying my argument much further.

• • •

OUTSIDE IN MARINE'S car, all the hooch I'd consumed seemed to catch up with me at once—my vision was doing the dip-and-twirl before she could even turn on the engine. She got a cigarette going and told me not to sweat it—with a smoke in her hand she could accomplish any known task.

We wove along several side streets, my stomach pitching with every turn, and in a few minutes we were in front of my building. I had the spins so bad that I skipped the cheek kisses, muttered good night to Marine, and stumbled out into the cold.

Right away the spins redoubled. I dreaded the task of climbing up to my hot, cramped apartment, but I had to get to a bathroom. I found the sidewalk, lit a cigarette I didn't need, and almost toppled backward. For a solid minute I stood there laughing at myself.

That was when I spotted it parked down the street: a black luxury sedan, idling with its headlights off.

I had a bad hunch it was a Mercedes.

A minute later I was inside my apartment, leaning back against the locked door. I remember not being able to think around the pounding in my ears, reaching for the light switch but stopping, holding myself still as the room swayed from side to side.

And that was all.

MIGHT WE SAY EVIL DEEDS?

I woke up with my face pressed against the cold porcelain base of the toilet. There was a warbling megaphone sound coming from somewhere nearby. I pried myself off the floor and checked my bedroom window: legions of demonstrators, all heading east toward Place Graslin, just as they had the weekend before. I remembered then what I'd told Léo, but all I could think about now was the category-four hangover spreading through my body. I needed to take drastic action for myself, and fast.

I threw on some clothes and headed downstairs to the street, hoping to push through the flocks of protesters to the Marché Plus, across the plaza. But the crowd was thick. My headache had entered blinking red status, and so I started weaving my way up the sidewalk, looking for an opening to ford across. Then, in some random stroke of bad luck, I spotted Patrick, Joël, and Julien coming down the sidewalk with the crowd.

They saw me before I could steer away. When we reached each other, Julien took me by the shoulders like a long-lost brother.

"He's alive! He survived the Caps Olympics, and now he comes to march."

We stepped clear of the crowd. Joël was talking loudly on his cell phone, and Patrick was wearing the wet smile of an early-afternoon beer buzz.

"But you're headed the wrong way," Patrick said. "Unless you're against us."

I had no defense. Joël handed me his bottle of water, and the four of us took a side street, bypassing the demonstrators in order to smoke Patrick's joint. Julien fell in stride beside me.

"You know what this *manif* is all about, right?" he asked.

I looked at him skeptically. This was the first sober attention I'd gotten from Julien since he'd returned from his business trip in December, when I'd first met him. The one time I'd asked him about the trip, he'd looked at me sideways, as if I'd crossed some delicate line between us. My mind shot to the kiss in Julien's hall-way, then went out to Nabec's cottage.

Only then did I recall seeing the Mercedes the night before. It made my stomach wrench.

"Did you understand my question?" asked Julien.

"Yeah," I said absentmindedly. "Something to do with the student *surveillents* losing jobs."

"That's only the half of it," Patrick said. "We've got elections coming up. One-third of the National Assembly will be up for new representatives, which is enough to shift the balance. Eight months from now, Jeff, we may have a government that approves of some of these ridiculous antiterrorist bills. Which would do a real number on people coming into and leaving France—tourism, see. Not to mention private businesses. One of the parties even wants to send troops to Iraq. So the demonstrations are basically to tell the Prime Minister—"

"To get fucked!" said Joël, who'd finally hung up his phone.

We cut down Rue Le Blanc, which runs parallel to Rue Verne, where the demonstrators were funneling into Place Graslin. I took the joint from Joël and hit it once before handing off to Julien, who passed it back to Patrick. The hash scrambled my reasoning almost instantly but took a ton of weight off my head.

"Wait," I said. "Can't people keep it from happening by voting?"

"Not as simple as that," Julien said. "Here's the thing: we've got a multiparty republic, and a couple of those parties are in bed with outside organizations. Like the CIA—"

"Nobody knows that for sure," Patrick interjected. "But your country has more influence than you probably think, Jeff. They've got big money interest in the Middle East. Which is bullshit."

Patrick flung the spent joint into the street. I could hear amplified voices rallying the crowds two blocks over. The noise made my skin tremble.

We rounded the corner of a little side street called Guist'hau, which gave onto Place Graslin, and entered the fringes of the *manif.* Before us stretched a sea of protesters, at least a thousand of them crammed into Place Graslin, a chaotic mass of pumping fists and signs with antiwar and antinationalist slogans on them. In the center of the roundabout were three white minivans, rear doors flung open, megaphones and cabinet speakers lashed to their roofs. Around each van stood a clutch of young men in hooded sweatshirts and red knit hats.

We pushed our way across Place Graslin toward the opera house steps, where we'd get the best view of the chaos, and after a solid ten minutes of bobbing and weaving, we'd gained a position on the pillared platform of the opera house. I watched the spectacle in awe, feeling the noise deep in my chest and combing the crowd below for signs of Léo. Patrick's hash had helped my hangover settle into one of those sporadic headaches—painful, but not as bad as I'd anticipated. Though I had a hard time following what the guy on the mic by the minivans was carrying on about, I found myself getting riled up anyway, cheering and pumping my fists with Patrick and the others.

Eventually I spotted Léo. He was down in the center of the

roundabout, his big purple scarf draped around his neck like a pet snake. He and several others were standing near the minivans and handing flyers out into the crowd. I watched as a tall, olive-skinned kid pushed his way toward Léo and said something into his ear. After that Léo seemed to be giving him instructions, pointing back toward the vans. It made me chuckle to think of Léo in charge of others, but only because he'd mostly related to me with his poor English, which made him sound like a kid with a third-grade education. I wondered how old I seemed to people like Patrick and Julien.

Soon the demonstrators started clearing out. I stayed with Patrick a few minutes more, then said my good-byes and headed over to the central tram station at Boulevard Cinquantes Otages.

SOLÈNE AND HER friend Elise were exactly where Solène said they would be, in a smelly hipster café called Rhythm with a girl named Melanie. After some awkward cheek kisses with all three, I ordered a beer and for the next few minutes deeply regretted coming. Patrick's hash hadn't quite worn off. I was having a hell of a time forming slick sentences in French. And more than once, as the four of us blundered through small talk, I caught Solène watching me. I even noticed the waiter, who looked about my age, giving me the raised eyebrow. It put me on the defensive. Just because I was hanging out with students outside of class, it didn't mean I was up to risky business. And Solène wasn't even a minor—last fall in the cafeteria, she'd made it perfectly clear to me that she'd already turned eighteen. Anyway, it didn't matter to me, and I didn't care if it mattered to anyone else.

The soccer stadium loomed over an enormous crammed parking lot at the easternmost stop of the east-west tram. Even before we'd reached the turnstiles, I could feel the skin-quivering rumble of the soccer fans' cheers. I followed Solène past the roaring squads of riled-up soccer fans and up to our seats, and for the better part of the first half I sat still, drinking in the mad spectacle.

Even though the game was far more intense than the *manif* in *centre ville,* I found myself mingling the two events in my mind, imagining we'd all come here to blow off the steam we'd built up in town. During a break in the action, Solène recounted the fierce rivalry between the two teams, and while she spoke I had to lean in close to hear her. Her breath smelled like cinnamon and beer. She was wearing more eye makeup than usual. I noticed how blue her irises were, shot through with streaks of gold. I could see the brown roots of her hair. She dyed it blond and wore a slender gold chain around her neck that held a charm of a heart the size of a raindrop.

"You can't wait to tell the class that you got the American assistant to come here," I said.

She shook her head and smiled. "It could be a secret, if you wanted."

Finally she looked me in the eyes and stayed there until the moment grew heavy. Then something happened down on the field, and around us the crowd erupted. We all stood.

A player had broken free and was dribbling the ball into a clearing toward the goalkeeper. The player with the ball shuffled it from one foot to the other, then fired it over the keeper's hands into the goal. I threw up my hands and cheered, and right away everyone nearby, including Solène and her friends, turned on me with betrayal in their eyes. I sat down fast, realizing that I'd cheered for the visiting team.

After that, the home team started taking a shameful beating, allowing two more goals, both of which, as best I could guess from the looks everyone was giving me, were entirely my fault.

At halftime, Solène and I headed down to the lower levels for beers. We tried sneaking into the pricey seats, but got caught and retreated up the walkway to a balcony that overlooked the multitude of cars in the parking lot. I told Solène about the Caps Olympics, and she shook her head, grinning as if she herself had been burned by the game plenty. We smoked cigarettes and wound up talking about Corbières. Then, after making fun of several of her profs, she fed me the dirt on some of the boys in our class, and our conversation landed on Léo. When I asked about his running around with these local political groups, she acted uneasy with the topic, saying something about Léo's big heart, his passion for social change. Which I had plenty of respect for, I told her. I also told her how he always came at me sideways, as if he had something to fight with me about.

Solène blushed. "Here's the thing," she said in French. "I think Léo likes me. Not just as a friend, if you know what I mean. To me he's a good friend, a very good friend—but nothing more. He's gotten really involved in this political fundraising group lately."

"What kind of fundraising?"

"You know, all sorts of things." Solène looked away. "I used to help them out—all things through the school, though."

"That's cool," I said. "Is it just students, or are there *surveillants* and profs helping out too?"

"Depends," she said. "Some profs help. You know M. Dreyfus? He helps, I've heard."

I said nothing to that at first. "Doing what? He's a strange one."

Her eyes flashed to mine and she smiled. "Yeah. It's all that hair, I think. He's nice enough."

I was already impressed by how easily she and I were talking, now that we were alone—we moved in and out of English naturally, more easily even than Françoise and I did. I bought us another round of beers, nursing mine and wishing halftime wouldn't end. Still some guilty part of me was overly conscious of the fact that I was Solène's teacher. Whatever fondness I felt toward her, I knew, whatever hint of attraction there was, would have to stay at arm's length. She was just a kid.

ON THE TRAM back into the city, Solène and I squeezed in close to each other. The second half of the game had been a drag, and Elise and Melanie had taken off early, after the visiting team had scored another two goals. For several stops, Solène watched me and I pretended I didn't notice.

Finally she said, "You could walk me home. My house is near the stop."

"It's a dangerous neighborhood?"

"No—but you could meet my father."

It wasn't the fishiest offer I'd gotten in France, but it was definitely top five. I scrambled for a clever excuse.

"Your father wouldn't want me to show up uninvited."

"He is not like other fathers," she said. "He's quite interested in foreigners, too."

I knew I could refuse and get away with it. But I was feeling just loose enough now to meet a student's dad—aside from Paul and Juliet, Lucien's parents, I'd met none.

"Just come and have a beer with him," she said. "You can practice your French."

I gave her a nervous smile, trying to figure whether she'd take it the wrong way if I said no.

"Fine," she said. "It is a very dangerous neighborhood—horrible and dangerous."

She laid a killer smile on me as the tram slowed for her stop, and at the last second I climbed off with her. We cut south into a well-manicured neighborhood of town houses and brick apartment buildings, lacquered mailboxes and big plastic trash cans at the ends of the driveways. The cold air was making dreamy yellow halos around the streetlights, and as if some unspoken agreement had passed between us, our hands touched, and then our fingers laced together, innocently, as naturally as if we'd known each other for ages.

SOLÈNE'S DAD, THIERRY, was a tough-looking guy in his late fifties with a stiff smile, thin black hair that reached his shoulders, and the thick neck of a weight lifter. After a sturdy handshake and a deep look in the eyes, he led me through the short entryway into their living room, where stacks of newspapers and magazines lay strewn over the couches and floor. He went to the kitchen and came back with a beer for Solène and a Calvados apiece for us. Then he invited us out to the back patio for a smoke.

After a bout of small talk, Thierry complimented my French, a formality I'd already learned to distrust. But Thierry wasn't using an accent typical of the region; his was tricky, jumbled and nuanced, like Bruno's at the Rougerie. When I told him that I lived in west *centre ville*, Thierry grew suddenly interested.

"You catch any of that so-called *manif* earlier this afternoon?"

"Funny you ask," I said. "I joined in."

He gave me a suspicious look, as if I'd just said something wrong.

"I went with some friends," I explained. "Not the best of reasons, I suppose."

"And what would be the best of reasons, M. Delanne?"

"I don't know. Opposition to French involvement in a crooked war."

Thierry stroked his chin and muttered something I didn't catch. I asked him to repeat it, but missed his meaning again the second time.

Solène translated for me: "He says that sometimes such things may be organized for good reasons, but not by good people. It's a French proverb. He likes very much *les aphorisms*."

Thierry smiled at her, nodding as if he'd understood and approved.

"That's true," I said in French. "Though the opposite may be true as well—bad reasons, good people—right?"

Thierry smiled again and nodded, though I couldn't be sure if he was humoring me or just showing his appreciation for wordplay. He looked nothing like a language lover; he had the thick, callused hands of a man more invested in his muscle than in his mind. His weathered T-shirt and blue jeans, like his accent, also gave off a blue-collar vibe, though he had an intense, somewhat insane look to his eyes, as if he were troubled in the psychological sense.

When the conversation went dead, Thierry turned off the patio lights and gazed up at the night sky. Solène watched him closely, and the bond between them seemed to radiate in the darkness. Solène said something about the bathroom and went inside. Without missing a beat, Thierry turned on me.

"You are my first American, M. Delanne."

"To do what?"

"Not to do—to speak with me. I've never said more than a few words to one."

I tried to separate the way his words sounded from the way he'd said them. He didn't seem half as uncomfortable as I was.

After an uneasy silence, I said, "So what do you think? Am I *that* different?"

He shook his head and gazed back up at the stars.

"You're aware that Americans are not very popular in France right now, aren't you?"

"Sure." I wondered where he was headed. "Some Americans aren't very popular with Americans right now, either."

He chuckled. "You've learned good French, M. Delanne. I say this sincerely."

I asked him to call me Jeffrey. We sipped our Calvados and smoked. I glanced through the patio doors into the kitchen. Solène was on the phone.

"I have a confession." Thierry's tone suddenly changed. "Solène talks about you very much . . . and I asked to meet you personally."

I froze, dreading what I imagined would come next: *Keep your dirty American hands off my daughter,* or *If you ever hurt her . . .* both of which I'd suffered through plenty in high school and was not eager to hear again. But Thierry was winding up for something else.

"I owe you a warning," he said, looking me hard in the eyes. "As an employee at Corbières."

Now I could read his expression better. He was genuinely concerned.

"I have a number of friends," he started to say. But his whole manner of speech had changed. He was speaking very slowly now, watching me carefully as if to make certain I was following every syllable. "I mean to say that I know men who know many things, Jeffrey. I worked as a detective for thirty years. It is not my job anymore, but I have kept certain . . . acquaintances."

My heartbeat rose into my ears. "I don't understand," I managed.

"You spoke of attending this so-called *manifestation* today in *centre ville*," he explained. "And I've no doubt that your motives were innocent. But you must not assume that the motives of others—the people in charge of staging such spectacles, for example—are as innocent as yours. In fact, it would be a big mistake to assume that much."

He moved closer and lowered his voice. "It would likewise be grave to assume, Jeffrey, that even your students are entirely innocent or naïve. Certainly you know that Corbières is special in Ste-Térèse because its *proviseur*, Georges Brule, is running for National Assembly—and because he supports this new business of replacing student *surveillants*. He is almost certain to win, and many parties in France are anxious about it. But what you may not know is that this puts special national focus on this part of the region— on this city, and on your school."

After a minute of painful silence, I said, "I still don't see what this has to do with me."

"It would take much too long for me to explain it all. I only wish to warn you, Jeffrey. Not everything in Ste-Térèse is as it seems. Be very careful during these times. This city is full of dark corners. Some people at Corbières are playing with big trouble. Some students, even, have been misled into believing that their futures depend upon one political movement or another—you'd be surprised how far some would go when they feel that their futures depend on it."

When he said that, I took a sudden accidental gulp of air. In the dark, with his thin black hair falling over his neck like a hood, Thierry looked a lot like a devil.

"It would also be convenient," Thierry said, "for certain interested parties to have a foreigner—an American, especially—upon whom they might pin their, might we say, evil deeds."

My vision swam several quick laps. Did Thierry show this much concern for every foreigner he met in Ste-Térèse, or had he somehow smelled Nabec on me? I remembered the Mercedes I thought I'd seen the night before, and at once I was sure of it: the image looming there in my memory was real—Nabec had sent for me again.

Then came a flood of frantic thoughts. How I might be prosecuted in a French court of law. How I'd gotten into trouble writing bad checks in Arizona. How that poor Brit bastard had pleaded with me. How I'd watched Nabec's goon wallop him, and how, in the residual daze, I'd taken Nabec's money for it. For a terrible grinding instant, I was ready to tell Thierry everything. But no. Absolutely not. There was no way Thierry needed to know about it—he was talking about something else altogether.

"I'm not talking particulars," Thierry said. He seemed now to be watching me closely. "I just have a nose for these kinds of things. And friends. That's all I'm saying. Don't be surprised if someone comes to you, let us say, with a proposition, and asks if you wouldn't like to be involved. Even something as straightforward as a *manifestation*. I want you to stay out of trouble, Jeffrey. These aren't the best of times to be a foreigner in France. Especially an American."

We were studying each other's eyes when Solène joined us again. She'd changed into a pair of purple pajama pants and a tattered gray sweatshirt.

"You're not still talking about that *manif,* are you?"

"No, not at all," Thierry said. "I was just telling your friend here that if he ever needed help, he should call me." He reached into his pocket and handed me his business card: THIERRY DUVIN, it said. CONSULTING.

"Those were going to be my next words," he added. "That you should call me, before anyone else, if something happens."

"Don't scare him, Dad," Solène said. "He doesn't have any reason to be afraid, nothing bad is going to happen to him."

"No, of course not. This is just in case. He sees that—right, Jeffrey?"

I nodded and tried to smile.

"And now I'll say good night," Thierry said, stepping to the patio door. "It was very nice to meet you, M. Delanne. Is this name not French?"

"No," I said. "Though my great-grandfather—"

"Please come by for dinner sometime. I make a mean beef tartar."

He shook my hand and went inside. I spent a jittery minute standing in silence with Solène.

"I've got to go," I said.

"He does not mean to scare you, Jeffrey. It is just his—how do you say?—his habit. He is a sort of police. Retired police. Sometimes he takes things too seriously."

I nodded, but could feel the nerves twisting up in my face.

"Not at all," I said. "I actually enjoyed talking with him—he's a cool guy. I'm just exhausted. I had a horrible hangover earlier. I've got to get some sleep."

I didn't care whether or not it sounded convincing. I needed to go somewhere secluded and rinse my mind of Nabec. And I needed to stop thinking about that Mercedes.

Solène followed me inside. "He likes you. I can tell."

"Oh, I like him too. And I had a good time at the soccer thing. I'll see you in class, okay?"

At the front door she gave me the kind of penetrating gaze that sometimes turns into a hug. But even though we'd made a strong connection earlier, I stepped away from her, mumbling a good-bye in one language or another and hurrying out the front door into the cold.

AS IF I HAD TWO MINDS

I holed up in my apartment all the next day, feeding myself heavy doses of cognac and the blues. I knew Thierry couldn't be wise to what I'd done for Nabec. But I couldn't shake the paranoia he'd planted in my head. If only I hadn't gone to meet Thierry, I kept telling myself. But what would that have changed? The problem still lay festering before me. I couldn't deny that I'd seen that Mercedes parked up the street after Julien's party, and I couldn't escape the horrible dread of seeing that Mercedes again—Nabec wasn't through with me yet.

Monday's classes sloughed by, and of course my students wouldn't participate. In the halls between classes, kids I didn't even know seemed to be giving me scornful glances, pointing and whispering as I passed. All day long the profs' room was abuzz about the forecasted *manif* this coming weekend, an even bigger demonstration that would explicitly protest Brule's right-wing, pro-nationalist political party.

It wasn't until Tuesday morning that life at Corbières took a sharp turn.

It was about a quarter till eight, still half dark on Rue Corbières.

I rounded the corner to find more than half the lycée standing outside, the street so congested that the school's front entrance was blocked. I started pushing through the crowd, thinking it was just some malicious early-morning fire drill. But halfway to the front doors I saw a white minivan parked at the cross street. A couple of heavy police-style blockades barred the lycée's front entrance, and behind the blockades a handful of older kids wearing red knit hats and goatees stood on a little makeshift rostrum. All around them the lycée kids seemed to bounce with excitement. As I wove my way through, handfuls of blue flyers traveled back into the shuffling crowd. Lucien, Paul's son, was standing near the front. I pushed up beside him and grabbed his arm.

"What's going on? Am I supposed to stay out here with the students?"

"Pas de classe," he said. *"C'est la grève jusqu'à neuve heures."*

By *grève* he meant a French-style boycott—not exactly a *manif,* but not a parade either. I still couldn't see how a band of teens led by some charged-up university kids could legally hold off lycée classes for a full hour. I asked Lucien who the guys were at the entrance.

"Former *surveillants,*" Lucien said. "The law goes into effect today. They lost their posts."

Léo's skinny head was moving toward me through the crowd, his long purple scarf wrapped around his throat. He looked perturbed. When we reached each other, he handed me a flyer.

"Come on," he said without looking me in the eyes. "They'll probably let you inside."

"Hey, I saw you handing out flyers at the *manif,*" I told him. "I didn't know you were helping the organizers."

His eyes caught mine. "Not really." He gave me a wary look after that, as if I'd let some sworn secret out of the bag. "Just with little stuff, nothing really."

I followed Léo up to the blockades, where one of the ex-

surveillants asked for my ID. I showed it, but only after Léo mumbled something to him did he pull back a blockade for me.

In the profs' room, everyone was standing around with blue flyers. Paul, whom I hadn't had a chance to talk with since his dinner party—since the night I'd ridden out to see Nabec—was hobnobbing with a few other profs at the other end of the big oak table.

"Think of all this as a formality, Jeffrey," Paul told me, once I'd made it over to him. "Something that simply must happen."

I could usually count on Paul to give me the lowdown on local and national politics. He was a good-natured but frustrated politician at heart, and he had a gifted, inspiring way with words, though you couldn't guess it at a glance. His lips were large and clumsy. Atop the arch of his nose was an exceptional eyeglass trench, which with his glasses off gave a botched-makeup impression, and more often than not he wore a perplexed look, as if in his long hours of reading he'd reached a state not of enlightenment but of mystification. He was also one of the shrewdest, friendliest men I had ever known, and even though he tended to preach, I felt I could trust him like family.

He showed me a few key phrases on the flyer and told me that as newly laid-off employees of the city's lycées, the *surveillants* were within their rights to boycott. They'd chosen Corbières first, on account of Brule, its *proviseur,* a position somewhere between superintendent and city councilman.

"This *surveillant* business is only the tip of the iceberg," Paul added. "Brule's party supports drastic antiterrorist and national security legislation. They also have little concern for minorities and immigrants, and practically none at all for the Arab question."

I'd crossed paths with Brule maybe twice. He kept an office adjacent to the main lycée office, but was probably there only two or three days out of the week. He was an intimidating, statuesque figure with silver hair, a bronze face, and the kind of Zeus-like gaze that assured you he was willing to devour your soul, if matched with a suitable Bourgogne. I asked him why Brule didn't just shut down the boycott, if he had so much pull in the city.

"Let's just say that Brule is craftier than he looks," Paul said. "Playing along keeps votes. And keeps enemies at bay."

I thought about what Solène's dad had said about Corbières and its students. I wondered how many enemies Brule had right here on his own territory. Françoise, with whom I usually had coffee on Wednesday mornings, appeared suddenly beside me, looking as if she'd slept on the floor of the smoking room overnight.

"Change in this country happens slowly," said Françoise. "Often when your back is turned—so watch your back closely."

"How is everyone so sure he'll be elected to Parliament?" I said.

"It's a powerful party he's in," said Françoise. "And some people think he's a sort of hero, because he's taking a bold stance on national security. But these people don't know what bloody awful laws will be passed if Brule and a few others in his party win seats this year. They don't know what liberties they stand to lose, you see, or what will happen to private business, among other things. Anyway, they certainly don't know that he's a bloody fascist."

Paul bit his lip. "Jeffrey doesn't need to hear that."

Françoise said, "Of course he does, that's nonsense. Of course he does."

I watched the two of them exchange narrow looks. When Paul checked his watch and excused himself, Françoise dragged me into the smoking room, which was crammed with profs leaning against the teaching assistants' lockers and huddled around the espresso machine. Françoise explained to me in English that what she said was not necessarily common knowledge in the community: when he was younger, Brule had worked as an administrator in a highly selective national security division of the government. His move to the education sphere, she claimed, was strictly political and had worked well to win him an enormous voice in both Ste-Térèse and the Loire region, districts handpicked by his party, which included other ex–National Police bigwigs, men who'd forged long-term ties with outside governmental agencies.

"Why doesn't everybody know this?" I asked.

"Not everyone in France reads the news as closely as they'd have you believe, Jeffrey. Ask Patrick about it sometime, if you're ready for an earful. He knows all about Brule's history, his views on antiterrorist legislation, even his stance on private business, I'd wager. Enough to blow your mind."

THE *GRÈVE* BROKE up at about ten minutes after eight, and I spent the nine-o'clock hour trying to channel my kids' energy toward conversations in English about the strange event. I used the same routine during my eleven-o'clock, but found myself either fighting for their attention or shouting at them to wake up. About midway through that class, I lost my cool with one of the boys in front, who'd fallen asleep and had made an impressive drool puddle on his notebook.

"Come on, people," I said. "It's not like I can cancel class just because school got boycotted for ten minutes."

Léo raised his hand. "M. Henri cancel za class."

"M. Henri has a contract that runs the rest of his life," I said. "And he's French."

At that they all started whispering to one another, until Margot, a typically cooperative girl who was always drawing deranged flowers on her hand, threw me a curveball: "Would it not show the appreciation for French culture to do as the French do?" she asked.

A smattering of giggles in back. But Margot didn't look like she was joking, and Léo was glaring at me now as if I'd betrayed not just his homeland but his family's religion.

When the bell rang, I nixed the homework I'd planned and packed up my stuff as fast as I could. Solène was waiting out in the hall. Her eyes looked washed-out, her face pale and tired. She spent long hours with books, I knew. I admired that.

"What's up?"

"I'm sorry I didn't stop them," she said.

I tried to act as if I understood what she was talking about. "It's okay."

"No," she said. "It's not. Before you came in, they were talking about giving you trouble. Purposely. I don't know why Léo says the things he says." She hesitated a moment. "I think those guys he's been helping out do not like you. Or Americans with jobs in France. Or something."

I gave her a confused look, figuring I'd heard her wrong. What the hell did Léo's protest buddies care about me? I was working for peanuts as a temporary foreign assistant.

"Just don't tell him I said anything," she said then. "My brain isn't right today, I should have stopped them. Sometimes I feel as if I had two minds."

I gave her a big accidental smile: she couldn't have worded my own problem more precisely. It struck me as highly ironic, too, that I'd found such a kindred spirit in a student. She was a kid, sure, but she seemed to have an understanding beyond her years. I imagined her father, Thierry, had taught her that rare youthful self-determination. I'd spotted a strong resemblance, the same steadfast honesty in Thierry's eyes, and now again I found myself tangled up between attraction and guilt.

"Let's just forget it," I said.

She nodded and took off, and I watched her walk away, feeling as if she'd just stolen something from me, though I couldn't say what that was.

IN THE SMOKING room, I stashed some books in my locker and found two handwritten notes. One was from Paul: in the confusion, it said, he'd forgotten to invite me to see a small local production of a play with him and Lucien that Saturday. The other note wasn't addressed or signed: *Did I say or do something to deserve the silent treatment? Waited for you yesterday . . . now I leave it to you.*

No doubt the second note was from the needy Sicilian hand of Amelia. I'd caught her creeping into Corbières before—she was friends with Rigoberto, our Spanish assistant from Paraguay, who'd worked at Lycée Dubois, where she now worked as an Italian assistant, two years prior.

I'd always been confused by Amelia's loneliness. She was a pleasure to behold—short but nicely proportioned, brunette and very young, with a pair of dazzling green eyes and faint patches of freckles on her cheeks. She shouldn't have had any trouble finding attention elsewhere. It was her third year in Ste-Térèse, and while she'd made lots of friends over at Dubois, most of them were students a few years younger than she. The one and only night I'd kissed her, she'd told me that she wasn't into younger guys. She'd also said that she had a thing for Americans.

AFTER LUNCH I slipped out through the front doors of the lycée and fired up, watching the students come and go and trying to remember when I'd stopped caring, when the satisfaction of instilling knowledge in young people had dried up. I wondered why I'd ever imagined that I could be of any service to them, and I realized what this kind of thinking meant: I needed to find a new line of work.

But more than that, I needed to figure out how to stay clear of the work I'd done for Nabec. I needed to do something more than just sit around and hope it would go away. Problem was, I didn't know what that something more should be.

I finished my cigarette and lit another, and before that one was half gone, I saw a short white man with a dark frizzy Afro cross Rue Corbières, round the corner, and head up Rue Gigant away from the lycée. He had on a wrinkled gray trench coat and was packing a brown leather satchel: Dreyfus in the flesh.

I took it as a revelation, and took off after him.

At the end of that block, Dreyfus went right toward Boulevard Le Clerc, heading south at a fast clip. I broke into a jog, and by the time I reached the corner and was sure I was within earshot, I yelled Dreyfus's name. He didn't turn back but crossed the boulevard, doubling his pace.

I doubled mine, following him south on the other side of the wide boulevard. At the next plaza he veered east again. I crossed to his side of the street, and soon we were approaching Place Malraux, just up and over from the bustling Place Graslin. I ran full-tilt to Place Graslin and saw Dreyfus enter a pack of pedestrians, making his way around the rim of the roundabout. By now I was sweating like a fugitive, but too close to let him give me the slip.

When I saw a break in the roundabout traffic, I ran for it again, dodging three lanes of traffic and cutting across the grassy center of Place Graslin. I reached the other side of the roundabout and yelled his name.

This time he stopped, turned, and looked straight at me from across the street. There were three lanes between us, cars whipping past. I could see him, and I knew he could see me. I waved my arms over my head. But his expression remained ice-cold, almost dumbfounded, as if he were a blind man looking at the shadow of a ghost.

When there was another break in traffic I hurried across. But Dreyfus wasn't anywhere in sight. The S-21 Gare bus was pulling off beside me to my left. To my right, the glass front door of a little boulangerie was closing behind someone in gray. I checked in the boulangerie and the tiny *tabac* shop next to it: no Dreyfus.

But now I was ready to chase that bastard all the way to hell.

A cab had pulled up where the S-21 bus had been. A woman in a black fur coat climbed out and I jumped into the backseat before she could get the door closed. The S-21 had made it a full block now and was signaling left. I got out a twenty-euro bill and waved it at the driver.

"*Suivi cet autobus,*" I said. "*C'est le S-21, au Gare. Vite, s'il vous plaît. Vite!*"

The driver gave me an amused look. *"Ce n'est pas un film, monsieur,"* he said. *"Je peut vous ramener quelque part, mais c'est tout—c'est pas un film, tu vois?"*

"Just do it!" I said, tossing the twenty into the front seat.

We followed the S-21, though not very closely. As we neared the train station I felt a flood of bitterness toward Dreyfus, the slippery son of a bitch. Why would he ignore me on purpose?

In the station's front parking lot, I flung open the cab door, leaped out, and pushed my way past a row of people waiting to board the S-21. The bus driver started shouting at me, but I climbed on anyway and inspected his bus. There were maybe ten passengers still on board, but no Dreyfus.

In the train station lobby, some few hundred people were trying to get around one another, lining up at ticket machines and blocking a clear passage to the train platforms. I cursed aloud—it'd be impossible to check every platform.

I stepped out into the cold, cursing Dreyfus. I'd just lost my only chance at getting a straight answer. And blown twenty euros.

I HEADED WEST toward my neighborhood on foot, passing the *médiathèque* and hiking up to Place Théâtre. I peeked into the windows of the Rougerie, but the only guy I recognized besides Bruno was Michel, whose anti-American bullshit I wasn't ready to contend with.

Then, as if misfortune had smelled my failure and decided to go double or nothing, I came around the corner and saw it idling in front of my building: a black Mercedes sedan.

My thoughts scattered, then landed in one pile: *Run for it.*

I headed fast around my side of Place Théâtre toward the Marché Plus, fighting the urge to look back, and kept moving down the street toward Place Graslin. The air had grown colder and the streetlights had begun to blink on. There were enough people on the street that if Nabec's goons tried to force me into the car, I could make a big scene. But I barred the thought—I couldn't let myself think that way. Not yet.

Anyway I didn't need to look back—I could feel that Mercedes rolling down the street behind me.

I remembered an Australian pub called Le Boomerang, just down the street at Graslin, which had a back patio that opened onto an alley.

I crossed the street and against my better judgment finally glanced back: four cars were waiting to enter the roundabout, the last one a black sedan.

My stomach pitched. I ducked into Le Boomerang and hurried around back and up a few steps to the patio doors. The doors leading out were locked.

The barman was behind the boomerang-shaped bar, stacking pint glasses in tall rows beside a giant Jagermeister dispenser. I asked him in French if I could take a beer out on the patio.

"Patio's closed," he said in Anglo-French, without even looking up.

I glanced out the front doors, the windows of which were too darkly tinted for me to see through. There were five others at the bar. Two small groups on the upper level in back. Everyone with imperial pints of pale beer. I bought a Foster's and moved with it to the back edge of the bar and closed my eyes. Gradually my heartbeat slowed. It was over. They had me cornered. Even if they didn't come in for me, even if I bellied up here until closing, they'd still intercept me outside my place.

I guzzled the beer and bought another. I started thinking about riding out to see Nabec, giving him a final, unequivocal no. But at the thought of sitting with him, listening to his reasoning, his eloquent voice, his intense way with words . . . I knew I had to resist. A sudden rush of nervous energy started twirling at the base of my skull and moved down to my shoulders and arms.

I sucked down a cigarette and realized that I was clenching my fists and mumbling aloud. The barman was watching me. He said something my way in English.

"Huh?" My eyes fastened on the man's large black eyebrows. Had he said my name?

"You all right?" His accent was more British than Australian.

"Yeah. Don't mind me." It felt strange speaking English outside of the classroom. I couldn't figure why it hadn't felt as strange with the Brit out at Nabec's cottage.

The barman glanced at my pack of smokes. I pushed the pack across the bar, and he took one and fired up. An old Bob Dylan song about being stuck in Mobile had come on the jukebox. Right now I would have traded a vital organ to be stuck somewhere else, even Alabama.

I looked down and realized I was wringing one fist hard against the other. The barman was eyeing me again. I waved him over.

"Here's my problem," I said. "I met this girl. A Sicilian, if you know what I mean."

The barman's bushy eyebrows rose with his smile. "I know *quite* what you mean."

"Long story short," I said, pointing to the front door. "I can't go out that way."

He nodded again, still grinning. "Why don't you say so the first time, mate?"

I asked him if there was a phone. He pointed over to the wall by the front doors. I went over, inserted my phone card, and typed in Françoise's home number—she lived nearby, and I was willing to bet she'd help me without needing too many details. But there was no answer. I cursed, put down the phone, and tried again. Again no answer.

My second beer was only half gone, but I felt a nagging urge to make a move. I was close enough to the front doors to see out the windows, and I couldn't see any black Mercedes. It was too risky to call Paul, I knew—he'd want to know the details, and I wasn't ready for that. I decided I'd have to show up at Françoise's apartment unannounced.

As I passed back through the bar I gave the barman a nod. He followed me up to the upper level with a big ring of keys and opened the patio door.

"I owe you one, mate," I said. He grinned and locked me out.

I crept across the patio and down the narrow stairs into the alley. The Mercedes was idling in the dark alleyway with its lights off, maybe six yards to my right.

My stomach seized. A thickset man in a black suit came around the car. He opened the back door and gestured inside, as if we'd arranged to meet in this dingy, narrow space between one street and another—as if I hadn't just run from him.

"He requests your presence," he said in French. "It is quite urgent."

"I don't *quite* give a shit," I said. "Take my phone number. Tell him to call me."

He gave me a blank stare, then slowly shook his head. I stepped away from him toward the alley entrance. Another goon entered the alley from the street and stopped, blocking my way. He had a wooden cane with a brass handle as big as a doorknob. His little eyes were aimed directly at my chest, his expression as steady as stone.

"This is fucked up," I managed. I stepped back toward the bar patio.

"Le Monsieur sends his apologies," the one with the cane said.

"Fuck that, this isn't right."

His partner took another cautious step my way. The one with the cane raised his weapon.

"There is no other choice," he said. "This is what he wants me to say."

YOU WILL FIND IT
NOWHERE

Nabec was wearing a silk pin-striped suit with a beige tie and a pair of gold cuff links that I was ready to bet could cover my student loans. As before, his hair was neatly combed, his face immaculately shaven, his expression calm, contemplative, and cool. Behind him stood the same broad-armed bodyguard. But this time in the corner of the room lay an assortment of power tools and piles of chair-railing and crown molding and such. The place smelled a little like lumber and freshly cut wood, an odor I'd loved until now.

As soon as I sat down, Nabec slid a cigar from his pocket, lopped off the tip with a gold cigar clipper, and situated the extravagant thing between his lips. He poured us each a Porto, pushed a glass to me, and rotated the cigar three times before his bodyguard stepped up and torched its business end. Once the smoke cleared, I caught Nabec's eyes studying mine.

"This has got to be the last time," I said, more out of discomfort than courage.

"Sure, Jeffrey. If you wish it to be."

"I do." I hesitated. "But how . . . how can I be sure of that?" I stopped and steadied my breath, marshaling all my nerve. "And why am I being brought out here against my will?"

Nabec took the cigar from his mouth. "You can be sure of what I tell you, Jeffrey, because I am telling you it. And you've been brought when you have because I have needed you at these times. As I told you before, fear will only distract you. Soon our business here will be finished."

I realized that I was clenching my fists. "I've just got to know that this ends tonight."

Even as I said it, my guts coiled. Nabec didn't answer. He puffed his cigar and watched me for a long minute.

"*Qu'est ce que l'expression americain,*" he said finally, "om ease where you ang za hat?"

He was just changing the subject. But I sensed that the old man was insecure about his English. And I wasn't eager to find out how easily those insecurities could turn to malice. Anyway, I knew what it was like to be sensitive about speaking another language, even if I had a far better handle on his than he had on mine.

"Not bad," I said in French. "It means that home isn't a lofty idea. It means that home . . . that home is a practical reality."

He puffed his cigar and let his eyes move to the ceiling. "I like this expression. I heard it yesterday in an American film. I listened to the phrase several times, searched my dictionaries, yet its meaning still escaped me . . . but *a practical reality,* I see, yes . . . though I myself have no lofty ideas about home, none at all."

He lowered his eyes onto mine. There was something new there now, something almost sad.

"You see, Jeffrey—" He hesitated, glancing at his bodyguard. "My parents were murdered when I was very young. I was sent to boarding school in Switzerland and was never at home, really."

For the first time his words sounded clumsy in his own mouth. It was as if he'd never confessed such a thing in his life. I took my eyes from him and sipped my Porto.

"Then your home is where you keep your things, your daily stuff," I said, still not wanting to set him off. "Home is wherever you're most comfortable. Wherever you hang your hat."

Nabec grinned. "I wear no hats, Jeffrey."

He refilled my glass, this time pouring the rich crimson liquid to the brim.

"You regard the United States as your home, do you not?" he asked.

I thought hard about that. He was asking me to confide, as he had.

"Sure," I said. "I grew up there. My parents, they're divorced, but they still live there. They raised me there. I guess it's more of a home than anywhere else."

"And why did you leave, Jeffrey? If you don't mind my asking."

I did mind his asking. But only because I wasn't sure anymore of the answer.

"I don't know. To experience another culture. To improve my French. I don't know."

When our eyes met again, I realized that I was lying—and that he sensed it.

"That's not true," I said. "I'd lost my connection with it. I'd lost my perspective. And I was looking for a new one. An older one, you know, one that maybe came before the one I was raised to have. But it wasn't my home. Not like it was for everybody else. It was just a convenience, and I knew it. I don't know how it happened to me . . . I guess I don't wear hats either."

We drank in silence. A minute afterward, I'd almost forgotten where I was.

"Cigarette?" Nabec asked. When I nodded, his bodyguard placed a pack of Philip Morris Lights on the table and left the room.

"Home is where we are protected from those who wish to harm us," Nabec said, once his man had shut the door. "Nowhere else. And there is no home without freedom. In this sense, home is the condition of absolute freedom, is it not? It is a condition man can only create for himself. This is where politics becomes complicated. For businessmen, freedom of this sort comes at a high cost, just as the freedom to speak, and the freedom to know the truth, for most, have come at the cost of revolution and sacrifice—of murder. But I give little preference to one *nation* or another, Jeffrey. Nations, corporations, universities—all these are businesses. Do not let them fool you. They make homes for themselves at the cost of excluding others, hiding truths, and killing.

"What I mean to say is that with me, you would always have freedom and protection," he concluded. "Even if it doesn't seem so. As long as you are loyal to me. As long as you tell me the truth."

It was an invitation to cross a line, clear enough. And for a moment, the notion of such a place seemed awesome, even as my better instincts resisted; aside from the tools and lumber piled behind him, aside from the table in front of us and the unfinished room where we sat, we seemed to be in some barren, stripped-down state of exile, far away from the hang-ups of civilization, free to choose our own boundaries, free to speak and act exactly as we wished.

I was wrong, of course. Later I'd realize just how much. I'd gone in there mentally unprepared, unarmed, totally vulnerable. But in the moment, as I sat before him and searched his dark eyes, I felt my own reasoning veer wide, rationalizing, grasping for ways to explain my own dark impulses. He was so much older, after all, so seasoned in the ways of the world. And what did I really know of the legitimacy of foreign governments, of foreign businesses, of foreign laws? What did I know of morality, outside of the country where I'd absorbed a particular sense of it, outside of what I felt in my gut, which in that moment was abandoning me, pulling my mind in two directions at once?

My hands shook in my lap. Nabec took his eyes from me and for a long moment seemed lost in thought. I imagined he was trying to remember what it was like to be younger, to be as conflicted as I was—what it was like before he himself had crossed that line, before he'd discovered what it was like to be absolutely free.

"I cannot help you with your beliefs about right and wrong," Nabec said then. "But know this: we live in worlds that we create for ourselves, and none other—worlds governed by our own actions, by our own declarations of freedom. All else is illusion. If it is prison that you fear, or death, then stop fearing this instant. Loyalty in my business, Jeffrey, is repaid by loyalty, which is more than we can always say for the business of governments, is it not?"

Right away part of me said *yes . . . but no!* All of this was beside the point. Even if I understood him, even if he was half right, I had to resist. He'd forced me to come here, after all, and now he dared to talk about things like freedom in absolute terms.

"What do you want from me?" I asked.

Nabec leaned forward. "A name. My client in the next room knows of a name. I want you to persuade him to tell you it. And I want you to go to him and do it alone."

I kept my eyes from his. Even if I said no, I realized, he'd still make me do it. He only wanted to give me the illusion of choice.

"And what if . . . what if he won't tell me it?" I asked.

Nabec smiled, lowering his eyes. "What you will find, Jeffrey, is that the fear of pain, with cunning yet intimidated men such as these, motivates more than pain itself."

I hesitated again, finding my voice at first unwilling. "And then you'll let me go? For good?"

"Yes, Jeffrey. Then, if you wish, I will send for you no more."

The next question on my mind was the obvious one: *And what if I say no?* But I was too afraid to cross that line with him, too scared to break the illusion he'd tried to create. I guzzled what was left of my Porto and stood.

Nabec stopped me before I could make it out the door.

"Use caution, Jeffrey," he said. "This man is both a traitor and a liar. The name he knows he will not wish to tell. Remember that he does not know what I know. Only I know the larger picture, only I can know what to do with the smaller pieces as I gather them. And so, for you, it is essential that you learn to sort this man's truth from his lies."

We exchanged a long, terrible gaze. I nodded and stepped out.

THE MAN IN the room to the left was gagged, his arms and feet tied to his chair. He looked tougher by far than the first client: heavy shoulders, leathery face, wide, sweaty forehead, and an overgrown flattop. There was electric lighting in the room now, two bare bulbs high in the ceiling, their wiring loose and dangling over the timber joists. I shut the door and pulled over the other chair, but didn't sit right away. The guy looked determined to fight me to the death. But I knew showing fear wouldn't get me anywhere.

"I'm only going to say this once," I said in a hard voice. Then came an idea. "There are three levels to what's going to happen to you. First, I'm going to untie your gag and give you a chance to tell me what he needs to know." I paused, searching the guy's eyes. "And if you don't tell me what we need to know, we'll have to go on to the next level, which is going to be much, much more painful than the first."

Once I'd said it, chills ran through me.

"As for the third level," I said, "I'm not even going to talk about that until the time comes. But let me make clear, before we start, just how easy this is: you give me a name, and you get free-dom." I paused again, concentrating on my delivery. "Just think about that: freedom. It's the most valuable thing in the world. No money is worth as much—no possession, either—and you're in for a world of hurt if you turn it down."

As I removed his gag, his eyes didn't budge from mine. I stood in front of him and gave him a moment before squatting at eye level with him.

"It's all he asks," I said. "A name, and you're free. It's a good fucking deal, my friend."

The man gave me a mocking smile. "You can take your deal and shove it."

His accent was American, and Southern. I tried not to show my surprise.

"Where are you from?" I asked.

"Can't see how that matters much."

"Can you see how much it matters that you tell me that name?"

He raised his sweaty eyebrows and leaned in. "You better fucking believe I do—more than you know, I'll tell you that much."

"How's that?"

"'Cause that man you're working for is gonna just turn around and sell the name to some bad motherfuckers. That's how."

I let myself smile at that one. "Do you have any idea how far-fetched that sounds?"

"Go ahead and fuck yourself," he said. "You oughta know better than to believe that fucking Arab. But maybe I'm giving you too much credit."

I studied his face. He was Texan, I was willing to bet: stubborn as hell and a smart-ass to boot.

"Sounds like you're ready for level two, then," I said.

"Bring it on, buddy."

We gazed at each other for a minute. He kept himself dead still.

"You don't get it, do you?" I asked. "You're *fucked* if you don't tell me the name."

"*You* don't get it. I ain't telling you shit."

I stood up and ran my fingers through my hair. I was in far worse shape than the first time.

"You realize that this puts us both in a tight spot, right?" I asked. "I mean, you realize that I'm only doing what I have to, right?"

"Am I supposed to feel sorry for you, son? 'Cause that ain't gonna happen, neither."

I felt the urge to take a swing at him now, just to knock off the edge he seemed to think he had on me. I held down the anger, but I knew I had to get out of that room.

"Fine, then," I said. "Good luck staying alive."

I left the room, shutting the door behind me. Nabec's personal bodyguard was standing in the front doorway smoking.

"Qu'est ce que tu fais, il l'a dit?" he asked, wanting to know if the Texan had fessed up.

"Non," I said. *"C'est impossible."*

The bodyguard shook his head and frowned, pointing back to the room. Our eyes locked. I didn't make any attempt to conceal my rage. Now I knew I'd read the situation right: I wasn't going anywhere until I got what Nabec wanted.

I cursed the goon to his face. He shrugged. The fury started to burn in my face and shoulders. He smirked, with a cocky satisfaction in his eyes, and something broke loose in me.

I threw open the door to the left, rushed at the Texan, and got right in his face. His whole body tensed up, his eyebrows pushed together, and a couple of veins rose on his forehead.

"You know what?" I said. "You *deserve* to have these guys kick the shit out of you."

He was breathing through his nose, watching me, trying to get a read. "Fuck you, partner."

I cocked back and slapped him hard across the face. It felt good, like something I'd wanted to do since I'd arrived in France. No—all my life.

The Texan turned his head with the blow, but I wasn't satisfied. I hit him a few more times, open-handed, until my hand glowed with pain. Afterward, the Texan raised his head and licked his bleeding lower lip. He still had the obstinate look in his eyes, minus some of the cockiness.

"I'll bet that makes you feel pretty tough, don't it?" he muttered.

"Tell me the name."

"What part of *fuck no* don't you understand?"

I reeled back and punched him square in the teeth. As his flimsy wooden chair tipped backward, his eyes grew wide. And I just let him fall.

When he landed, his head smacked the concrete floor with a heavy thud. He didn't move for a solid minute.

My rage turned frantic, a frenzied minute passed—I was afraid to check the damage done. I paced up and back, then squatted beside him, worried I'd busted the poor fucker's skull. Finally the man opened his eyes. He closed them immediately afterward, grimacing from the pain.

I stood. My eyelids were quivering from the adrenaline pulsing through my face.

"Hurts, doesn't it?"

The Texan just lay there, his breath coming in groans. I crouched and pulled him upright in his chair, struggling with the weight. A thin stream of blood was making its way down his stubbly chin. He could hardly keep his head up.

I paced once around him, summoning what was left of my self-control. I'd never hit anybody like that before. It felt shamefully invigorating.

"Now listen close," I said. "It's not just you that's in trouble. You've got to fucking tell me. For our own good."

"You wouldn't of done that . . ." the Texan muttered between breaths. "Not if you knew what I know . . . fuck, man, it's a matter a safety—"

"It's just a name. And then all this'll be over—then you'll go free. Don't you see that? You're bringing all this on yourself."

His eyes grew wide. "If you really believe that, son, you're a fucking dumbass."

I put a little more into the second punch. It hit his nose and sent his head whipping back, and his chair tipped backward again.

His face clenched as he went down. The back of his chair made a loud smack. But I knew his head had hit the floor hardest. This time his groans faded into a steady whimper. This time, watching him squirm around in pain wasn't as shocking, even though my hands still shook. My ears were ringing. My vision seemed to twitch. Next thing I knew, I was yelling at him.

He cursed me and jerked sideways, his chair falling over on its side, leaving his back toward me.

I squatted behind him. My fists were throbbing, but I couldn't feel the pain yet.

"You don't get to decide what's safe. All you get to do is tell me the fucking name. So the two of us can get the hell out of here."

"You gonna break my fucking skull over it?" he mumbled. "You ain't even . . . you don't even got a clue who you're doing this for."

I moved around him, crouching where we could both see each other. Blood streamed from his nose down his throat and onto the floor.

"You're right, Tex. I just want out of here. Can't you see I don't have a choice?"

He started to jerk from side to side, as if he could somehow up-right himself.

"I don't double-cross my country," he said between his teeth.

"Your country?" I stood and cursed him. None of this seemed real. "Just tell me the fucking name, man."

There was a ringing coming from somewhere far off. I went around behind him again. The guy knew the name—he was one word away from ending all of it, and I was on the verge of losing the last ounce of my cool.

What he said next was all it took: "A coward is what you are . . . a fucking *traitor* coward."

I took a step back, kicked, and watched my foot strike the spot where his hands were lashed together behind his chair. He howled before I could see what I'd done: one of his fingers had taken the full force of the kick and had broken sideways and back. Now it stuck out at an unnatural angle from the hand.

I stepped away and felt an enormous wave of strength in my chest.

"I told you—" I yelled. "I fucking warned you—I tried to tell you, man."

I paced up and back for a minute, trying to shut out the man's wild moans. But I'd already taken it this far, I knew—there was no going back.

I squatted behind him. "Tell me the fucking name. I'm going to make it hurt, don't you see?"

I touched the toe of my boot to his broken finger. He wailed.

"I'm gonna keep making it hurt until you tell me," I said. "So tell me the goddamn name!"

He cursed me. I pressed down on the broken finger with my boot, and he screamed.

"Jesus fucking Christ, man . . . my goddamn hand . . . I'll fucking tell you."

I tilted him upright and backed away. He was practically hyperventilating, his whole face quivering. For a second I felt some compassion. It seemed to plead with me from a great distance. I shut it out and looked down at my hands. They were spattered with his blood. It looked strangely natural. I made a fist and cocked back.

"It's Bradley," he blurted. "Kenneth J. Bradley. He's a U.S. senator. From Utah, I think."

I stood for a long minute studying the Texan's eyes. He wasn't lying.

"Nevada," I said. "Kenneth J. Bradley is a senator from Nevada."

"Whatever—he's a goddamn U.S. senator, and he's supposed to be here in France this week, and that means that soon as the Arab hears his name, Bradley's up shit creek."

The adrenaline began to drain from my arms and legs. I could feel the pain rise across my knuckles. The rage stayed steady.

"You don't know that," I said.

"Sure I do . . . that's what I been trying to tell you: I worked for him. Not Bradley—the fucking Arab."

Our eyes locked. "Bullshit."

"Take it or leave it . . . I'm just telling you how I know . . ." His voice trailed off into groans. As much as I fought not to believe him, something told me the Texan wasn't lying. And I was so troubled now that I needed a seat. I put the other chair where I could sit and still watch his face.

"Prove it," I said.

"Can't, really," he grumbled. "Started a couple years back, when all this terrorist shit started getting bad out in Afghanistan."

I poked a thumb at the door. "You're talking about him, Nabec?"

"That's exactly who I'm talking about."

He held my gaze now, still didn't look to be lying. My heartbeat slowed. Even though I remembered Nabec's warning, my confidence was betraying me—I didn't know whom to believe.

"What did you do for him?" I asked, hoping to catch him in a lie.

"Little bit a everything. Brought him information, mostly."

"Directly to him, or through an interpreter, like me?"

The Texan cocked his head at me. "Straight to him, buddy. *T'as pensé que je parle pas français?*"

I froze and for a long moment, as my heart burrowed down into my stomach, I doubted my own ears. "You speak French."

"What did he tell you?" he asked in French. "That he needed you to translate my Texan English into French for him? Sly old bastard."

"Shit," I said aloud, without meaning to.

"Shit is right," said the Texan. He spat a wad of blood and phlegm over his shoulder, most of which wound up on his shirt, then lowered his chin and grumbled to himself, clearly trying to manage his pain. "That motherfucker . . . had you fooled, didn't he? That's why I was . . . I was trying to tell you, son. It's why none of this is safe . . . for you or me or anybody."

"That doesn't mean that a U.S. senator is in any trouble."

The Texan laughed. "You really don't have a clue what he's actually doing with the information he gets, do you?"

"No," I said. "And I don't want to. I'm done here."

I stood. But I'd lost my nerve. I could feel some powerful fear rushing in, alongside plenty of guilt, now that the adrenaline and manic energy were making an exit.

"Sells to both sides," the Texan said. "Doesn't give a shit which—whoever'll pay most, probably. My guess is he's been selling to a few terrorist cells here in—"

"I don't want to hear it." I headed for the door.

"Him and those goddamn crooked shoulders of his. Always sitting around with his fingers lined up on the table like some goddamn praying mantis."

"I said shut up."

"I'm trying to help you, kid. Us. All's I'm saying is you never know what he'll do to Bradley, or for Bradley: the Arab's only out to make money, and I held out on him, on account of I'm an American, and that's how I wound up here."

For a minute as I stood frozen by the door I couldn't break free of the Texan's gaze.

"You're just trying to fuck with me for smacking you around," I said.

"Go on over and tell him, then. But keep your eye on the news, see if something don't happen to that senator. You know who Bradley was, don't you? S'posed to be an ex–CIA man, coming over here with a few others to meet with French Parliament members, trying to get them to do Lord only knows what. Man like that'll do a lotta bad for the people paying the Arab."

I didn't want to believe him. But I couldn't see what other motive he might possibly have for saying what he was saying. I opened the door.

"Give yourself another week," he said. "But I'll tell you right now, a couple weeks'll be too late—I'm serious as I'll ever be. You think guys like him last as long as they do trusting people with their dirty work, then letting them skedaddle?"

I stopped in the doorway and watched the man lick the blood off his lips.

"You ever stop and think about what happened to the interpreter who came before you?" he said.

My lungs suddenly collapsed. I studied the Texan's face. He wasn't bullshitting.

"Think the one came before you is still on his payroll?" he said. "Think he's mopping up sunshine somewhere in the Caribbean, paid like a banker to keep his mouth shut? See, I started thinking about it not long before he turned on me." Now he was gazing past me out the door. "Ain't never seen the man in public. Sure, he talks like he's as free as a hummingbird. But you ever once seen him out in the open, talking with other folks? I bet it's only his goons and people like us that see him. He don't trust nobody, other than those men out there, with his real name—'cause it ain't Nabec, I'll tell you that—or with what he looks like, or what kind of Porto he drinks. Know what I'm saying?"

I froze. "What kind of Porto *does* he drink?"

"Ain't trying to trick you, son. I'm trying to save your ass."

"Then tell me what kind of Porto he drinks," I said.

The Texan leaned in and lowered his voice. "Isabella something," he said. "Dudn't say on the label, but he'll tell you if you ask him. Masked face on the bottle. Tiny red masked face. I remember that for sure. Tastes pretty goddamn good, too, if you ask me. But then, I ain't much of a wine man myself."

I shut the Texan inside alone and stood in the front room with my hands on my knees, concentrating on my breathing. There was a light at the end of the hall to my left. Furniture and stacks of lumber and a back door. But I knew I couldn't make a run for it—that would have been like asking to be tied up and gagged with the Texan.

I wrung my hands and wiped the blood off them. Some dread rose up in my throat, then settled. I headed for the room to the right.

NABEC HAD A tired but pacified look on his face. I gazed at the bottle of Porto on the table. Its label was facing me. It had a sinister red mask on it, but no name.

"Working with hooligans is not easy, is it?" Nabec asked.

I shook my head no. My ears had started to ring again. When Nabec told me to sit, I obeyed.

We drank in silence. My heart was beating hard against my chest. I realized that we were alone again—no bodyguard, just us and the Porto. He filled our glasses and rekindled his cigar.

"Do you still wish to be finished with this work, Jeffrey?"

"Yes."

"Then I will honor my promise," he said.

My eyes met his. They seemed dead cold. It was my turn to talk now, but I was scared speechless.

"You have something to tell me," he said after another moment.

"Yes," I said. The ringing in my ears stopped.

Afterward I could give no good account for what came over me. Maybe it was just another idiotic manic impulse. Maybe I actually thought I could evade Nabec with an outright lie, or maybe I'd somehow swallowed part of my fear. Either way I couldn't play along anymore with his fucked-up information game—not if it meant fingering an American senator.

"The name is Brule," I said finally. "Georges Brule."

A half second later, I deeply regretted lying. But it was too late—the deed was done.

Nabec reached into his jacket and took out an envelope. He pushed the envelope across the table and stood.

When I stood, my knees could barely adjust to the weight of my own body.

"I love that Porto," I said, half to verify the Texan's claim, half to break the heavy silence. "What's it called? I'd love to pick up a bottle of it somewhere."

Nabec raised one eyebrow, lifted the bottle, and appraised it like an heirloom.

"It is called Speciale," he said. "Isabella Speciale. But you will find it nowhere."

ASSURE ME YOU'VE UNDERSTOOD EVERYTHING

After that I started sweating like a snitch on parole. I'd show up at the lycée sweating, sweat profusely during class, lie in bed sweating all night. And not just because I was worried about what might befall Brule—I had a hunch that once Nabec found out I'd lied, he'd send his goons for me one final time.

I massaged my sore fists and bit my fingernails down to nothing, paced a thousand circles around the trunk in the center of my room. On the trunk sat Nabec's envelope: two five-hundred-euro bills, double what I'd earned for the first job. Part of me was ready to find Nabec and tell him the truth, to explain how afraid I'd been—to throw myself on his mercy before he could find out the truth.

But that was impossible. I'd done myself in, and there wasn't any way to undo it.

I called in sick on Wednesday, went in on Thursday, but came straight home afterward, pulling the drapes and collapsing in bed. I was tempted to talk with Françoise about it. Or else Paul. Or else I could track down Dreyfus and see what kind of message he could pass along. But the only way to do any of that, outside of an awkward phone call, was to hang around in the profs' room, where for some reason my remorse felt ten times heavier.

Thursday night I got bold and went down to the main foyer building. On the TV were disturbing images of a riot in *centre ville,* which at first I took for historic footage. As it turned out, the riot had happened that very afternoon: shots of Boulevard Cinquantes Otages blocked off by a legion of students, plugged-up tramlines, jammed traffic, protesters on top of cars—all on account of this recent *surveillant* business. More than I'd realized, these disgruntled university students commanded an enormous influence on lycée kids throughout the city.

Students from all five lycées in Ste-Térèse's *centre ville* had joined in, the reporter said—some fifteen hundred protesters in all. The police had detained more than thirty university and lycée students. They were confident that the demonstration-gone-bad had been plotted by the same organizations in charge of the *grève* at Corbières and the city-wide march a week before.

Asleep that night, I dreamed that I'd participated. Léo and I were stuck in the middle of a shifting, furious mob of students. He tapped me on the shoulder, climbed up on one of the cars where there were already several kids, and started shoving the others into the bloodthirsty crowd below.

FRIDAY MORNING I found some more courage and headed to Corbières early, convinced now that the only way to free my mind of Nabec was to find Dreyfus and have him pass along a message—what Dreyfus had started, he could finish. He also owed me a big explanation: he would tell me why he'd set me up with crooks, even if I had to force it out of him.

But of course Dreyfus wasn't anywhere around. My paranoia turned into impatience. I took to questioning people in the profs' room about Dreyfus's whereabouts, even cornered a few profs I knew outside the profs' computer lab: no dice. Then I slipped into the low-key bathrooms down by the *surveillants'* office to towel the sweat off.

Richard, the prof of letters who'd been at Paul's dinner party, was at the sink. When I asked him about Dreyfus, he claimed to have seen him on Monday.

"Though it might have been the Monday before," he said. "Why do you ask?"

"He's got something I need . . . and I forgot to give him my number."

Richard dried his hands and studied my eyes.

"He's not here very often," he said finally. "You do know he works in Lourange, don't you?"

I didn't know that, but I wasn't going to say so. "He still works *here,* doesn't he?"

"Mais oui, mais oui."

Richard checked his watch and made a move for the door.

"Has he been sick or something?" I asked.

"To be sure, M. Delanne, I am no authority on M. Dreyfus's health."

What Richard didn't know was that he was one wisecrack away from losing some teeth.

"Tu connais pas l'expression 'nobody likes a smart-ass'?" I asked all in one breath.

The jab went over his head but appeared to get across my irritation.

"Mais oui, mais oui," he said, before shuffling away.

Back in the profs' room I wrote Paul and Françoise each a quick note, requesting a word with them but not specifying why, and dropped the notes in their lockers. I stepped back out into the hallway, worried sick, and realized that I'd let myself get too worked up—I felt responsible for Brule's safety. Which meant it was time for a drink.

A group of older students made their way past me in the direction of the front doors. Solène and Elise were lagging at the back of the group, and when they saw me, Elise waved hello and kept on toward the front doors.

Solène stopped. We exchanged the cheek kisses, which had somehow ceased being awkward between us, even on school grounds. In her arms were a few books and a short black peacoat like mine, and her pupils were dilated, as if she'd just stepped out of darkness.

"You're sweating," she said. "You okay?"

"Long story. I'm fine."

I felt suddenly needy. She lowered her eyes.

"I still feel bad that my dad gave you a scare that night."

"No worries," I said. "It was time for me to go anyway."

"He said he likes you. He would like to invite you for dinner."

The prospect of seeing her dad again made me grow instantly cold inside. My patience felt scoured raw. Much as I liked Solène, I was fresh out of pleasantries. The silence grew heavy.

"Where are you off to?" she asked.

"Was going to stop in at the Rougerie, this little place just up the street."

Solène looked confused only for a second. "Oh, that little bar?"

"My second home."

Now we'd entered a trust, I knew; there were few students I would have told that.

She checked her watch and cursed. *"Il faut que je pars."* She reached and squeezed my hand before heading for the front doors.

I watched her walk off and felt newly charged with motivation. The main lycée office would be open for another fifteen minutes—maybe they could tell me where to find the mysterious Claude Dreyfus. I headed down the hallway in that direction, but the minute I stepped into the main lycée office and saw Rochefoulin, Brule's henchman administrative assistant, looming over the counter that separated his sacred space from the rest of the world, I lost my French.

Like Brule himself, Rochefoulin was inordinately tall, though he carried his weight like a peacock—heavy shoulders back, nose in the air. He also had a tricky Parisian accent, which I suspected he laid on even thicker for guys like me.

I waited patiently for Rochefoulin to acknowledge my presence. He was thumbing through some papers with one hand and nibbling from what looked to be a plate of sardines and mayonnaise with the other. Finally he looked up, only to glance immediately back down at his paperwork. I had an urge to smack the sardine out of his hand.

"M. Delanne," he said, without making eye contact. "Something I can help you with?"

I couldn't remember anymore how I'd planned to go about it. "Yes . . . if you would."

"I am preparing to leave for the day," he said. "Surely you didn't come in to watch me eat?"

When he glanced up, I gave him my best smile. "Of course not. I just have one question."

"And what question could you have, M. Delanne, before I leave for the weekend?"

Finally he gave me the eye contact I was hoping for. But I could smell the man's breath, along with his determination to be an asshole.

I laid it all on the line: "Would it be possible for you to give me M. Dreyfus's home telephone number?"

Rochefoulin took off his spectacles and raised an eyebrow. "No, M. Delanne, that would be very, very far from possible. How else could I be of service to you?"

He was leering at me now. I was one degree of heat away from leaping the counter.

"M. Rochefoulin," I said. "There was something we were working on, Dreyfus and I, outside the lycée. He hasn't been here much lately, and I don't have his phone number. Why is he never here?"

"M. Delanne," Rochefoulin started, then he rattled off an explanation that I would have needed a written transcript to decode—mostly jargon-rich bullshit about lycée protocol. I caught the final word clearly enough: he ended his explanation with the word *Brule*.

Right away I said, "Oh, M. Brule is not necessary. No need to bother him. That will be all."

But Rochefoulin had already lifted his phone.

"*C'est M. Delanne,*" he said into the receiver. "*Oui . . . Il a demandé le numero de téléphone de M. Dreyfus, il dit qu'ils ont travaillé ensemble. Oui . . . Oui, toute suite.*"

I'd already gotten a hand on the door. "I'll leave you to your sardines, Rochefoulin."

"You are not to leave just yet," he said contemptuously, phone still in hand. "M. Brule will see you now."

"As I said, I really don't wish to bother M. Brule. Anyway—"

"And as *I* said, M. Delanne, M. le Proviseur awaits."

I knew enough not to piss off the overlord of the city's lycée network. After all, talking to Brule was the least I could do; I'd already put him in more danger than he'd be willing to believe. I shook my head at Rochefoulin before heading into Brule's chamber.

IT WAS A long, narrow room, dimly lit and decorated in somber beiges and blues. Brule was sitting at the far end, behind a large rosewood desk. A massive window covered with translucent cream drapes made the wall behind him seem to glow like a blank cinema screen. He was on the phone, but his eyes were on me. His expression softened some. He smiled and waved me over to the silk-upholstered armchair across from him. When I sat, my throat went instantly dry.

Brule said something into the phone in a language I didn't recognize, and then hung up.

"Well, let us see," he said. "It is Jeffrey, is it not?"

His voice was musical, rich, the kind of stuff you hear on learn-to-speak-French recordings.

"Yes, yes," I said. "But I had no intention of bothering—"

"Good, Jeffrey, perfectly well and good. I asked M. Rochefoulin to send you in because he mentioned that you came to inquire about M. Dreyfus. Is this so?"

He said Dreyfus's name carefully, dragging out both syllables. As I remembered all that Paul and Françoise had said about Brule—that he was a big political figure in waiting, a missile ready to launch into the big time—what was left of my shaky courage slithered off to rot.

Brule held himself like a statue, as if he were made of three or four Rochefoulins. His hair was silver, his face severe and tan—the deep copper kind you can only get in the tropics. And while there wasn't a trace of meanness in his expression, no sign whatsoever of falseness between his eyes, I knew the man, with a single phone call, could have me deported in the matter of an evening. Why had I worried about the man's safety? Of all the names I might have given Nabec in lieu of the right one, Brule's now seemed the most secure. What would a crook like Nabec do to Ste-Térèse's proviseur of schools?

I decided to level: "Dreyfus found me a little side job. I need to speak with him about it, but he's never around."

Brule studied me for a long moment: a flawless PR face. I hoped to God he wouldn't ask me about the so-called side job. He broke our gaze and poured a tiny packet of whitish powder into an empty glass, topping it off with water from a fresh bottle. As he stirred the powder in, Brule glanced up and caught me watching.

"Do you take vitamins, Jeffrey?" he asked.

"No. I mean, sometimes. When I remember to."

"A word of advice: start remembering. Every day. I myself prefer them in a powder. A habit passed along to me by my late grandfather, a distinguished colonel in the gendarmerie."

I wasn't sure if he was attempting small talk or just changing the subject, both of which were fine by me.

"Okay," I said. "I'll start remembering to take my vitamins."

When I started to get up, he said, "Please, please, Jeffrey. Sit down and be comfortable."

"But it is the weekend, monsieur, and I should allow you—"

"Good, Jeffrey, all well and good. But relax, please. Before the weekend begins, I would like to know something."

I sat and used my shirtsleeve to wipe the sweat off my forehead. "To know something?"

"Yes, Jeffrey. You understand why we can't give a prof's phone number to a foreign assistant, don't you?"

"Yes, lycée rules, of course," I said. "It's impossible."

He took a long drink from his vitamin concoction and pursed his lips. "Yes, well said, but . . . in this particular case, Jeffrey, I'm going to make an exception."

I felt a wave of relief. Brule cut it short: "Out of curiosity, Jeffrey, what exactly did M. Dreyfus tell you about himself?"

"Not much." I hesitated, unsure what he was after. "He used to live in the States. Studied English and French. And American film. He's quite the Woody Allen fan."

Brule sat back and bit his lower lip thoughtfully, as if I'd given him something to chew on.

"Yes—Woody Allen," he said finally. "Of course. A wonderful filmmaker. Films much the same, but wonderful nonetheless . . . and did M. Dreyfus tell you about his own work?"

"No. I just assumed he taught—"

"English, yes—he teaches English here. But he did not tell you what he does in Lourange?"

"No," I said. "But then of course I wouldn't know . . ."

"You say he lived in the States. Did he tell you where?"

"It was Minnesota, I think."

"Yes, yes, of course. Minnesota—yes."

Long silence while Brule nibbled his lip intently. He killed his vitamin water, placed his elbows on the desk, and carefully laced his fingers together. His eyes and face were like granite.

"Tell me, Jeffrey. Do you like France?"

"Absolutely. It's very—"

"And you plan on staying in France, I take it."

"Perhaps," I said. "If I can."

He took a small notebook from his desk, leafed through it, and scribbled a number on the back of a spent envelope. He handed me the envelope somewhat ceremoniously.

"I would like to help make that possible, Jeffrey. But there is something I want you to do for me." He stopped short, searching my eyes.

"Yes?"

"I want you to come and see me after you see M. Dreyfus again."

I'd had zero intention of asking him to keep me there any longer, but curiosity got the better of me.

"Why?" I asked.

Brule searched my eyes. "Let us say that I keep an eye on all my visiting profs. And my foreign assistants." He gave me a well-polished smile. "But Dreyfus has remained surprisingly detached from us here—he hasn't once paid me a visit—which is quite unusual for visiting profs. So if there are things you learn from—or about, mind you—our M. Dreyfus, I would like you to come here and inform me. He is . . . very private, too private for a professor here at Lycée Corbières. Can you do that?"

I hesitated. "Of course—sure. Yes, sir."

"And this also means that you mustn't inquire about M. Dreyfus to others, and of course you mustn't tell him that I have inquired about him. It must be a . . . an agreement between us."

"Agreed, then." I stood.

He stood too, but with a nervous expression. "You've absolutely understood? Assure me you've understood everything, Jeffrey."

"Absolument," I said. *"J'ai tout à fait compris, monsieur. Tout à fait."*

TOO MANY SAPPY ROMANCES

I carried a beer and a shot of Bruno's rotgut cognac into the empty back room of the Rougerie to process the odd encounter. Brule was even creepier in person than his reputation suggested, and it was pretty obvious that he was holding out on me—maybe even flat-out lying. Either way, what he'd implied about Dreyfus wasn't helping the little man's case. My thoughts kept worming back to what Thierry had said about Corbières: every day since my talk with him, the place had gotten more haunting.

But I realized that I wasn't just haunted by these unknowns—I'd begun to fear myself. I'd crossed a line and could still feel the aftermath, the gradual acceptance of my own violence. Forgetting about it wouldn't undo it, and now that I had Dreyfus's number, it was time to try to fix what I'd screwed up. Not for Brule's sake—he'd be just fine—but for my own.

It was five minutes till happy hour, and I still had the better part of a beer going. I went back up to the bar and got Bruno's attention, pointing to the pay phone near the front door.

"It works?" I asked. I'd never even considered using the ancient thing before now.

"Depends on what you're using it for," Bruno said with a chuckle. He was in one of his rare playful moods.

"I mean can I call somebody on it?"

"Depends where you're calling."

"Damn it," I said. "Can I call Lourange on it?"

He said yes, that the phone usually worked for in-city calls, and started pouring me a beer.

"This one's on me. You seem like you need it, my man."

Evidently I was on his A-list since I'd covered my tab. But I was tired of him always having one thing or another to hold over my head. Fucking bartenders—same all over the world.

"I've already got one," I told him.

"That's never been a problem for you before." He let loose another hearty chuckle, but stopped when he saw my scowl.

The phone was the old-style kind without any slot for your calling card. I typed in the code on my card, got nothing, did it again and got the busy signal. When I typed my number in a third time, only to hear an automated operator claim that my card was out of minutes, I slammed the phone receiver down, snatched my coat off the rack, and headed for the door.

Right then Marine pushed in with Angelique and a bucktoothed young lady whose name I could never remember. Even in my flustered state I could see no reason to refuse the cheek kisses from Marine.

"You're leaving just before happy hour?" Marine asked. "You must be losing your mind."

"And he's trying to leave a free beer on the bar," Bruno cut in. "Slamming down phones, storming around. You better make him drink his beer before I dump it on his head."

I shot a glance at Bruno and narrowed my eyes; I would have liked to see him try. But with Marine there I felt my temper flag. I glanced back and forth between them. They were making an obvious attempt to cheer me up—almost too obvious. But they were right—I needed company more than anything else.

A FEW HOURS later I was having Bruno refill the tall five-liter spout pitcher of beer, which we called *le giraffe,* for the table in back. Happy hour was over, the endurance drinking begun. Julien and Joël and several others were there, but my eyes kept landing on Marine. I caught her glance shift my way off and on, and soon I let the confusion of loud music and talk become a blur of forgetting— about Brule and Dreyfus and Nabec, about everybody who wasn't there with me having a good time.

By the time Patrick and Michel showed up, I was half bent and in no mood for their newest sociopolitical spiels.

I slipped up to the bar and ordered a cognac. Marine was sitting a couple of stools down. We made eye contact and held it for a long time, until Angelique moved out from between us, heading for the bathroom. I felt a wave of desperate courage, and slid over onto Angelique's stool.

"When do I get a rematch in Caps?" I said.

Marine laughed and poked my hand with a finger. "You're not very good at losing, are you?"

This was more than a little ironic coming from Marine, who would race you to the front door and back for the pure competition of it. Her hair was down and her face seemed to glow beneath the dim lighting over the bar. I caught her looking over my shoulder into the back room, and my mind scrambled for something, anything, to say. I realized only then that I'd misgauged my beer intake and was already feeling sloppy. My desperation felt like hunger, but I was in poor shape for flirting. Suddenly the tangle of music and voices started fucking with my head.

"You know, you never told me how you and Julien met," I said.

"What?" she called back over the noise.

"You and Julien—how did you meet?"

She shrugged. "Here, I guess . . . it was a really long time ago."

She was making it sound like a crime she was ashamed of, and I told her so.

"I guess I read too many sappy romances when I was a girl," she said. "But whatever. You can't have everything the way you want it."

I looked her in the eyes. "Yeah, but you can have some things that way, right?"

"What?"

"I said you can have whatever you want, Marine, and you know it."

She smiled, then pressed her lips together in thought. I could tell now that, like me, she was teetering on the verge of drunk.

"I just wish . . ." she started to say. "Sometimes it's like I'm not even there when he's around." She lit a Marlboro Light and looked down at her full drink, a whiskey something. Then she killed it in two expert swigs.

"That's the one thing I can't understand about him," I said. "He's the luckiest guy in here, but he doesn't seem to know it."

Solid eye contact. She seemed to be reading me. She looked away and said, "There's nothing I can do about it." Angelique had come back and was standing almost between us now. "And there's nothing you can do about it, either, okay?" Marine added suddenly.

I tried not to react but probably didn't do a strong job of it. There had been more between us over the months than just harmless flirting. It angered me that she and I knew exactly what to talk about but could never get around to it. In the same instant I realized that all her power to curb my hotheadedness had disappeared.

"Of course not," I said. I gave Angelique her stool back, guzzled my cognac, and waved Bruno down for my tab, thinking I'd better get home before I got in a fight with my aching fists.

As if my luck could get any worse, Amelia, my so-called Sicilian girlfriend, and Rigoberto, the Spanish assistant at Corbières, were coming into the bar on my way out.

Amelia inspected me like a younger sister. "Look at you, you're all sweaty."

She was slurring, botching the French. Rigoberto, too, seemed to be swaying—they were both as drunk as peasants. I announced that I was leaving.

Amelia clutched my arm. "But we came here to find you."

"You're a little late." I cast a glance back at the bar. Marine's back was turned. I dug through the pile of coats on the rack and extracted mine. "I can't stay. It's been a bad night, that's all."

I glanced back at Marine again. She was watching now. She looked away. I decided I'd had enough of this shifty company and pushed outside into the cold.

Amelia was close at my heels. "What's wrong with you?" She had a pained look on her face.

"Just let me go, will you?" I said.

She stepped toward me with a longing look in her eyes. "It's this new job, isn't it? You haven't been the same since that night you told me about it."

She was talking about Paul's dinner party. "I don't want to talk about it. Just let me go."

"Why do you shut me out? All I want to do is make you feel better. Whatever it is, it's not as bad as it seems."

She slipped her hand inside my coat. We stood on the corner, shivering. The air seemed to be empty of everything but the cold and Amelia's hungry eyes.

I took a step back, felt myself wobble, stopped. Under her long, slick leather coat Amelia had on tight black pants and a low-cut purple top—a full-tilt prowl suit.

She moved closer and reached for me, and a second later she was kissing me hard on the mouth. Between kisses she stood on her toes and whispered in my ear—something about going back to my room, then something saucy about gymnastics.

"It could be so dirty," she said. "I know just what you need."

We were still in plain view of the Rougerie's big front windows. For a second I got the spins, then I began to wonder if Marine might be looking out from inside. We moved out of the way against a brick wall around the corner. Amelia drove a hand down the front of my pants.

"I'll make you forget everything," she said. "Everything but me." Then with her other hand she pulled my face to hers and laid on me the sloppiest kiss I could remember since my junior-high days. I got her shirt untucked and fought with her bra while she moaned and mumbled in Italian.

"Let's go somewhere warm," I said.

Inside my room I steered clear of Amelia's careless kisses and stripped off her clothes so fast that she seemed confused, standing there in the darkness in nothing but a pair of red panties. Then she was in my bed on her back, and instead of pulling them down, I tore off her underpants and flung them across the room. She taunted me in what English she knew, clutched me around the neck, and bit my shoulder, hard. I almost slapped her, but instead I rolled her over on her stomach. She clenched at first when I entered, then relaxed, reaching back, reeling me in tight and pressing her face deep into the sheets.

When it was over, we lay shoulder to shoulder in my tiny bed and gazed up at the ceiling, panting in silence as if we'd just survived a train wreck.

Later, after I'd dozed and woken up still drunk, I found her snuggled against the wall with all the blankets. I felt the urge to

take her again, to wallow deeper in what could only be more regret, to give myself over entirely. Instead I left her lying there and
burned the next few hours roaming the streets, full of rash rebel-
lion and madness. Almost hoping that Nabec's black Mercedes
would come for me now. To get me out of this place. For good.

NOTHING HEROIC ABOUT
SITTING IN JAIL

After getting back and finding Amelia gone, I slept till noon then tried the number Brule had given me, listening to ten or twelve rings before hanging up. I tried twice more before shoving the slip of paper back in my wallet, only to find the card Thierry, Solène's father, had given me that night after the soccer game. More and more he was looking to be my best bet. As much as he'd spooked me with his strange-things-are-afoot talk—even if Brule was in no danger at all—I might need an ally like Thierry, someone who had some friends on the legal side of the law.

I paced around the room for a while and then reluctantly dialed Thierry's number. After the third ring, a young female voice answered. But I wasn't in the right gear to talk to Solène. I hung up without a word.

I sat down on the bed and massaged my knuckles, still sore from punching the Texan. It was hard to tell what was making me so deeply suspicious of Dreyfus. Part of it was obvious—his elusiveness, combined with the fact that he'd connected me with an Arab mafioso. But there was something more to him than that. He wasn't as absentminded as he'd led me to believe. And while I had no proof, I was beginning to think like Brule: Dreyfus was too shady to be exactly who he claimed to be. Which meant it was time for me to stop sitting around, and to do some investigating.

Down in the main foyer building I conducted a little online research. All the professors' names and photos were on the Corbières website, including those of visiting profs, but Dreyfus's name was nowhere—he wasn't even listed on any of the Lourange online yellow pages. Thierry Duvin's stats were easy to find. He'd received a prestigious lifetime service award several years back from the Police Nationale. His record was listed with several dozen other cops, all marked "retired." He'd worked in a branch called DST, a counterintelligence unit known for having never been infiltrated by a foreign agency, according to a news article. He was a sort of hero in the war against crime, as best as I could tell, and knowing this made me uneasy as hell, given what I suspected about Nabec.

Back upstairs I poured myself a tall drink from the bottom of a bottle of cognac and contemplated the telephone. Finally I dialed Dreyfus's number again, only to lose count of the number of rings. I didn't call Thierry again. Part of me knew I was only stalling, but some other, more desperate part of me clung to the belief that I might be able to tidy up the mess on my own. I was afraid, too, that Thierry might take my story to some cops who would neither be my allies nor see things my way.

What I didn't see was that the longer I waited, the more difficult gaining allies would become.

That evening I went with Paul and his son Lucien to see a small-time production of *Les Liaisons Dangereuses,* which I had a hell of a time following. The room we'd been corralled into was roughly the size of my high school cafeteria and heated like a sauna. At intermission I fled to the little vestibule, where the air was cooler and cheap cold wine was being served, and for the remaining hour of the play I sat between father and son, dabbing my face with a hanky and trying not to think about Nabec. But, trapped there with my own nagging conscience, I couldn't keep from turning the conundrum over and over. So what if I got through to Dreyfus and had him pass along a message to Nabec? Even if Brule was in no danger, and even if Nabec had found out I'd lied and still wasn't going to come after me, I still had to tell somebody in authority about what the Texan had said about Senator Bradley. Which meant I had to tell someone, even at the risk of bringing more trouble upon myself—the mess had grown too large to tidy up alone.

After the play, Paul invited me to his home for a drink, and all the way there in his station wagon, Lucien wouldn't shut up about the riot in *centre ville* on Thursday. Apparently a few Corbières kids had been arrested for vandalism and assault, among them my mysterious student Léo. Big surprise. But Lucien was making the whole thing sound valiant, like a coup of historic proportions.

"There's nothing heroic about sitting in jail with an assault charge against you," said Paul.

Paul had heard from another prof at Corbières that Léo was being held in jail over the weekend because he hadn't cooperated with the cops. It wasn't the first time he and a few others in the activist group he ran with had had run-ins with the law; last summer he and two others had been caught sneaking out of a condemned building in the old warehouse district in east Ste-Térèse. When the cops brought them in and questioned them, Paul said, not one of them would breathe a word, and somehow they'd been released with minor slaps on the wrist.

That was all it took for Lucien to lose interest in the topic. At their apartment he headed straight to his room. Paul said it was just a phase he was going through, and broke the seal on a bottle of bourbon. I had a hard time keeping my eyes on Paul's. I'd left that note in his locker a couple of days back, saying that I needed to talk with him, and now I felt too ashamed to open up. Even though now was the perfect time to confide, an all-too-familiar stubbornness had risen up in me, mostly because I'd already made up my mind during the play to take the problem to Thierry first. Besides, Paul's opinion mattered too much to me. He was often quick to judge, and as I sat there drinking whiskey with him, I realized that I didn't know how to explain in French what I'd done for Nabec. Not to him, anyway. After another drink I stood and told him I'd take the tram home. Paul followed me to the door.

"Is everything okay, Jeffrey?"

Our eyes met, and for a second there I almost caved. "For now," I said, managing a smile.

"If you're having a problem, I could give you my attorney's phone number."

I shook my head. "I just have to tend to a few things, that's all."

"What about the note you put in my locker? What's wrong, Jeffrey? I want to help. You've got to let people help you."

I couldn't say why, but when he said that, something in me snapped.

"No, I don't," I said. "I don't have to do anything." We exchanged an intense stare. Then I took my eyes from his. "Thanks, Paul. For the whiskey, for everything . . . I'll let you know, okay?"

Outside I wondered if I'd just shut a door that might not easily reopen. I started walking, but hadn't made it five feet when I heard footsteps behind me.

I spun. In front of the building beyond Paul's stood an old man with a cane and a bag of groceries, struggling with his building door.

"Need some help?" I asked.

The street was deeply quiet. It was just the two of us and a dim streetlight. It was probably no later than ten, but there were no cars or voices—not even a gust of wind.

The old man's eyes were wide with terror. His paper grocery bag shook with his arms. He looked at me as if I'd just threatened to maim him—just stood there, frozen, with a heart-attack expression on his face. Then he crouched, carefully and without taking his eyes off me, and set his groceries on the ground.

I stepped back, and as soon as I did, the man began fumbling frantically with his keys.

I said: *"C'est cool, monsieur, c'est bien cool."*

I pictured him rushing inside and claiming he'd almost been mugged. I wasn't in any shape to sort probability from paranoia, so I headed fast up the street toward the tram stop, forcing myself to laugh it off. For a second there, I'd been as spooked as the old man. I wondered where the jumpy old bastard had been shopping this time of night, why such an easily frightened soul would go out after dark at all.

Just as I had that thought—in the same instant, not a hair between—I heard a noise that made my mind go blank with fear: behind me, at the other end of the block, a car gunned its engine.

I didn't have to turn around, though I did anyway. As plain as day: a black sedan barreling down Paul's street toward me. My stomach squeezed into a tight knot. *Jesus,* I thought. *How soon till I can walk the streets without seeing a goddamn Mercedes.*

It was hard to tell how much time whipped by—I might have hesitated. But then I broke into a run, crossing the first intersection and hustling across the empty plaza to the tram stop, thinking it best to put myself in a crowd of people.

The plaza was deserted.

I shot a glance back down the street. The black sedan was pulling up to the intersection, slowing but not stopping.

My heart leaped into my throat, and I hurried across the tram tracks with its beat pounding in my ears. A few stops down, I could see a pair of tram headlights. They approached infinitesimally.

By the time the tram docked at the stop before mine, the black sedan had circled the roundabout of the plaza to my side of the tracks. Now I could see the silver glint of the car's circular hood ornament.

Another glance at the tram: it was leaving that stop, nearing mine. I closed my eyes, and every organ in my body seemed to groan: *Nabec is onto my lie and returning for payback.*

When the tram screeched into my stop, I knew the Mercedes had pulled up behind me. I didn't check to see—I waited for the sound of car doors slamming, the sound of foreign voices calling my name, and prayed for the tram doors to open. When they finally did, I jumped inside.

I held my breath until the tram doors closed. We were moving again. I checked in either direction: no goons in black suits.

I found a seat and fought to settle my breathing. There weren't but eight or ten people in my car, every one of them looking at me as if I had blood down the front of my coat. I took it off, clutched it in my lap, felt the sweat cascading down my back and arms and legs. Here was a good reason to perspire—or was it? After all, how many Mercedes sedans could there be in a city of half a million? A few thousand? And how many of those were black?

As we slowed for the next stop, I gripped the plastic seat under my legs. My hands were slippery with sweat, and when the doors opened it took every ounce of will in me not to scream.

No one boarded our car at that tram stop. Or at the next. Or at the one after that—though my terror at each stop was the same: a sudden loosening in the guts, followed by a sharp ringing in the ears. Then the tram doors closed me in safely again.

At the fourth stop, a short man in a long black trench coat got on and sat directly across from me. Bald and pudgy in the face, he looked like one of the guys who worked at my post office. We stared at each other. His face was sweating too. I could count his facial pores in a glance.

I tore my eyes away from his. He was a nothing, a nobody, a warm body covered with clothes. I needed to think with my mind, not with my keyed-up impulses. I needed to stop thinking like a crook.

By the time we reached the central tram station at Boulevard Cinquantes, my heart had finally slowed, though I couldn't stop sweating.

The southbound tram I was on stopped just as the westbound tram was pulling in. More at ease now, I got off, hustled over, and boarded the westbound. Now I was starting to think I'd fallen victim to simple paranoia. It wouldn't have been the first time.

I rode until Place Médiathèque, then got off and stood still on the platform until the tram pulled away, gazing across the wide, empty courtyard that led up to the media library. Nothing but paranoia. Nothing a drink and a cool shower couldn't fix.

I crossed the dark concrete courtyard. A quick nip of something at the Rougerie, I thought. Surround myself with people. Talk it up. Laugh it off.

I hadn't made it halfway across the courtyard when the Mercedes showed up in the cross street. It turned fast into the courtyard and gunned its engine, its bright round headlights blazing across the dark lot.

I threw up my hands out of instinct. The Mercedes screeched to a stop maybe a dozen yards away. Its passenger door swung open, and out jumped one of Nabec's goons.

As he moved toward me, he reached into his jacket. I took a step back, stopped.

The gun was black and tiny in his hand. The Mercedes's headlights glowed around him. I braced myself for a blow, and then my vision sharpened.

The man was holding a hand out to me. Like an escort. My own private chauffer. As if to say, *Don't fight it—it's time to come home.*

BY THE TIME we'd turned off the highway onto the road that led to Nabec's cottage, I was all out of sweat. All I could think about now was Nabec's cold, dark eyes, that fierce gaze, the intensity of his eloquence. I wondered what smooth words he'd use to remind me that I'd violated his trust.

We pulled to a stop at the end of the drive. The Bentley wasn't there. Our engine didn't shut off, but my door opened. I got out and stared Nabec's goon straight in the eyes.

"Le Monsieur is running late?" I asked.

Rather than answering, he gestured down the path to the front door of the cottage, taking me by the arm as we walked. A bolt of rebellious electricity shot through me. I held down the rage.

The light in the front room was off. The door to the left was closed, and there was no light coming from the room to the right. I shook my arm free and made for the door to the right, but the goon grabbed my elbows and yanked me backward. Before I could react, he'd kicked open the door to the left and shoved me through the doorway.

As he tied me to the interrogation chair I saw the gun harnessed under his arm and knew it was idiotic to fight back: even if I made it past this one, there'd be another waiting outside.

Once the goon had my arms and legs secured, he turned off the light and shut me in the room alone.

FOR A TERRIBLE stretch of time I wasn't sure if I was hearing my own breath or the syncopation of mine with someone else's. I could smell something funky hanging in the cold air—body odor, something rotten or burnt, like singed hair. Was this what death smelled like?

I tried to remember a time when I'd been in a comparable fix, but I had no frame of reference outside of the time I'd gotten arrested in Tucson, not long before I'd come to France. It had been the first time as an adult that I'd actually hoped my family might provide some kind of leverage—my dad worked as an agent for the border patrol in Nogales, and had since before I was born. No big secret, but it was a fact I'd kept from whomever I could back in Arizona, something I'd told no one here in France. Between that and my criminal record—misdemeanors, though I hadn't exactly been free to leave the country when I boarded the Paris-bound plane in Phoenix—over the last six months some small part of me had felt that I'd been hiding skeletons.

And there you had it: not the whole reason I'd left the States, but the darker end of it. And now the guilt for every crooked thing I'd ever done seemed to congregate as I waited for Nabec in the cold darkness, ruminating over all that had led me here.

My life up to that point seemed now like a pit that I'd dug intentionally for myself—as if I'd gone out of my way to seal my own doom.

I could hear mice scratching and scuttling around me on the floor, creeping up to my shoes and scurrying back to the shadows, impatient for me to die. I kept telling myself they weren't rats, kept telling myself that any second the door would open. That old Nabec would walk in, and then it would be my turn to be persuasive with him. And then he would let me go.

But I knew it wouldn't happen that way.

When the door finally did creak open, I was out of my mind with desperation, ready to fight, play docile, say whatever—anything to get out.

The light came on and a slim, dark-haired young man stepped in. He closed the door softly behind himself, and as I recognized him my stomach rolled: it was Rafa, the young Arab who'd met with me in Lourange just before everything went to hell.

I started talking fast. "This isn't cool, Rafa. I made a mistake, I'm ready to tell you what I should've told him, so let's be civil about it."

Rafa folded his arms and grinned. "You're damn right you made a mistake, Delanne."

He was wearing a dark suit, the side pocket of which bulged as if it were stuffed with gloves or a scarf. He pulled the other chair over—the same one I'd used during two interrogations—placed it in front of me, and took off his jacket, situating it neatly on the chair back.

"He should give me a chance to explain," I said. "Come on. Let's be cool."

"He's finished talking with you, Delanne. You fucked up. You lied to him. Can you understand how much that hurts? What about how utterly stupid it was?"

"Let me explain—"

"Don't make me gag you, Delanne. I'd enjoy that too much."

I held my tongue. The skin on my face started to twitch. Rafa sat down, reached into his jacket pocket, and brought out two tight rolls of red cloth.

"Granted, you were led into this," he said.

My thoughts tangled. I wasn't sure I'd heard him right.

"Drafting you for those interviews was his decision," he said. "And he had to make that decision, for business' sake. This is what he wants me to say."

"Fuck his business—" I started. Rafa's glare stopped me.

"You want to blame somebody, Delanne, blame your own people. Blame this stupid war they're starting. None of this would be necessary—you wouldn't be necessary, Delanne. You think for a second we'd be in business with those fuckers if your people hadn't taken it too far—if they weren't taking it too far now? Anyway, you weren't fit to polish his shoes."

I knew better than to ask him to tell me what the hell he was talking about. I understood enough: he was talking about the parts of Nabec's fucked-up business I wasn't privy to. But I couldn't see what any of that had to do with my so-called people. Rafa had unraveled one of the rolls of red cloth and was wrapping it slowly and carefully around his left hand.

"You're right," I said. "I fucked up. But it's difficult in another language—"

"Let's not get too far ahead of ourselves." Rafa was grinning now. "There'll be plenty of time for the two of us to see things eye to eye, Delanne. You see, le Monsieur, he's a sort of . . . a student of human nature, if you will. And he's been kind enough to give me certain freedoms this evening. I plan to make thorough use of those freedoms, Delanne."

Once he'd finished wrapping the first roll of cloth around one hand, he started with the other. My vision sharpened. I couldn't gauge how much hurt I'd be in for, but the thought of it made the blood race to my brain. I was enraged, yet somehow invigorated. When Rafa finished wrapping his right hand, I flexed with all my force against the ropes around me. Not an inch.

"Ever done any boxing, Delanne?" Rafa asked.

"Now hold on—"

The first punch hit me square on the mouth. I saw a constellation of colors and felt my chair tip backward. Rafa caught me by the shoulders, stopping me, and my eyesight came back crystal clear. My lips tingled, then burned. Every ounce of fear I'd been feeling before gave way to rage.

Rafa stood there grinning at me. "I'm sorry, what were you saying?"

I tongued my split lip. "I was saying *go fuck yourself.*"

He threw an overhand right that landed flat on my left jaw and made my skull snap and rattle. I emitted an involuntary groan, and at once my ears started ringing. There was plenty of blood in my mouth now, and I thought *to hell with it:* no amount of fawning was going to keep this guy from walloping me anyway. I gave Rafa a toothy smile.

He leaned forward calmly, fists on his knees. I remembered seeing the scar above his eyebrow that day in Lourange. Now it made sense, along with the marks on his hands that I'd taken for ink stains: Rafa was a fighter. Which meant he could make it hurt much worse.

"Okay," I said. "What do you want me to say?"

Rafa's eyes grew wide. "Good, good, Delanne. You're starting to listen. So let's have it. Who have you told about what le Monsieur has had you do out here?"

I hadn't seen that one coming. Out came the truth: "I haven't told anybody, man. Nobody."

"*Nobody?* How am I supposed to believe that?"

"I wasn't exactly proud—"

The next blow hit my nose. My chair tipped back, but he caught me by the shoulders again. I closed my eyes until the stinging in my nose went numb and shot up into my forehead.

"Wrong answer," said Rafa. "You're not taking any of this personally, I hope."

I grinned again. "Of course not. I just didn't take you for the jealous kind, Rafa—were you afraid I'd be your replacement?"

He gave me a left-right combo, followed by a left hook that made my vision cut out for a few long seconds. I felt as if I were falling. Then the blood came pounding back into my temples.

"Jealous of what?" I heard his voice say from somewhere in the fog. "A fucking American who can't decide whose side he's on?"

I got hold of myself, raised my head. The light seemed to flicker above us, but soon my vision refocused. Rafa was standing before me in ready position, breathing heavily through his nose with his lips pressed together. He wanted to knock me over and kick the shit out of me. I was starting to think that might come sooner than later.

But he wouldn't get the chance.

There were suddenly voices outside the room—arguing, frantic voices. Then there was some scuffling, followed by a knock on our door. Rafa slipped out and shut the door fast behind him.

A long minute or two passed. More panicked voices. Then everything got confusing: more arguing out in the main room, foreign-accented French, another language I didn't recognize, another voice in French—an older man's voice, but not Nabec's. Then another long minute or two of excruciating silence while my face throbbed with pain.

I started turning over all he'd said about Nabec and his so-called business, how much it really mattered to Nabec that my country was about to start a war, and what any of that had to do with me. After another minute came a bang on the cottage's front door, and I thought I heard shouting outside. The doorknob jiggled. I heard orders in native French, and after a few seconds came another bang.

Then the door to my room flew open, and standing in the doorway were two gendarmes, pistols aimed at my chest.

AN HOUR OR so later they were marching me down a narrow linoleum hallway to a cell block in the Lourange city municipal jail. No formal charges. No explanations. No clue as to how long I'd be detained. I'd been fingerprinted and given sheets and some toiletries, and that was all. On my block there were some twenty dark jail cells that faced a public area. One of the deputies led me to the last cell and slid the cell door home behind me, the sound of which was mortifying.

In the darkness I could just see a tiny steel toilet and a short bunk bed, the lower level of which was empty. I slung a sheet across my new bed, lay down, and stared up at the sagging coils.

Finally I'd made it to hell. My face hurt too much to give a damn.

EARLY THE NEXT morning our cell doors unlocked automatically and slid open for breakfast. The other prisoners were weary-eyed, yet acted like overworked office personnel, strangely at home and miserable in their oversized jumpsuits. During the meal—a rock-hard roll, a mealy red apple, and a bowl of coffee that smelled like cinnamon and mud—I studied the other inmates in snatches, careful not to stare. None of them looked remotely like Nabec's goons, and Rafa wasn't anywhere among us. There wasn't a mirror around, either, though I didn't need one to know that my face was roughed up pretty bad. I had a rip-roaring headache now. And a ton of unexpected esteem for boxers.

That whole day I holed up in my bunk with one of my cellmate's paperbacks, an unlikely romance that helped send my imagination off, which I needed more than any sort of physical comfort. I knew my situation was grim: tied up in the French penal system as a foreigner on a temp visa, I'd have to jump through more hoops than a circus monkey to see freedom. They'd also want to know what I'd been doing in that cottage.

During our soggy dinner of overbaked potatoes and stewed meat, a few of the inmates tried to draw me into conversation, but the last thing I wanted was to be unveiled as an American, a fact my accent might give away. I kept my answers brief and monosyllabic, and looked each of them in the eyes for no longer than an instant.

Back in my bunk, I'd almost finished the paperback romance when my cellmate came in and asked me point-blank where I was from.

"Canada," I said.

He got a cigarette going, caught me eyeing it, and handed one over.

"Young Canadian like you," he said, "you're back on the street in a week. Unless you did something despicable, what?"

His laugh broke into a foul emphysemic cackle, which disturbed me so much that I crushed my cigarette out, half-finished. When he was done coughing, he took another huge drag off his smoke, the ash of which was fully two inches long, and told me that they'd just turned on the TV. I'd be a fool to sit in my bunk during TV time, he said—it was our highest inmate privilege.

He left me in peace, but not a minute later a big commotion broke out at the end of the block. Scrambling out of my cell, I found the inmates gathered in a horde and hollering at the TV, which was chained to a high platform on the other side of the cell-block bars.

It was tuned to the news. On the screen were images of explosions and street fires, missiles flashing across the night sky—the first pictures I would see of my country bombing Baghdad.

I joined the rest of them in front of the TV. After the initial surprise, they piped down and we all watched in silence. Most shook their heads in somber disapproval. But I saw plenty of veneration on those faces as well. It was a thrill to watch anything burn from behind bars.

WHAT MANNER OF
MAN HE IS

The next morning I hadn't quite finished chiseling through my breakfast when one of the deputies came around and called my name, instructing me to take the crap they'd issued me up to the cellblock entrance.

The deputy led me down a narrow corridor and into a cluttered office with no windows. He muttered something I didn't quite understand, then ordered me not to touch anything and shut me in there alone.

Soon as I sat down, my eyes darted around the room, hunting for useful objects, though I couldn't have said what for. Then a whiskery detective in a wrinkled brown suit barged in with a mug of pungent coffee. He leafed through a manila folder at his desk and then looked up flabbergasted, as if my very presence were suddenly an outrage.

"I'm gonna make something very clear before we release you," he said in a gravelly voice.

He glared at me for a minute but then seemed to change his mind, getting up and walking around behind me. He leaned over my shoulder and placed a cool, dry hand on my neck.

"I don't know what you were up to out there in that cottage, Delanne," he whispered. "But I know you're not innocent, and if it were up to me, I'd bury you so deep in shit that it'd take you the rest of your miserable life to get back home."

I looked straight ahead, reminding myself that he was a cop, that it was the same all over the world—cops spook people for a living.

"You don't belong here, Delanne," he said. "Not in this city, not in this region, and not in this country. I don't know how you got here, but we'll be watching you—you can count on that."

He went back around to his desk, sat down, and gulped his coffee. Even though I knew it was just a routine, it was doing a number on my nerves. I started to say something in my defense.

"Keep your fucking mouth shut," he cut in. He scratched his whiskery jowls. "We know you have a contract at Lycée Corbières that lasts another two and a half months. And we know you're in room 228 at the Foyer International in Ste-Térèse. So let me make this perfectly clear: when your visa is up at the end of May, if we find you anywhere in France, I will make sure—personally, Delanne—that these people who took care of your release don't interfere with my busting your ass."

He put his coffee down and grimaced, as if he were already sick of it.

"And I don't wanna hear about you going anywhere until that visa is up," he added. "Except to the train that will take you to Charles de Gaulle and back to the States. Or else I'll come get you. Personally. Do you understand what I'm talking about, Delanne?"

I was boggled, not sure if a man could loathe a complete stranger so intensely, or if this one just needed to quit caffeine. I fixed my eyes on him until he was finished, wondering if and how Nabec had taken care of my release—I couldn't see who else might have.

Five minutes later I was standing outside, as free as an orphan, suddenly starving for something decent to eat and as many stiff drinks as my wallet could manage.

I decided to get back to Ste-Térèse first, but wasn't halfway to the Gare de Lourange, which stood maybe two hundred yards from the police station, when a navy Peugeot with tinted windows slowed beside me.

The driver's window came down. "Excuse me, would you like a ride?"

I glanced at the driver—he'd used English, but I didn't know him—and picked up my pace. I was finished putting up with bullshit.

The Peugeot coasted alongside me.

"Are you not the American, Jeffrey Delanne?" asked the driver, this time in French.

My neck went hot. I stopped and faced the man. He had a long tan face, a sloped forehead, a dark mustache, and aviator sunglasses. I'd never seen him before.

"Fuck off," I said.

I walked on. The Peugeot coasted alongside.

"Would you not like to know how you were released, M. Delanne?" the man asked.

He'd switched back to English. For a second I thought he might be another detective, maybe even a fed. There was no one in the car with him.

"You've got the wrong guy," I said in my best French accent. "Name's Jean-Marie."

"Well, Jean-Marie, I'm a friend of a friend—a good friend."

I started walking faster. I didn't care how he'd discovered my name, and I didn't care to hear his theories as to why I'd just been released. I was finished getting into strangers' cars, fed up with the cloak-and-dagger business.

When the man said something about wanting to help me, my patience went red.

"I don't care who you are," I said. "Get your goddamn car away from me."

He braked a few feet up, pulled his shades down his nose, and smiled at me as I walked past. Another car pulled up behind him, its driver plainly impatient.

"Look, Jeffrey. I know who you are. I'm here as a favor to our mutual friend, M. Dreyfus."

Hearing Dreyfus's name made me stop on a dime. "Dreyfus is *not* a friend of mine."

I started walking again. He coasted alongside. The car behind his honked twice.

"Come on, Jeffrey," the man said. "Would not a friend of yours get me to wait outside the police station for you, to offer you a ride? That sounds like a friend to me, Jeffrey. We're all friends here. Now get in."

I could feel my legs slowing down. If this guy could take me to Dreyfus, I'd be one step closer to being finished with Nabec—finished with the whole mess. And Dreyfus still had to answer for lining me up with a crook in the first place.

The driver of the car behind his leaned on his horn.

"You don't seem to understand what M. Dreyfus has done for you," the man said, unfazed and still coasting alongside. We were sprinting distance from the train station parking lot.

"You mean the trouble he got *me* in? Or didn't he tell you about that?"

I'd switched to English without thinking. He seemed to follow me just fine.

"Okay, Jeffrey. But Dreyfus still wishes to see you now, to talk with you, to explain himself and give you advice. You might be interested in knowing what manner of man he is."

He had his sunglasses off now, and was studying me closely.

"You need help, Jeffrey," he said. "Have you seen your face? Come on and get in."

I stood there for a long minute, searching the man's eyes while the next car blew its horn. Then I climbed into the backseat.

• • •

WE DROVE OUT of the city, first on the *autoroute,* then onto a few winding country roads. As we moved deeper into the country, my breathing quickened—we were entering the same dreary woods where Nabec's cottage had been. Here and there I checked the driver's expression in the rearview mirror. He was acting as if we were out on a pleasure cruise. But soon I recognized a familiar road sign. A familiar intersection. Part of a torn-down fence followed by a sharp left turn.

My stomach jumped and seized, and I felt a jolt of adrenaline. We were headed for Nabec's.

I went for the door latch—which was locked. The driver sped up suddenly. Without thinking twice, I threw my arm over his seat, slinging it around his throat and pulling him back against the headrest.

"This is when you tell me what the *fuck* is going on," I said between my teeth.

He was doing a champion job of keeping the car at speed and on the road.

"Let me out now!" I yelled.

He took one hand off the wheel. It dawned on me that if he belonged to Nabec, he'd be packing a gun. I tightened my hold anyway. The car swerved.

"Don't . . . be stupid," he managed.

When we rounded the next curve going way too fast, I loosened the headlock—he was one stubborn son of a bitch.

We were coming up on Nabec's driveway, and then we blew past it.

I let go of the guy and sat back, breathing hard while we drove the next few miles. The driver seemed unusually okay with the fact that I'd just attacked him. I muttered a half-assed apology, but didn't feel compelled to explain myself.

When we slowed and turned onto a long gravel drive, the guy

said, "There is nothing to be afraid of, Delanne. I've done just what I told you I would do. Now I'll wait and take you home after you've spoken with M. Dreyfus."

His tone made it sound like a threat. We came to a stop at the end of the drive, where in the middle of a grove of knotty evergreens sat a square stone bungalow, like Nabec's but tinier. I asked him if he'd be so kind as to unlock my door.

He faced me, grinning. "*Calmez-vous, Jeffrey*. You have arrived on the side of the good guys."

WE'D PULLED BETWEEN two navy Peugeot sedans exactly like the one we were in. When my door unlocked I climbed out quickly and checked the surrounding countryside, trying to gauge how long it would take me to walk back to the highway, where I could hitchhike back to Ste-Térèse.

The driver's window came down. "Dreyfus is inside, Jeffrey. Go in through the front door."

I did it reluctantly, but before I could get there, a man in a blue serge suit stepped outside. He was as big as an NFL lineman, hulking thighs and shoulders, neck like a cinder block. When our eyes met, he dropped his chin and muttered something inaudible. I spotted a tiny black cord running from his ear under his shirt collar, and I could see a rather obvious gun bulge under his jacket.

The realization hit me like a brick: more fucking cops.

I stopped in my tracks. But the giant held up a hand, as if to cast some sort of spell on me. We exchanged hard stares. I didn't dare run—the man could clearly outsprint me, with a twenty-yard handicap, and I wasn't in the mood to be tackled—though my gut was telling me to get as far away from this neck of the woods as I could.

Before I could say anything, Dreyfus stepped out through the front door. He looked nothing like the Claude Dreyfus from Corbières: this one was clean-shaven and wore a sharp charcoal suit and red tie. He'd even tamed his Afro.

He came over and took my hand and started pumping it as if I were a returned war hero.

"At last we meet on the other side, Delanne. Ouch—you must have taken *quite* a thrashing."

I snatched my hand away from his. "You're a fucking cop? Is that what all this is about?"

"Well, yes, but first things first. Congratulations are in order, Jeffrey—you did splendidly."

Here was the long-awaited punch line. I was even hotter about it than I'd expected. I took my eyes from Dreyfus's and gazed across a clearing in the woods, trying to fend off the fury.

"You owe me an explanation," I said. "You owe me a big motherfucking explanation."

Dreyfus cleared his throat. "You're confused, that's all. You're not seeing—"

"Used, by a pig," I said—louder, so his man could hear me.

A flash of anger showed on Dreyfus's chubby face—he was easily prodded. He started to say something, but his cell phone stopped him short.

"Non," he said into the phone. My mind went back to Nabec's cottage. The torment, the lost sleep, the violent impulses. All leading to a tidy beating from Rafa and a couple of days in the slammer—all because of the man standing in front of me.

I felt like knocking him down and kicking him in the ribs, right in front of his behemoth sidekick.

"Oui," he was saying into his cell. *"Oui, et je dit* non *alors. C'est clair? Bon."* He hung up and frowned at me. "Walk with me, Jeffrey."

I humored him and walked back with him to the driveway, where a few other suited men in trench coats had gathered by the cars. There was a row of tall pines behind them, long pine needles decorating the grass all around.

"Tell me this, Dreyfus: How the hell are you a teacher at Corbières?"

This drew a big grin. "That's a whole different matter, Jeffrey—and none of your business. I have only brought you here to offer you encouragement, so do not make me regret it."

I imagined my hands shooting out and grabbing him by the lapels. But I had enough wounds to nurse already.

"You got me thrown in jail," I said. "Two days ago I was tied up in Nabec's cottage, playing punching bag for one of his lackeys." I pointed at my face. "*You* did this to me, asshole."

Dreyfus's face went rigid. "You're confused. Nobody forced you to do this. And the worst of it is over, anyway—if you follow my instructions."

I was willing to bet that the worst wasn't over. But that wasn't what was eating me.

"All this just to set the old guy up?" I said. "To make me into your prize witness? Do you know what he does to people? You put me in big-league danger, man. I could have been—"

"Come now, Delanne, you're a smart young man. You can imagine the way these things work. You were in that jail cell for how long? *Un jour, deux?* Small price to pay, to be in Nabec's trust. All you must do now is face him once more . . . in a different context, most likely. So prepare yourself."

I searched Dreyfus's little eyes. He was hedging, twisting the truth to make it fit.

"But why me?" I asked. "Did you look at a lineup of foreigners and then say, 'That one, let's fuck that one over'?"

Dreyfus's eyes grew wide. "Now have this straight, *mon ami*—" He stopped himself and took a deep breath. "I am not asking you to understand my job. This case is not an easy one. This man has certain . . . advantages. And in my line of work we take extraordinary measures."

I glanced at the men over by the cars. They weren't looking my way, but they were silent—listening in. I shook a cigarette out of my pack and fired up.

"A fucking Arab gangster," I said in French. "Do you know what he was having me do?"

Dreyfus placed a finger over his lips and lowered his voice. "Prudence, Jeffrey. He paid you, did he not? I might have left your stinking ass in jail."

He had a point. But I couldn't understand why he didn't want to know what Nabec had had me do, if I was supposed to be used as some kind of witness against him.

"So what the hell am I supposed to do now?" I asked. "I've got cops offering to escort me to the airport in May, and ordering me not to go anywhere until then. You've fucking ruined me."

At that I detected a smile on Dreyfus's face. It was all I could do not to take a swing at him.

"It is you who have ruined yourself, Delanne." He stepped away and opened the back door of the nearest Peugeot. "We're done talking. I'll contact you about the next step. Don't go anywhere, except to work—you must continue going to Corbières. Pierre over there will take you home."

"Incompetence," I barked at him before he could get into his car. "You have to trick foreigners into doing your dirty work? Fucking French incompetence."

More outrage flashed in his eyes—just what I wanted.

"Now you calm down, you little prick," he said. "Or else I make your life into hell."

"You won't make my life hell," I said. "Not if you want me to keep playing your little game."

Dreyfus laughed, glancing quickly around at the others, who were all watching closely.

"You'll play my game whether you like it or not," he said coolly, and in French.

He stepped my way and put his hand on my shoulder, dangerously close to my neck.

"Sleep it off, you look like *merde*. But you must continue to go to work. Do not make me send Pierre to escort you there. You would not like that."

He climbed into the car, chuckling. "If you leave town, I will have you found and thrown in jail. This is something in which you have no choice. You must continue going to Corbières every day, life as usual. One must keep up appearances, after all. I will contact you when the time comes."

He shut himself in, but his window was lowered a few inches. I couldn't hold back.

"And what if I tell Brule that he's got an undercover cop working at his school?"

"Now, Jeffrey." Dreyfus's glare was baleful, poisonous. "Understand me here: that would simply be bad for your health."

ONE WEIRD SON OF A BITCH

When Pierre stopped his car in front of my place, I got out and told him to rot in hell.

"Ah, Jeffrey," he called back. "You and I may very well have our day. We'll see then if you are brave enough to take me around the neck."

He pulled away before I could think of a wise comeback. I stood on the street for a minute or two with a cigarette. Fuck comebacks—it was time to do something. I headed upstairs to my room and dialed Thierry's number. He picked up on the second ring.

"It's Jeffrey," I said. "We need to talk."

Long silence. "Okay, Jeffrey. How about tonight at nine? I'm going out now."

I took a beer with me into the shower and afterward checked out my face in the mirror: slightly swollen nose and bottom lip, a faint yellowish bruise under my left eye, and some redness on my left cheek. I looked like a strung-out, spoiled version of myself.

I dozed for a few hours and woke up feeling like summer garbage. Down in the main foyer building there was a note in my mailbox: *Meet me at the Rougerie at six?—A.*

The clock said ten till six, a coincidence, though I was willing to bet she'd meant the day before. It didn't matter—I didn't need her around to watch me drink.

I found the Rougerie deserted except for Bruno. He had his ancient black-and-white TV behind the bar tuned to the news, and with the sound off, the place was as silent as a tomb. I shook Bruno's hand and ordered a Pelforth draft with a bourbon chaser. Not a half-minute later, Amelia and Patrick rushed in from the back, followed by Françoise, Marine, Joël, and Julien, all of them singing "Joyeux Anniversaire."

I didn't have the heart to tell them that my birthday wasn't for another week.

Bruno opened a few bottles of Beaujolais and poured glasses for everyone. When it was time for a toast, the salute went out not just to me but to Julien. I caught his smile and raised my glass to him—I'd find out later that his birthday was tomorrow, and that somehow Amelia had found this out and coordinated something with Patrick.

I killed my drinks, paid brief attention to a glass of wine, and started feeling like my old self.

Not for long. People kept asking about my face, wanting to know whom I'd tangled with, and how, and why. And bringing it all back home in the meantime. I said it was a long story, and left it at that. Because it was painfully clear to me that I was worlds away from these people now—I couldn't relate on a conversational level with them anymore, couldn't imagine any of them hearing my story and actually buying it. Now, rather than the usual urge to pull my usual Irish good-bye, all I felt was the urge to smash something priceless.

Julien stopped me on my way to the bathroom.

"You should have seen when they surprise-birthdayed me about an hour ago," he said. "Almost messed my pants. But really, who'd you get in a fight with?"

"Long story, man. Some other time I'll tell it."

He pretended to punch my sore jaw. "You gotta keep those hands up, partner." He held up his hands a few inches from either side of his face, ducking and bobbing his head like a boxer.

"Come tell us the story tomorrow night at my party," he said.

I nodded, but thought *not a chance.* It was fine that he was warming up to me after three or four months of keeping me at bay, but it was a little too late. Back in December when we'd first met, he'd seemed pretty curious about me, for roughly an hour.

Soon a clutch of fresh drinkers crowded in for happy hour. Amelia cornered me and tried mothering over the swollen parts of my face. I told her if she didn't quit it I'd leave.

"Don't be an asshole," she said. "Have another drink. It's your fucking birthday."

"It's not even my birthday. And since when did you know Patrick?"

Her eyes flashed to mine. "I don't. And I know your birthday isn't until next week, but I'll be gone next week—I told you that Friday night. Spring vacation's next week, remember?"

I couldn't remember her saying anything like that, and it made me hot to think of all I might have told her in my soused state. I was mad, too, about forgetting our upcoming vacation—in a few more days the lycées would have a full week off for some kind of French ecclesiastical holiday. And I wasn't supposed to go any-where, which reduced my vacation prospects to lolling around in my apartment with a paranoid thumb up my ass.

The clock caught my eye: almost eight. Françoise came over and reeled me back to the table in the back room, where the rest of the gang had assembled and was now taking part in some kind of drinking game with three soiled decks of playing cards. Françoise had clearly overshot her wine quota by several: her lips and teeth were stained purple, she had a mean case of hiccups, and her head was wobbling around like a newborn's. But I wasn't going to give the old woman a hard time.

She forced me into a seat beside her and tried speaking English, but couldn't hold more than four words together. A Beatles song came on the bar stereo and everyone started singing along at an obnoxious volume.

I myself had a one-track mind. I leaned in to question Françoise: "Did you know Claude Dreyfus was a cop?"

She closed one eye and reared her head back defensively. "Not now, Jeffrey, not the time."

"You knew it, then?"

She hiccuped, closed her eyes, and started shaking her head to the rhythm of the music.

"You knew he was a cop?" I repeated.

"Jeffrey!" She took a long drag from her cigarette and reached for her glass of wine. "Some fings not now—"

She hiccuped again, this time so violently that some of her red wine splashed out of the glass in her hand and onto her lap.

I looked over at Marine, who was sitting on her other side. Marine gazed at me for a long moment, but tonight I wasn't in the right gear for her come-hither-you-can't-have-me ritual. Amelia was over with Angelique, throwing darts, her back to us. Joël was sitting across from me, singing to the music with Michel, who as usual was all smiles but probably itching for a pointless debate.

I put my hand on Françoise's wrist. "Do you even know what I'm talking about, Françoise?"

"Oh . . . Jeffrey." She set aside her glass, looked down at her lap, and started pawing at her skirt. "Bloody fuck. Who in bloody hell did that?" Then she threw back her head and burst out laughing.

I decided I'd had enough of these people. Patrick intercepted me on my way up to the bar to pay. His eyes were red with hash and watery with drink.

"I wanted to tell you something," he said. "About the Italian."

"Amelia? She's Sicilian."

"Italian, Sicilian—she's fucking weird." He glanced over at the dartboard and Amelia. "I couldn't tell you earlier. But she came in here two nights ago and started acting like we were old friends. I mean, I met her like once, right?"

"Right," I said, hoping the conversation would end there.

"So I just thought I should tell you. Somehow she found out about this surprise birthday thing we were going to do for Julien, and she told me your birthday was coming up. That's how we knew to include you. I mean, you never told us it was your birthday."

"It's not. Not till next week. But thanks, Patrick. Have a good night."

"Thing is," he said, placing a hot hand on my shoulder, "she started asking questions about Marine, like there was some kind of woman jealousy thing going on. I told her something about you and Marine being just friends. Then she said something about Julien, and we talked about him. I didn't know she knew him . . . kind of weird."

"Did you tell Julien?"

"Earlier. He said, 'You mean that crazy green-eyed bitch Jeff knows?' I don't think anybody likes her, Jeff."

"Count me in," I said. I shook his hand reluctantly, then went up to the bar and asked Bruno what I owed him.

"Hell," said Bruno. "More than I'm worth, I'll tell you that, my man!"

"Seriously," I said.

"Seriously to you. Happy birthday, kid."

"It's not my birthday yet," I said, pushing a twenty-euro across the bar.

He raised his eyebrows as if I'd said something offensive, and pushed the bill back.

"We'll let it slide," he said. "But don't come in on your real birthday begging for free ones."

That was about all it took. If I'd been as drunk as everyone else, I would have aimed for his front teeth. When someone beside me touched my arm, I nearly jumped out of my shoes.

Marine was standing there wearing an expression that I couldn't have cracked with the help of a dozen detectives.

"I don't care if that Italian girl sees me talking to you," she said.

"Sicilian, and we're just friends—not even that, really. Have a good night, Marine."

She put her hand on my elbow. "Julien and I broke up, Jeffrey." I looked her hard in the eyes, but felt nothing but bitterness: great timing. I glanced at the clock behind the bar. Eight fifteen.

"I'm sorry to hear it, Marine. But I have to go."

"We were having problems," she said suddenly. "I just thought you should know."

Her eyelids looked heavy, but I had no pity left in my heart.

"Can we talk about this later?"

"It's what I said the other night, isn't it?"

"No," I lied, remembering our talk a couple of nights before, and how she'd made clear that my chances with her were essentially nil. "I've really got to go, Marine. Have a good night."

I pushed the twenty Bruno had refused back across to his side, dug my coat out from the pile around the coatrack, and stepped outside without even a glance back at her.

Julien was outside talking on his cell in German. When he saw me he said something in French and hung up.

"Where you going, partner?"

"Nowhere," I said, searching for a way to shift the topic. "I forgot you spoke German."

Julien narrowed his eyes but still looked jumpy—sweaty forehead, clenching jaw, wide eyes.

"Work stuff," he said.

I started to go, but stopped. "What exactly do you do, man?"

"Just stupid shit for a newspaper—stupid newspaper shit."

"Which paper?"

Julien's eyes tick-tocked. "The *Journal.* But don't get me wrong—I'm just an assistant, and it's monkey work—bullshit monkey work, stupid newspaper shit. Look, where are you going?"

I studied his eyes. I was about to take a big step in going to Thierry with my heap of woes, and I didn't want the whole world to know. Anyway, Julien was the last Rougerie person I wanted to talk to—I didn't care to hear his side of the unfolding Marine drama.

"Nowhere," I said. "Have a good one."

When I turned away, Julien grabbed my arm. I shook out of his grip.

"What's your problem, man?"

"Just hold on a second."

He jerked a hand up between us, as if to introduce something monumental. Then his cheeks swelled—he seemed deeply troubled by something in his stomach—and he let loose the most abominable belch I'd witnessed since college.

"My one gift," he said.

"You know, you're one weird son of a bitch."

He grinned. "You got that right. And you don't even know the half. Have a happy birthday."

"It's not my fucking birthday, Julien. Good-bye."

As I walked off, he called after me, "See you at the party at my place tomorrow night, then?"

"Sure, sure," I called back.

"I'll take that as a yes! I'm holding you to it, Jeff. Don't do anything I wouldn't do!"

Even several buildings down, I could feel his weird eyes following me.

NEVER WILL BE SOME
PIDDLING DETECTIVE

On my way to the Place Médiatheque tram stop, I did some important rehashing. Clearly both sides were yanking my chain: Nabec hadn't needed me the way he'd claimed, and Dreyfus had something else up his sleeve. But Dreyfus hadn't given me instructions beyond staying put and going to work. That meant the gig wasn't over yet—maybe Nabec wasn't quite finished with me. If so, it was safe for me to become a paranoid wreck.

Now going to Solène's dad felt like my only option, my only chance to dodge the shit storm I could smell heading my way. If only I'd known that the storm was moving in from more than one direction.

The tram stop was empty except for two young guys, one huddled against a nearby pay phone and the other waiting down at the other end of the line. Both kept glancing my way, and with every minute their glancing made me jumpier. Finally the tram pulled in and I got a solid look at them from its headlights: they were both fair-skinned, baggy-jeaned, and couldn't have been much older than my seniors.

I rode two stops east, walked ahead five or six cars, and jumped off at the last second at Place des Ducs, in front of the chateau, one stop before the Ste-Térèse train station. As their tram car passed, I saw both kids standing side by side, staring out the window at me, as if they'd both just become buddies. The next tram pulled in a few minutes later, but I let it pass and grabbed the one after that. I was at Thierry's place in another fifteen.

Solène opened the door on the second ring.

"You're here," she said.

I felt as if I'd rung the wrong doorbell, though of course I hadn't.

"Sorry to just show up like this. I actually called this morning and arranged to talk with your dad—for some legal advice."

"He told me, Jeff. Come on in."

I hesitated in the doorway. Her curly blond hair was piled on top of her head, and I could tell she'd sunk some quality time into her eye makeup. Her tight zip-up hooded sweatshirt said COLLEGE on the front, and the terry-cloth shorts she had on looked a lot like underwear: lithe naked legs, smooth bare feet, toenails painted orange.

I shot a glance down the street the way I'd come, almost ready to run for it. She waved me in behind her.

Inside, with the door shut behind us, I was even more on edge.

"It's just that he's not back yet," said Solène.

The house seemed different from before—slightly warmer, dimly lit, soft music coming from a farther room.

"God, Jeff, what happened to your face?"

I felt myself blush. "It's nothing, seriously."

"Did you get into a fight?" She reached to touch my face. "You did—with who?"

"Shouldn't I leave and come back later, Solène?"

"That's silly. Dad expects me to stay with his guests until he gets home—it's normal."

I was still stalling in the entryway. "I thought sure he told me nine o'clock."

"Nine means ten to him. He has a great mind that's not so great with numbers." She seemed to sense my discomfort and switched to English: "He'll be back sooner or later."

Sooner or later. An expression I'd taught her class the week before. I pretended not to notice and followed her into the living room, choosing an armchair and picking a newspaper from the pile of them on the coffee table—today's *Journal.* Almost immediately I remembered Léo's arrest.

"Hey, did Léo get out of jail yet?"

Solène looked up suddenly, as if I'd mentioned something forbidden.

"They let him go this morning, but he has court things to do now."

"What the hell was he thinking?"

"I don't know," she said. "I really don't know anything else about it. You want a beer?"

"I'm fine." My eyes landed on her legs. I looked away. "Honestly, I can just sit here and read until your dad gets back."

She went into the kitchen and came back with a bottle of 1664 and a glass. I tried to act interested in a front-page news article from the Sunday edition about the riot in *centre ville.* Toward the bottom of the page, a few names I didn't recognize had been underlined with a red pencil. Without looking up at her, I thanked Solène for the beer and drank from the bottle. She retook her seat in the armchair facing mine. At once I could feel the heat from her eyes. She cleared her throat and told me in French how frustrated she'd gotten earlier with some English reading. I looked up and became locked in an awkward gaze. Her lips parted. She seemed to be expecting something.

"Do you read much in French, Jeffrey?"

I looked down at my newspaper. "Some."

She came around the coffee table and sat beside me on the couch, leaning in to take a look.

"One of Dad's," she said, referring to the paper. "He's doing some private investigation thing."

"I thought you said he was retired."

"He is," she said. "But he was a detective, so he knows all sorts of people. People ask him to help them . . . Hey, I meant to ask you something about the other day, Jeff. What was wrong?"

Our eyes met. She seemed a dozen times more at ease than I was. "What other day?"

"When we talked in the hall. You looked as if something awful had happened. I can tell when you're frustrated, you get this look in your eyes."

I looked into her eyes. "Oh yeah. The other day." She was talking about the day we'd crossed paths, just before I'd gone to the lycée office and had gotten wrangled into talking with Brule. So much time seemed to have passed, she might have been talking about a day five years ago.

"I had a lot on my mind," I said.

There was a colony of sweat migrating down my back now. I could hear the music more clearly. It was coming from upstairs—a Coltrane song called "Moment's Notice" that I'd been in love with since high school. I turned the newspaper to the next page, fighting to keep my eyes away from Solène's bare legs.

"There always seems to be too much on your mind," she said. "Sometimes in the corridor you look lost."

I took a big swallow of beer and met her gaze again. "I'm a long way from home."

She smiled. "Why did you leave there?"

I put the newspaper down and thought hard about it. "I guess sometimes you just need to go somewhere."

More intense eye contact. Her eyes had something firm and fixed in them, a youthful determination minus the naïveté you'd expect.

"I know," she said. "But doesn't it sometimes feel like there's nowhere to go? Nowhere new, I mean."

"There isn't anywhere new," I said. "That doesn't do away with the impulse to keep looking. That's my problem. I'm always making it so I have to leave." Something came to me then. "I guess I thought I'd find what I was looking for here. Maybe not something new, but something older."

Solène nodded. "It's all place-names. You go to place-names, and when you get there or stay long enough, it feels the same as anywhere else. That's how it was every time I left St-Térèse with Mom, anyway." She gazed off. For the first time I noticed a faint birthmark on the left side of her neck, just above the collarbone.

"I think it's because we're the same wherever we go," I said after a minute.

We didn't look at each other now, didn't need to; we'd stumbled onto something without planning on it, an answer made up of a thousand more questions.

She stood. "I want to show you something."

I didn't get up until she was at the stairs.

"It's up here," she said. "It's just a photo, come on."

On the second floor she turned right, down a short hallway. I stopped in the doorway of a tiny bedroom with lavender walls and a low ceiling, a single bed with a dresser at one end and a narrow desk and a computer at the other.

She went to the computer and turned off the music. Then she crouched, took a framed picture from under her bed, came back and handed it to me: a photo of a woman in her mid to late forties, full cheeks, large eyes, and curly blond hair like Solène's. The woman was smiling, her arms spread wide. Behind her lay a dark ocean streaked with waves and a fantastic pink-orange horizon.

"My mom," Solène said in French. "Her birthday was a week ago. Would have been. She liked to travel. She took me all over western Europe, Spain especially, where my brother lives. It was always a mission for her, you see, one quest after another."

I smiled and moved the photo into the hallway light.

"My thirtieth birthday's next Thursday," I said.

We stood in the doorway, looking at the photo in silence.

"We used to go to that beach every year for her birthday," she said. "Near La Rochelle. It was always cold and rainy. Three years ago, I took this picture. It was evening, the first time that the sun ever came out—it came out just before it went down."

Solène's lips were pressed together in thought. "You hide this from your father?" I asked.

"No," she said. "Dad keeps plenty of photos of her around. He dealt well with it. At least after the first few months he did. We both learned together, I think. To understand it."

I wanted to say that I hadn't learned to understand a goddamn thing about death.

"I'm sorry."

We hugged—it seemed fitting, standing there talking about her deceased mother. Her heart was beating so fast that mine picked up speed. I moved to step away from her, but she didn't let go.

The picture fell to the carpet, and I held her slender back as she kissed me. Her lips were confident and full. Her tongue made a circle around mine, brushing against my teeth. I pulled away and said something in English that an instant afterward I couldn't remember.

She leaned back in, but I took hold of her wrists and held her a safe distance away. We were both breathing heavily and gazing into each other's eyes. I realized then that I was willing to do anything for her—anything but that.

A second later an electronic pulse seemed to jolt the entire house, followed by a low, machine-like grumble. I leaped into the hallway like a soldier under fire.

Solène started laughing. "It's just the garage door, Jeff."

"Sounded like a fucking earthquake." She laughed again.

"It's not funny," I said. She seemed to know that I wasn't just talking about the garage door.

• • •

I HURRIED DOWNSTAIRS and threw myself on the couch. Thierry came in from the garage.

"Welcome back, Jeffrey. Sorry if I'm a little late."

He was wearing a sharp gray suit and a white dress shirt with no tie. A panic-ridden minute whipped by. He was an ex-detective, after all, and I hoped he wouldn't suspect that I'd just kissed his daughter.

Solène came downstairs, paused where her dad couldn't see her, and gave me a mischievous smile and the old finger over the lips. She was wearing the same sweatshirt, but had slipped into a pair of tight faded blue jeans. She ducked into the kitchen and spoke with Thierry in hushed French. Then Thierry came out with a pair of heavy-bottomed rocks glasses and a fresh bottle of Jack Daniel's.

Solène wasn't far behind. "Off to Elise's to study," she announced.

She headed past me and out the front door without looking my way. I bit my tongue, hard and on purpose.

Thierry poured our drinks with a stone-steady hand. We drank without meeting eyes.

"How about the patio for a bit?" he suggested. "Unless it's too cold for you. I find the cool air helps me think."

Outside, he kept the lights off and gazed up at the night sky. My breathing had slowed, but my stomach still felt balled up and jittery.

"All this cold," said Thierry. "Soon it will be over."

I knew he didn't want to chat about the weather. We lit cigarettes. He asked how things were at Corbières. I said fine, except for a few uncooperative colleagues.

Thierry chuckled. "I hear that."

He looked to be in a reflective mood tonight. I drank and looked across his tiny backyard, a well-kept plot of grass surrounded by a privacy fence.

"Something happened to your face," he said.

"I'd like to tell you about that."

"Something about what we talked about before?"

I fought off the urge to chicken out, and nodded. "I'm not sure where to start."

"The best place to start is at the beginning, is it not?"

Back in the living room, Thierry turned up the stereo—out of old habit, he said.

I told him about Dreyfus's offer in the profs' room a few weeks back, and as I spoke, Thierry didn't look my way. Neither did he budge or change his expression—not even when I told him about Rafa and the meeting in Lourange—until I said Nabec's name. At which point he let one eyebrow rise slightly.

I told him about the cottage in the woods between Ste-Térèse and Lourange, about the room to the right and the room to the left, about the info I was supposed to retrieve from Nabec's clients, and about how much I'd been paid to meet with each.

"And what place-name did the first man give you?"

I hesitated, but only for a second. "The old cathedral in the Bouffay."

Thierry faced me and did a quick but intense scan of my eyes before looking away. I told him about my third visit to the cottage, about getting beat up, arrested, and taken to Dreyfus.

"Claude Dreyfus," said Thierry with a chuckle. "I don't understand him—I might as well tell you that. That's another thing that makes Corbières so troubling. Did Dreyfus tell you anything else when he revealed his identity to you—anything at all?"

I was perplexed. I hadn't expected Thierry to be more interested in Dreyfus than in Nabec.

"No," I said. "Only that he wanted me to stick around, to testify against Nabec, I assumed. He said that it was almost all over, that I shouldn't go anywhere, that I should keep going to work and all that. But he set me up, see—he got me thrown in jail. And now I'm not supposed to . . ."

But Thierry wasn't paying attention. He'd zoned out and was staring up at a large black-and-white photo print on the wall, the image of a wooden pier stretching into some foggy gray water.

"Thierry?"

"What? Oh—of course. He shouldn't have done that. But we can assume that of Dreyfus."

Thierry sat back and nodded to himself for a solid minute. He was holding his cards close to the chest, which I should have expected—his ex-profession probably made asking a given and revealing a rarity. But it was starting to irritate me—it was my ass we were talking about.

"This Nabec," he said finally. "You think he has other helpers at Corbières—other than you, I mean—other assistants or students, maybe, kids Dreyfus sends his way, like he did with you?"

"I don't know. I rarely see Dreyfus around. He's slippery like that."

"Jeff, I might as well tell you that Claude Dreyfus is not just some cop—he's an agent who followed a supposed lead last year into Corbières. Did he say anything about Corbières?"

It was clear to me now that Thierry's questions weren't aimed at helping me so much as at satisfying his own curiosities, whatever those were. And I was having a hard time staying cool.

"No, but that's not my problem, Thierry. I'm trying to ask you if you know anyone who can help me with this."

Thierry frowned. "I'm going to help you, Jeff. But you've got to realize first that what you've gotten into is much larger than a couple of interviews you did for some Arab."

"I know that. He's selling information to terrorists or outlaws or whatever. That's what the second guy I interviewed swore to, at least."

Thierry began massaging his palms with his thumbs, as if they were labor-weary.

"Here's the thing, Jeff." He closed his right hand into a fist, then gave me an accusing look. "That cathedral was an important location for some people I know. Up until about a week ago. When its cover was blown."

I sat up. "How the hell was I supposed to know that? I got fucking strong-armed into it."

"The cathedral was a point of exchange," Thierry said, completely ignoring my outburst. "A rendezvous point for a few special investigators I know. It takes weeks to set up reliable points of exchange, Jeff, so valuable information doesn't get leaked. All I can tell you is that highly sensitive information was leaked because of that. If Nabec is getting similar info from the men he interrogates . . . Were there other locations you supplied Nabec with, any he seemed more interested in?"

"I didn't *supply* him with shit, Thierry. And I don't appreciate being treated like a goddamn double agent—"

"Calm down, Jeff. You're not being treated any way at all." We entered a stone-cold stare-down. "Let's smoke another cigarette."

We went outside and spoke in whispers.

"I just need advice, Thierry. Try to see this my way—I've been yanked around enough already, and now I'm just looking for straight solutions."

Thierry said nothing for a minute. "Whether you think so or not, you made the right choice in coming."

Now that I'd ratted out Nabec, a man whose profile was getting worse by the minute, to an ex-detective who didn't seem very concerned with my welfare, I couldn't exactly agree.

"Easy for you to say. You're not the one having to watch his back every minute. All you—"

"Jesus, Jeff. Stop it." He held a hand in the air between us. "Just give me a chance to collect my thoughts. I'm not going to leave you hanging."

He couldn't have chosen a poorer expression, but seemed unaware of that. He took a big drag off his cigarette and mashed it out in the ashtray only half gone.

"Okay," he said then. "I'm going to risk a guess—an educated guess, but still a guess. But what I tell you, you can't breathe to another soul—I'm going against protocol telling you anything. So you'll have to forget about whatever Dreyfus and this Nabec have promised you or threatened you with. You'll have to swallow your fears and enter a trust with me. Understood?"

I looked him in the eyes and nodded, even though I only trusted him as much as any other cop I'd known. No matter what he said, he'd still only tell me what he thought I needed to know.

"Let's go back inside," he said.

IN THE LIVING room, Thierry changed the stereo to an opera channel, cranked up the volume, pulled off his shoes and socks, and shed his suit jacket. Under his left arm was a chrome semiautomatic strapped into a leather shoulder harness. He unhitched the harness and tossed it with the gun into the armchair beside him, sitting back in the couch cushions and sighing as if he'd just relieved himself of an unearthly burden.

"What we're talking about here are international troublemakers," said Thierry. "Or at least people who do important work for them."

"Come on, I could have told you that a long time ago. But do you think the Texan was right about what Nabec's been up to?" I wanted badly for that to be the case—I wanted to know that by lying to Nabec, I'd done at least one thing right.

"That's hard to tell," he said. "This Texan might have been anybody. Let me tell you a thing or two about Dreyfus, Jeff. He's what we call a prodigal. Starting about two years ago—after the attack on New York—Dreyfus was supposed to be investigating a private group of international businessmen for the DST, a counterintelligence branch of the National Police. These businessmen were people who colleagues of mine thought were in business with jihadist cells here in France—selling them intelligence that would keep the cells one step ahead of DST activity. Let's leave it at that—beyond that we're talking classified stuff. But when it was suspected a year ago that they might be using kids to do some of their legwork—kids completely unaware of what they were actually doing, of course—the DST nationals assigned Dreyfus to go undercover and investigate a few lycées in the area. Simple as that."

Thierry's eyes met mine. He seemed uncomfortable telling me the truth.

"Since then," he continued, "undercover exchange points have been blown one after another, intelligence has leaked all over the place, and the closer our guys have gotten to discovering the whereabouts of these jihadists—the guys buying intelligence from these brokers—the faster those parties slip away undetected. So there's a glitch in the system. It may be Dreyfus. They think he's not just pretending to work for the other side—he's actually started doing it for real."

"I don't know, Thierry. Dreyfus was acting pretty damn sincere about getting me to help bring Nabec down."

Thierry hesitated to reply. "Let's just say that the stuff Dreyfus has reported hasn't exactly jibed with the stuff we've gotten elsewhere. But either way, Jeff, if this Nabec is who we're looking for, then you're involved, and you're in deeper than I could even begin to explain."

Thierry poured me another Jack. I started thinking about how, half an hour ago, I'd been sweating the harmless kiss his daughter had laid on me. I felt a wave of anger rise and curl up inside me.

"Fuck that," I said. "If it weren't for a dirty cop, I wouldn't be involved at all. This is complete bullshit. I can't even believe I'm hearing this." I stood up. "You can tell your people that they're hugely mistaken if they think I'm going to take the blame for their leaked locations."

"Come on, Jeff, you're not listening right—"

"You're the one who's not listening right. I didn't come here to ask you how to turn myself in—I came here to get some help stepping clear of it."

"And you *can* step clear of it. If you cooperate with us. That's how it works. I'm just trying to get you to see that it's not exactly simple. You'll be expected to do a thing or two."

At that, my eyes caught his. I thought I could see where he was headed: this was probably where he made his move to manipulate me.

"First, you'll have to stay at Corbières," he said. "Act like you're not planning to go anywhere. It's the best thing you have going. You're a teacher, you work with kids, and you've stuck with the job—this is what the DST will want you to do first. And you're a foreigner, and they'll understand that this makes you a little naïve. Even though as an American . . ."

"What about it?" I asked. Thierry shook his head. "Come on, so I'm an American. What about it?"

"Like I said the last time you were here. Americans aren't very popular in France right now, Jeff. But we can work around that. If you stay put and keep going to work."

"I've got luxury sedans chasing me around the city, people following me on foot." I told him about the two kids I'd seen trailing me on my way over. "I don't think I should stay in this town another night."

Thierry stood up, shaking his head. "Is that what you've had in the back of your mind? That you can just run off? You haven't been reading between the lines if you think—"

"And you're not reading the large print," I snapped. "I can't keep going through the motions because I'm not fucking safe, Thierry.

I've been cheated, beaten up, and given the runaround one too many times—"

I stopped when I saw a twinge of fire in Thierry's eyes.

"Thanks for the whiskey," I said, and started for the door.

Thierry came around the couch. "Don't you walk out that door, Jeff."

But all I could think about was the pounding in my ears. "Don't you try and stop me."

"You can't just ride off into the sunset here, my friend. Dreyfus will send a team of men after you—he's already shown you too much of his hand to let you off easy."

I stopped in the entryway and faced him, but couldn't think what to say.

"You've got to follow this through," Thierry said. "Take responsibility for your actions. And not just for yourself—*justice* demands it, Jeff."

My will broke then, but not because Thierry was right—I had to follow through, I realized, because I'd already shown him too much of *my* hand. I could see now that I had to play along, if I wanted to find my own way out.

"Justice doesn't have anything to do with this," I said finally. "And you know it. If your people know Dreyfus is helping crooks, they would've brought him to justice a long time ago."

Thierry responded by motioning to the seat I'd been using. I stayed in the entryway.

"That's not how this works," he said. "They don't have any hard evidence against Dreyfus. And most likely they're trying to get to the guys he's joined up with, these intelligence brokers—the same guys he was sent to uncover. It's normal for them to want to use Dreyfus to lead them to bigger fish. They've got to stop the people who've been spoiling their operations. And that's just all I can tell you, Jeff—it's the best way for me to explain it to you."

I finished my drink and thought, *What bullshit.* He could tell me plenty more, if he wanted.

"Come and have a seat." Thierry sat down and filled my glass half full with Jack. "You did the right thing in coming, Jeff. Come back and have a seat. You're in good hands now."

I went over and killed my drink in one deep, sour swill. Thierry gazed again at the photo on the wall, as if something new had appeared there, some revelation emerging from the misty water.

"Let me ask you something," he said after a minute. "Why do you think I asked Solène if I could meet you a week ago? Is this some kind of coincidence to you, us crossing paths?"

"Apparently not."

His gaze was sudden, paralyzing. "The DST have been watching you since you met with the man you're calling Rafa a couple of weeks ago, Jeff. They've been following Rafa, waiting for him to slip. And he hasn't—except to bring us to you."

After getting hold of itself, my mind shot to the night I'd gotten arrested at the cottage.

"Is that how the gendarmes knew to come to the cottage that night? They followed him?"

Thierry shook his head. "No—that was something different, that was a fluke. The gendarmes got an anonymous tip, they said. It's not out of the ordinary. All I can say other than that is that Rafa and the others who were there with you weren't booked. But that's nothing now—the place was sold this morning to a retiree from Marseilles. An old woman. That trail's gone cold."

I stood up again and ran my fingers through my hair. "Thierry, you've got to believe me. I'm just a teacher from the States, man, I swear to God."

"I know that, Jeff. I knew that the first time we talked. I had a hunch before that, but I had to meet you and find out for myself. And I'll do my best to convince the DST people I know of that. It was a lucky coincidence that Solène happened to be in one of your classes. Though not a very big one." Thierry paused and gave me a sympathetic look. "Come on, it's no reason to get paranoid. Trust me."

I looked at him now with unveiled disbelief. "I thought you were a *retired* detective."

"I am, in a way."

The dodge made me immediately hot again. "Jesus. Why did I even come here?"

Thierry lifted his drink, killed it, and set the glass down exactly where it had been.

"You came here," he said, "because you want to know the truth."

WE WENT DOWNSTAIRS to Thierry's office. The basement smelled like a locker room and was stocked with old, heavy-duty weight-lifting equipment. Unlocking a door in the rear of the room, Thierry waved me over and flipped on the light switch. I hesitated in the doorway. It was the office of a madman: hand-sketched flow charts, newspaper clippings, enlarged photos pinned all over the walls between maps of France, Spain, Algeria, and the Mediterranean. Above a desk covered with notebooks and periodicals were three shelves that swayed beneath the weight of dozens of hardbound record books.

"Excuse the mess," Thierry said. "I can't clean when I'm working."

He offered me the big office chair and pulled up a stool for himself. When I sat down, my eyes latched instantly onto a massive map of Ste-Térèse. On it were dozens of red lines scattered across and in and out of the city. I saw where Corbières was outlined in red on the map. He cleared some desk space, maneuvering the clutter piece by piece out of our way, as if one false move would disturb an organizational pattern he'd taken a lifetime to perfect.

Then he faced me, his eyes grave, his face wrinkled with concentration.

"Since my wife died, I've learned to take bigger risks, Jeff. If I tell you now that I am not, have not been, and never will be some piddling detective, you must simply believe me, okay? You must never ask what exactly it is that I do, or for whom I do it. Understood?"

I nodded. Then he held up a finger and sighted it like a gun. "And you must never, ever tell Solène what I've told you, or what I'm about to tell you."

"Okay, okay—don't worry."

He slid out the keyboard from the center desk drawer and typed in a series of codes, a process I did not watch, but that took several minutes, until the monitor in front of us lit up.

"If these pictures mean nothing to you, then I've made a bad guess. And you've got to bear with me if I don't explain."

As he typed in another series of codes, my heart slowly crawled into my throat. We watched in silence as his photo software loaded. Thierry typed in one more code, hit Enter, and an instant later two photos appeared on the screen. They were black-and-whites: mug shots of the two men I'd interviewed for Nabec, both of whom, I had a hunch, were no longer among the living.

TO SQUEEZE THE LIFE
OUT OF YOU

Before I could get out of there, Thierry pulled up four more photos: one of Dreyfus shaking hands with a fat man in a fancy overcoat, one of Rafa sharing a café table with Dreyfus, one of me climbing out of the Mercedes, and another of me sitting across from Rafa in broad daylight at the Lourange University café. I sat there like a man watching his dream house go up in flames.

"These were given to us anonymously," said Thierry. "The consensus was that you came here to work for these people. That's why I asked Solène if I could meet you—I didn't quite agree with the consensus, and now I don't believe it in the least. The others will take some convincing, though, Jeff."

"That's the guy who used me as a punching bag," I said, indicating Rafa in the photos.

"So Nabec had the same man who'd interviewed you rough you up, after he found out you'd lied," Thierry said. "What about these first two—Nabec had you interrogate them?"

I nodded. "He wanted a location from that guy and a name from this one, the Texan."

"You're sure that's your Texan?" When I nodded, Thierry stood and clapped his hands together. "I told them. I fucking told them . . . And what name did the Texan give you?"

"Bradley. It's a U.S. senator from Nevada. I was afraid I'd be endangering the guy's life, you know, so I lied and told Nabec the name he'd given me was Brule."

Thierry didn't seem interested in that. "I fucking told them," he said again. "And they didn't believe it would come back around so easily . . . Bradley was a red herring, Jeff. Disinformation. That Texan was one of our contacts, up until about a week ago, when he dropped off the face of the planet. Not long before he disappeared, we had the name passed along at a few random exchange points, along with several other names and locations—to throw off these intelligence brokers and their jihadist partners, see. The cathedral was a legit location, but we weren't sure if things were being leaked there. And as soon as your Texan disappeared, I told my guys he was one of the leaks—I told them, but they didn't buy it. And this Nabec had him tied up?"

"Tied and gagged." I told Thierry how the Texan had convinced me that Nabec wasn't to be trusted with Bradley's name. Then I told him about how the Texan had spoken French, in order to prove that I was heading for deeper trouble. "But he didn't tell me that he'd been working for the cops."

"Of course he wouldn't," Thierry said. "But it serves him right. You can't work both sides for long—eventually it catches up with you."

"So who's the other guy?" I asked. "The Brit."

Thierry gave me a grim look. "Was, Jeffrey. Was. We found his body last week. We haven't found our Texan's body. Not yet, anyway."

I was silent for a long moment. "I got information from them, and then he killed them. He turned around and fucking killed them."

"We don't know that for sure," said Thierry. "If this Nabec is

our man—or one of them—this British fellow you interrogated
was probably nothing but a mercenary working for one intelligence
agency or another, probably knew very little. Nabec might have
freed him, like he told you he would, and the guy might have been
caught afterward and clipped by his own people. That's the way
this stuff works. Once you go over and your people find out, they'll
silence you to keep you from doing it again. We found the Brit's
body with no passport, unknown fingerprints: a wild card. We
don't know how he came about the information you say he had.
But if this Nabec character is one of the guys we're looking for,
and we can connect Dreyfus to him, then we might be able to implicate both of them in this man's death and start bringing the
house down. Don't you see? You've opened this whole thing wider,
Jeff. You should feel good about that."

I told him thanks but that I felt like doomsday. He put a
meaty hand on my shoulder. "Sounds like a job for Monsieur Jack
Daniel's."

"HERE'S THE THING I can't figure out," I said on our way upstairs.
"Why me, you know? Why did they need someone like me?"

Thierry chewed on that for a minute. "Hard to make an educated guess there, Jeff. Usually it's to make a scapegoat out of
somebody—in this case, you. But for what, and why you particularly, who knows? We could say safely, especially since you were
supposed to be translating for a man who didn't need a translator,
that this Nabec has something planned, something bigger than intelligence brokering, and maybe Dreyfus is playing along. Maybe
you were the easiest available guy, an American assistant working
right there at the lycée where Dreyfus was undercover. Maybe they
wanted to test you, feel you out, to see if they could get you to do
something more for them—to see how willing you were. You say
Nabec tried to persuade you, to reason you into joining him?"

I nodded.

"Maybe it was useful for him to have an American on his side," Thierry concluded.

I suddenly suffered a vivid memory of the second time I'd sat before Nabec. I'd seen something like honesty in his eyes, a genuineness that haunted me still. Why such a detailed routine, if I was only meant to be some kind of scapegoat, if photos of me with suspicious people were all they needed?

We were standing under the bright white lights of Thierry's kitchen now.

"Like I said, Jeff, now's not the time to panic."

"I don't know," I said. "I don't know if I believe that. What if they come for me again?"

"You'll just have to trust me. I'll get someone to keep an eye on you . . ." He stopped, seemed to be calculating. "When are you done with class tomorrow?"

"Two. A little after."

"Okay. I'll get somebody out there by then. But you have to keep going to work, keep being a teaching assistant at Corbières, where you're safe. And if Nabec's men do come for you, for Christ's sake go with them—you'll lead us right to him this time. That's what we need more than anything. And if you face this Nabec again, you've got to act like you'd sooner hang yourself than squeal to the cops—that's one thing they don't forgive. But trust me. We'll keep an eye on you outside the lycée."

A twinge of fear rose in my stomach, followed by a small burst of courage. Our eyes met. I realized that I couldn't enter the trust he was talking about—he was still a cop on a mission of his own, after all. But I had nothing to gain by letting him know my true feelings.

"I'm going to get you out of this mess, Jeff," he said, laying on the sincerity. "Our way. But whatever you do, don't trust Claude Dreyfus."

• • •

THIERRY DROVE ME home in his Saab. I locked myself in my swel-tering room and cleaned the place top to bottom, as if the next logical step would be to pack up my things and go, even though I knew I wasn't going anywhere. I lay down and tried to sleep. But my mind kept drifting to Nabec. Now I'd betrayed him worse than any of the men I'd interrogated. It was a betrayal that I felt in my bones, not in my mind, where I knew I'd done the best thing by finally taking action.

But how far had it gotten me? Thierry's hunches about Dreyfus were automatically suspect, because Thierry obviously had his own larger agenda, an investigation he wouldn't sacrifice just to save a guy like me from the noose. And, anyway, what reason would Dreyfus have for using *me* in an illicit partnership with Nabec? Why lead me to believe he was out to bust Nabec? And what could any of this have to do with Lycée Corbières?

All that really mattered now, I decided, was watching my back from more angles than one.

WHEN I WOKE up the next morning, my thoughts ran straight to Solène's legs and the taste of her lips outside her bedroom. I lay in bed for a long time thinking of her in order to keep from thinking of anything else. Then I checked my face in the mirror. Some of the swelling had gone down. While the flesh hurt to touch, the pain consoled me: for what I'd done to the Texan, I felt I'd had it coming.

Outside, the fog was dense and low. I rounded the corner onto Rue Corbières and stopped. The street was jam-packed with stu-dents again. Only there were twice as many of them this time, with twice as many signs and banners, and everyone seemed lathered up and ready for a showdown.

As I threaded my way toward the front doors, I even spotted several profs in the mix, some of them carrying signs that protested the wrongful termination of university *surveillants*, others with signs that opposed the election of Brule to the French National

Assembly. It was nearly eight o'clock. A powerful energy seemed to buzz amid the fog over our heads, like the exhaust of a machine about to explode. My aim was to get safely inside the school doors before that could happen.

It took a maddening effort this time to reach the blockades up front. I waved over one of the organizers and showed him my lycée ID. He shook his head.

"An assistant? You have to wait like everyone else."

"No, I don't," I said. "I work here. Now let me in."

A belligerent glaze showed in his eyes. He was wearing a red knit hat like the others, but he was too young to be intimidating.

"Why won't you take part in our protest?" he asked.

"I'm a foreign assistant. I have to show up for work, which means you have to let me in."

"You're mistaken, comrade," he said. "We don't have to let *anyone* in. Except for that fascist Brule, who has his own entrance."

Behind me the crowd shifted suddenly to the right, then to the left, as if farther back a giant was pushing his way through. I turned and saw nothing but dense rows of students. Several of them glared back at me, bitterly, as if I'd gone over to the dark side. A protest chant broke out farther back. I leaned in close to the young organizer.

"Let me in, comrade, or I'll climb over you and let myself in."

"What did you say?" he asked.

"I said don't make me kick your scrawny—" I stopped, looking him in the eyes. The kid wasn't personally to blame, though I was willing to take it out on him anyway. I decided against it.

"Look," I said, "I'll lose my job if you don't let me in."

He cocked his head to one side. "As we have lost ours?"

That was all it took. I started to shove one of the blockades aside, but the kid leaned his weight against it. I probably had thirty pounds on him, could've knocked him down flat. For a second I thought he was about to take a swing at me. And I wanted him to, bad—I was sick of being pushed around and itching for a reason to break somebody's nose.

An older organizer rushed over to make the peace and let me through. But just as I stepped through the barricade, I got a firm shove from the line of students behind me. I dropped my bag and spun, hands open and legs spread. The organizers grabbed me by my coat and hurried me inside with my bag, slamming the heavy lycée doors behind me.

INSIDE THE PROFS' room, several teachers were already bustling around the big oak table, as if the entire student body weren't outside protesting the institution. I'd never been more relieved to be in that cursed Xerox line, though I couldn't think of any good reason to make copies. There were no students in the school, no future for me as a teacher. It all seemed like wasted paper and ink.

Before it was my turn, Richard, Paul's friend on the English faculty, appeared beside me at his locker.

"I wish those bloody kids would realize that they cannot win," he muttered in English.

"Can't win what?"

"You cannot win a fight against Georges Brule, the *proviseur* of schools. Why would he sign a document denouncing a law made by the same party that will win him his National Assembly position? It's obvious. The police will disperse the crowd, and once the students are back inside, they will be too damned excited to do any work, because they will believe that they have changed the world, when they have only fallen behind another *demi heure*."

Richard said all of this while shuffling through the pile of papers in his arms. He smelled like bourbon and coffee, hadn't shaved in probably a week.

"Why doesn't Brule just call the cops now?"

Richard leaned in closer and lowered his voice. "Who knows what that fascist is thinking? He is a very mysterious man, be assured."

I glanced up the line at the Xerox. I was next, but the prof using it didn't seem to know how to manhandle the stupid machine.

"How 'mysterious'?" I asked Richard. He rolled his eyes and drew even closer.

"I have a distant cousin who worked with Brule when he was an administrator with the National Police. They called him *le Python*. Always waiting around the corner to squeeze the life out of you, my cousin says."

"I didn't know Brule used to be a cop."

"Not a cop, an administrator of some sort, it was a long time ago, deputy director of one affair or another." Richard hesitated, then leaned in even closer, so that it was just the two of us and his bourbon-coffee breath. "He is very supportive of antiterrorist bills in Parliament, incidentally. Bills not unlike those in your country, if I may say."

"But he still has friends in high places, right?"

"Of course, and enemies."

I remembered then that I was supposed to see Brule once I'd spoken with Dreyfus. I'd also forgotten to tell Thierry about the weird little deal Brule had made with me.

"But it's wisest not to speak of that here," added Richard. "And certainly not in French."

When it was my turn at the Xerox, the machine immediately jammed. This time I didn't hesitate to bring both fists down on its control pad.

Expecting to catch hell from the profs still waiting to make copies, I checked behind me. Strangely, all I got were somber nods of approval.

In another fifteen minutes the municipal police moved in and forced back the barricades, and just as Richard had predicted, eight-o'clock classes resumed thirty minutes behind schedule.

MY STUDENTS TRICKLED into the classroom and I let them carry on for another ten minutes, not seeing any point in hassling them, though when I did try to get them to review their idioms, they treated me like an ogre anyway.

It was a low-level class—all slackers, not a single redeemable character in the bunch. Even when I offered to dismiss them early, if they'd only work with me for ten straight minutes, they glared up at me in unison, as if I'd dumped a metric ton of work on them. A couple of the back-row boys started talking trash about me in French, and loud enough for everyone to hear. I considered sending them down to Brule's assistant principal, a stern, sharply dressed brunette in her late thirties whose name I could never remember, just to make examples of them. But I thought what the hell. I'd fought with these little bastards for six solid months, and if they didn't want to learn English, there wasn't much more I could do about it.

I called class to a close five minutes early, unheard of at Corbières, and then had a two-hour break until my eleven o'clock, a midlevel conversation class made up mostly of super-bright eleventh-grade girls. By the time I made it up to the right classroom on the fourth floor, most of the girls were already in place, squirming around in their seats and jabbering about the *grève*.

I got them working on a few exercises that required nothing of me. Then, with ten minutes left, the classroom door opened and in strolled two buzz-cut men in black suits.

I watched them take seats in the back row. Something in me erupted, and I stood.

"Now look . . ." I started to say. But making a big scene in front of the class would have been like doing it in front of the whole school—the way gossip traveled, I'd be explaining the matter to Brule in his office in less than twenty-four hours.

The girls started glancing back, whispering among themselves while those sons of bitches sat there motionless, staring up at me as if they'd come to be educated.

"Class is dismissed," I announced.

Several of the girls looked at me in disbelief. There were still another six or seven minutes of class time left.

"I said everybody get out of here—now."

When my students were gone the men stood and buttoned their jackets. Every French word I knew seemed lodged in my throat. The goon closest to the door went over and closed it. The other, a slope-shouldered man with a long face, took two steps toward me down the center aisle and stopped.

Finally I got hold of myself. "This is out of the goddamn question."

The tall one showed me his hands, a mock-peaceful gesture I wasn't ready to fall for.

"Your presence is requested, M. Delanne," he said in painstaking French.

It was the first time I'd seen Nabec's goons in broad daylight. Their eyes were steel cold.

"Tell him he can request my presence some other time," I said. "When I'm not working with kids. Now get the hell out of here before you cause more trouble than it's worth."

Neither man budged. The one at the door checked the hall through the glass.

"We come with apologies, monsieur," he said. "Sincere apologies. For your troubles. Your presence is nevertheless requested."

"I'll bet that's what he wants you to say, isn't it? Go back to him and tell him this: Where I work, here at this lycée, where I teach kids, is off fucking limits. Absolutely, end of conversation. I don't even know how you got in here."

I shouldered my bag and headed for the door. The man beside it spread his legs and opened his hands, crouching. The other moved an aisle closer and turned, sealing me between his partner and a row of desks.

I couldn't decide where to run: to the office, to my apartment, to the streets? I tried to remember if the room was in use the next hour. I was pretty sure it wasn't. And that these guys hadn't come to take no for an answer.

"Okay," I said. "I'll go with you. But we're waiting until the next period starts, when the halls are empty. Le Monsieur would agree to that, and you know it."

When their own eyes met, I knew I had them. "So get away from the door, would you?"

The end-of-period bell rang. For a few of the longest minutes of my life, we sat in the student desks, staring up at the blank blackboard. After the second bell rang we moved into the hall, slipped down one of the lesser-used staircases, and somehow made it outside without a hitch.

I could only pray that Thierry had put one of his men on my case sooner rather than later.

WHERE USUAL AND UNUSUAL INTERSECT, MY DEAR

*A**ttendez là*," the driver told me before getting out.

The Mercedes had stopped at the end of Nabec's driveway beside a classic-model Bentley. It wasn't the one I'd climbed into with Nabec—this one was sportier and cream-colored. I wasn't exactly surprised to be sitting outside the same cottage: it had already dawned on me on the way over that Nabec might be smart enough to trick the cops into thinking his cottage had been sold. I was learning to expect that kind of trickery from the sly old bastard.

My door swung open and I got out. Before me stood a man fully twice my size. He bowed and told me in melodious French to turn around and put my hands on the roof of the car. While he frisked me, the costly shell of that sleek Mercedes seemed to purr against the skin of my fingers, as if over the last two weeks, during our rides to and from the country, it had grown fond of my touch.

I said to the fat man, "You think I pack a gun to school? You know these guys picked me up at school, don't you? The place where innocent children go to learn math and science and such."

When the fat man was finished, he said, "Okay, monsieur. But if you had children of your own you would not refer to children as innocent."

I tried to return his smile, but my face wouldn't cooperate.

He led me around the front of the cottage and inside. It didn't matter how much courage I'd mustered on the ride over—one look at the dreaded place, and my knees wobbled.

I started across the front room to the door to the right. But the fat man grabbed my arm. When my legs buckled completely, he held me up. "Come on, man," I heard myself say.

Just then someone called from behind the door to the left.

"Pas de soucis, Delanne. Je prends pas la tête."

The voice was withered, feminine—the rich, seasoned voice of an elderly Frenchwoman. I glanced at the fat man. His face was too fleshy to read.

He nodded toward the door. *"La Madame vous attend."*

I steadied myself and went in.

THE ROOM BORE no trace of its prior self—it had been transformed into a sort of half-modern, mock-rustic luxury suite. Posh, wine-colored carpet. Slender floor lamps in each corner. Voluptuous love seats and fancy end tables. Mahogany bookshelves built into the walls. Its two windows, which only days ago had been boarded up, seemed to glimmer behind their sheer white drapes.

At the end of the room an old woman with a tall, stiff hairdo sat behind a broad mahogany desk. She was perched on a high-backed office chair and wore a warm, welcoming expression.

"There you are, Delanne," she said, waving me over. "Come closer, there's been no mistake, you will not be harmed." I was reluctant to move. She smiled and waved me over again. "You're in good hands, my dear. *Very* good hands, if I may say so myself."

I approached her, but stopped at a safe distance.

"My apologies for such a chair," she said, indicating a gorgeous leather armchair just in front of me. "It's an eyesore, but this place has been a work in progress, if you didn't know."

I took a seat, looking around the room in awe. I was too scared for words. I got out a cigarette and fumbled through my pockets for a lighter.

"Please don't smoke that," the old woman snapped. "What do you want? For me to keel over dead from your secondhand smoke? Mother of Christ!"

I shoved the cigarette back in my pocket and recited an apology. Then I noticed the corner where the forsaken fireplace had been. An elegant china cabinet stocked with crystal glassware of all shapes and sizes now stood in its place. It nettled me to no end.

"At last, the teacher from America," she said. "You don't look like any teacher I ever had."

After a flash of anger, the truth came out: "I'm not really a teacher, just an assistant."

"How charming. So are you crazy, or just stupid?"

"Not stupid," I said bitterly. "Maybe a little crazy."

She sat back, her lips curling into the slightest smile. "No, you're not stupid."

"Thanks," I said. "You're too kind."

"What I mean is," she said, apparently unaffected by my sarcasm, "you're not *dead,* are you?"

I hesitated, searching the old woman's wrinkled, hard-set face. "Not yet."

"Exactly—exactly, Delanne. Because dead is what you would be if you'd been stupid."

My skin went immediately cold. I gazed into the old woman's wild eyes.

"It's true," she said. "You shouldn't have lied to the Arab—that was *almost* stupid. I imagine he expected it, however. I might have expected it myself. How long did you presume it would take him to discover you had lied? In our business, Delanne, one must always double-check her facts."

I suffered another flash of anger. "I'm a little new to the trade, and I don't give a good goddamn about your facts. Why not just tell me what the hell all this is about?"

The old woman perked up in her chair, twisting her face into the most absurd expression I'd ever seen. She was extremely well dressed: black pin-striped suit, maroon silk scarf, hair gathered up into a sort of beehive. Although her skin was etched with deep wrinkles, it had a healthy olive tone to it. She wore gold rings on each hand, but no diamonds or stones—all gold on gold.

"Oh, the Arab knew the truth, young man," she said, ignoring my question. "As it turns out, the truth was a sham—disinformation, they call it. That's why you're sitting here now."

Her casual tone was giving me violent thoughts—it wasn't just the room we were in.

"How about telling me why the last time I was here I got beaten up and arrested? That seems to be pretty important, doesn't it?"

She frowned. "I see."

Without taking her eyes off me, she opened her desk drawer, withdrew a nickel-plated revolver that was as long as my forearm, and laid the thing carefully on the desk in front of her, as if it were an antique with delicate parts. I tore my eyes from it and concentrated on breathing.

"I know what you're thinking," she said. "'Mother of Christ,' right? It's a gift from the Arab. But look at it—the sheer power of such a thing. Especially in a nation where nothing of its kind is permitted. Now, I don't speak of violence, Delanne, no. I speak of anything but violence—I speak in fact of nonviolence, or at least its bastard son. You see, I'm under no obligation to use this beautiful, awful thing. And I won't use it, even though I have had the impulse many times during these last few days. Do you understand what I am saying, Delanne?"

I nodded, though all I could think about was taking the thing from her and holding it to her head, so she could feel the flip side of the power she was so fond of. I glanced back at the door. It was closed, but I knew the fat man would be standing right outside it.

The old madame reached again into the drawer and pulled out a leather pouch, from which she produced a pinch of blond shag tobacco and a rolling paper. In three deft movements she'd made a flawless cigarette.

She lit it and took a hefty drag, exhaling through her nose and grinning. Her teeth were so brown and vile that I looked away to hide my shock.

"You're taking everything too seriously, Delanne. I was only making a joke earlier—it flew over your head like a dove. Come on then, smoke up. You look like you could use six or ten."

I fished out my cigarette and lit up. It did nothing to quell my outrage.

"So what exactly does the Arab want with me?" I asked.

"Ah, the Arab," she said, sitting back. "He takes things far too seriously too. With his neckties and cuff links and weary eyes. Mother of Christ, I'll bet he has his bodyguard sleep at the foot of his bed!

"Look at this room, for example. That Arab was so wrapped up in work that he couldn't even give the place some ambience— couldn't even fulfill a simple request, one business partner to another, until the last minute. But this is why we work so well together, really. And it's beautiful in here now, isn't it? Something about the way the daylight spills through that window on an afternoon like this. I adore it already." She paused, studying me. "But I thought you'd be more angered by the other one—our pesky policeman."

At first I thought I'd heard her wrong. "So you know who Claude Dreyfus really is?"

The old madame slapped the desk and burst out laughing. "Do

we *know* who M. Claude Dreyfus is? My dear young man, we have no choice. You yourself wouldn't be sitting here if we didn't know about the so-called Claude Dreyfus. That's why your anger is misdirected. How he'd laugh at that one, the clever little toad. And how the Arab and I would pay not to be known by *him*."

Now I was fed up with being confused. "So Dreyfus knows about your intelligence business. He told me he was trying to bring you guys down. What the hell is he waiting for?"

The madame laughed again. "Surely you can see that he's not doing his job, Delanne. Maybe he likes us more than we like him."

"Bullshit," I said. "Why protect Dreyfus? He told me all about you."

"Did he now?" she asked, leaning over her desk and narrowing her right eye. "Let us say that when he discovered our business, he believed that we deserved blackmail more than a bringing down."

"You pay him not to turn you over to the National Police?"

She studied me cautiously, clearly deciding whether I needed to know.

"Let me tell you all about *him,*" she said. "He has for some time been washing money for other businessmen we know. When he found us, he offered us his services at a ridiculously high cost. Without an option to say no, you see. Such services go with the territory, Delanne. And so as partners, reluctant ones or not, we do favors for each other. That is how he referred you to us. And that is perhaps why he tried to deceive you about wanting to trap the Arab. M. Dreyfus has no intention of compromising his business venture with us, and so he probably has little desire for you, or anyone, to know of his true business."

"Aside from all that," she continued, "M. Dreyfus seems to think that since he is a policeman, he is indispensable. He is wrong about this—quite wrong."

Now I couldn't wait to tell Thierry about the money laundering—

maybe it would lead them to the evidence they'd need against Dreyfus.

"Well, shit," the old madame said suddenly. "Where are my manners? Armagnac, Armagnac. You take it, don't you? Please tell me that someone has introduced you to a fine Armagnac."

I nodded, though her phony hospitality made me want to reach over and smack her.

"You look like you could use a liter or two," she said. "Or three."

When she climbed down from her seat, I realized just how tiny she was—no taller than five feet, no heavier than ninety pounds, sopping wet. I could have thrown her across the room.

She went to the fancy cabinet behind her desk, produced a misshapen bottle of caramel-colored liquor, and poured healthy doses into two big snifters, pushing one across to me. Once back in her throne, she swirled her drink several times, then held it to her nose and frowned with concentration. I held down my anger and followed her lead. The booze reeked of enormous, high-octane wealth.

"When I've been drinking," she said, "I take it for granted that everyone else has been."

I watched her over the rim of my glass, guessing what she'd looked like when she was young: she'd been pursued by men for her charm, she'd commanded men so much that now she never doubted her influence over them—especially young ones like me. The thought burned deeply.

"But I did not summon you here to answer your questions," she said suddenly. "First item of business: apologies. Not because I enjoy apologizing for others, no, but because I believe that people should take responsibility for those whom they employ. It's not the first time I've been obligated to apologize for the doings of a man, I assure you. Nor the hundredth, for that matter. The Arab wishes to apologize for the . . . beating, as you call it. He was a little angry with your lie, Delanne, because he'd taken a liking to you. Even if he expected it, he took it somewhat personally."

"Then why did he let me get arrested? Wasn't the beating enough?"

The madame shrugged. "This is what the Arab wants me to say: he would apologize himself, but he is elsewhere on business. I'm usually the one who goes to Germany—his German is wretched, you see, and our clients there prefer me, for obvious reasons. It so happens that he is more useful to our partnership in France and Spain. But I think secretly he adores Germany, and anyway I spent the autumn months there with my assistant. But enough. Let us drink. To your future."

We tasted the Armagnac. It was far too complex to understand in a single sip. While she rolled another cigarette, I fought not to look at the giant gun between us—the temptation to reach for it was too great.

"All right, now let's cut the crap, madame," I said. "The second man I interviewed spoke French, so I know you guys didn't need any interpreter. You owe me a better explanation—"

"Young man, I don't owe you a *goddamn* thing—get that perfectly straight. And I will explain because it pleases me to. The interviews were designed to prepare you for our offer, but since you failed us by lying, we've had to change our approach. Now the Arab and I wish to give you one last opportunity to redeem yourself. Then your account will be cleared. How does that sound?"

It sounded pretty fucking good. But I wasn't satisfied.

"Tell me how," I demanded. "And give it to me straight, or you get nothing more from me."

"Ah, very nice—a good strategy, Delanne. Directly to the point—aim for the throat. Good. But all this depends on what role you are willing to play."

When I saw that she was only going to give me another runaround, I snapped.

"You know what?" I said, standing up. "I'm done playing roles for you and the fucking Arab, and after all I've been put through, I can't see how I owe either of you anything. You clear my account, and you clear it now—here and now."

I might have shouted the last part, and I might have moved a little closer to the old woman's desk than I should have. Because almost at once the fat bodyguard threw open the door and started to charge me.

The old woman held up her hand. "Everything is under control. Isn't it, Delanne?"

She was looking hard at me, her eyes wide and penetrating. I glanced at the fat man and back at her, then nodded.

"A sensible decision, Delanne. And in a way you have the right to be angry. I know how the police work, my dear. They make promises. And threats. They make you feel indebted to them. But then they shouldn't really concern you, Delanne. So forget their threats. Forget their promises. What I mean to say, Delanne, is, what if we made a promise of our own? An agreement?"

"I told you—"

"Delanne, you're clearly a determined, vivacious young man. But let me explain something about Dreyfus: he has become unnecessary. What I mean is, we wish to see him exposed."

I hesitated. Her choice of words in the French had me confused: I wasn't sure whether she meant exposed in the sense of being shown to be the double dealer that he was, or exposed in the sense of snuffed out—a distinction not always plain in the French. I doubted that she meant the latter. If what Thierry had said about him was true, cops like Dreyfus were untouchable, virtually impossible to kill.

Out came the truth: "Me too. But I'm finished dealing with him, and the Arab, and you—finished with all of it. I never wanted to be involved, until I was suddenly doing it—"

"An ancient story, is it not? *Until I was suddenly doing it.* How do you presume any of us began? There we were suddenly, born out of nowhere and charged with the burden of living."

"My burden is worlds away from yours, and you know it."

"Then tell me: How far will you go to be rid of your other-worldly burden? So you are in trouble with the law. What if I told you that we have friends who can make that trouble disappear?"

I took a big drink of my Armagnac, sifting through the layers of what she'd just said. I glanced back at the fat man, then surveyed the room, all the fine furniture and fixtures, and thought that I could still smell the sweat and blood of the men I'd met with here. It was a tempting offer. Because I believed that she and Nabec had the power and connections to absolve me. Which was more than Thierry had promised. But what good was a promise from these people?

"No," I said finally. "Absolutely not. I'm finished with this, and I'm finished with all of it."

She narrowed her right eye again. "I don't believe you, Delanne. Why? Because there's more to you, I can see that. There's more to you than even the Arab bargained for."

"And what *did* he bargain for?" I asked. When she smiled and shook her head, I scowled back. "Then why me? You can tell me that."

"Oh, come on, Delanne. Why you, why me, why him, her, us, them? What do you suppose? That every winner has no help from circumstance, and that every poor fucker in prison has only himself to blame? Moments, Delanne. People in shared moments, in shared places. People occupying the same ground—intentionally, coincidentally, however—where usual and unusual intersect, my dear. Shit happens as if there were no difference between the two. So you tell me—how the *fuck* can we know why?"

She was dodging the truth and we both knew it. I'd been tagged for some reason.

Another burst of mad energy pumped into my arms and legs.

"You want to know what it will take to push me farther?" I asked, fighting not to raise my voice. "Nothing. Absolutely nothing. Because I've already gone over the edge—I can feel myself going farther every fucking day. And I don't need you, or the cops, or the fucking Arab to help me with that. Not anymore. So tell the Arab thanks—tell him thanks a million. But I don't want his redemption—I'm done with him *right now.*"

The madame sat back and swirled the booze in her snifter. For a moment she seemed lost in thought. I stood there feeling my heart slam against my chest.

"Tell me this, Delanne—what exactly are you afraid of?" she asked. "Dying?"

In that moment I was afraid of absolutely nothing—all I wanted was to go ape-shit.

"Because if you're afraid of dying," she said, "welcome to the land of the living. The Arab won't kill you—I can assure you that won't happen. I'm only asking you to be willing to help us, when the time comes, to expose our mutual enemy, M. Dreyfus—and in our own way. What else could you be afraid of? Jail? How long do you think they can keep you in jail, Delanne, with us on your side? And what's a new future worth to you? Six months, a year? Sometimes progress takes sacrifice, Delanne. Or do they no longer teach such ideals where you come from?"

My breathing slowed. I tried hard to think beyond my own anger and sense of justice. She was extending something like protection for something like cooperation, and I knew the value of that. Even if I could never accept it. Still standing, I reached for my Armagnac and gulped it down.

"Such words don't surprise you from the mouth of an old woman?" she said quizzically. I shook my head. "Tell me, Delanne, how old do you think I am?"

Our eyes met again. She was eighty if she was a day.

"Fifty-nine," I said. "A distinguished fifty-nine."

When the old woman smiled, I looked elsewhere to keep from seeing those god-awful teeth.

"You will go places, my son," she chuckled. "And you Americans are not nearly as brash as you are made out to be. I myself do not see what all the fuss is about. You people can't be blamed for the actions of a foolish leader—not entirely, anyway. But I rather enjoyed your little outburst."

Now she stood. "I want you to have time to reconsider our offer, Delanne—it remains on the table."

Before I could tell her to go to hell, she held up her hand, just as she'd done to her fat bodyguard.

"And I'll give you a bit of free advice," she added. "Stay away from that lycée. Starting immediately. Understand what I am telling you. The man who calls himself Claude Dreyfus has plans for you—grave ones. So if you know what is good for you, you will go out of your way *not* to fall into those plans. Trust me, young man. Stay away from that lycée."

I left without saying good-bye. To date, it was my easiest exit from that place. Though walking out hardly felt like leaving.

MONSIEUR SCHOOLTEACHER ANYMORE

As soon as the madame's men dropped me off, I hurried upstairs to call Thierry. After a ton of rings, Solène picked up. My breath stopped short at the sound of her voice.

"It's Jeffrey. I need to talk with your father."

"He's not here," she said, an irritated edge to her voice. "He's supposed to be, but he's not."

I sat at my desk and stared out the window at the opposite building. "You said that's normal, that's just what he does, right? Says one time, means another."

She didn't answer. I realized then that she wasn't irritated at all—she sounded scared.

"He didn't come home last night," she said. "Which isn't normal."

I checked my watch. It was just after one. I thought about offering to meet her somewhere.

"Maybe it's nothing," she said. "Maybe he's helping someone with something that is taking more time than he planned. That's probably all. Can I give him a message?"

I considered that briefly, but said no. We both stayed on the line for a long, silent moment. I sensed that she might be pacing.

"Are you okay, Solène?"

"Yes, thanks . . . Yes, I'm okay."

I hesitated. "Are *we* okay?"

"What do you mean?"

I wanted to tell her that there weren't any hard feelings about what had gone down between us the night before. I wanted to say, too, that I hadn't exactly gotten her off my mind. But more than anything I was scared for her. I couldn't say precisely why. I just felt that by now I knew enough about what her father did—and enough about the city we lived in—to be spooked by just about anything. I thought about being tailed the day before and started worrying that someday Thierry's enemies might become aware of him, and follow him home. Maybe they already had.

"Do you have somewhere else you can stay tonight?" I asked. "If he doesn't come home."

"Sure."

"Then do it. Trust me, Solène. Thierry would . . . If Thierry had to spend some time away, helping a friend or whatever, he would want you to stay somewhere else until he got back."

After she promised that she would, I gave her my number and the number at the Rougerie.

"If I don't answer here, you can leave a message there and someone will get it to me."

I hung up, lay down, and dozed, dreaming of Amelia. In the dream we were kissing in her *foyer* room, and I wanted out of there so bad that I lied and said I needed to use the bathroom down the hall—the other *foyer* building, in real life, had closet-sized rooms with shared bathrooms in the halls. Next thing I knew I was running down the street shirtless. I kept throwing looks back, though Amelia wasn't following me, and then ducked into Le Boomerang—the same bar I'd run into when I'd tried to escape Nabec's goons. The same English guy was working the bar. Only this time, sitting on a stool with a full pint for each of us, was

Amelia herself. Leering at me. Shaking her head as if to say, *Did you really think I'd be that easy to shake?*

When I woke up it was after 2:00 a.m. and my body was covered with sweat. I went to the bathroom, washed my face, and checked my tired eyes in the mirror. More than anything, I wanted to get out of this town—away from the people who were out to ruin my life, maybe even just as far from my so-called friends.

But good sense kept telling me that Thierry's advice was the best thing I had going—that if I ran, I wouldn't get very far. I just wasn't sure how much longer I could bear to listen to good sense.

OUT ON THE street later that morning the fog had been pushed up by a bone-chilling cold, the dry, stagnant kind that sucks the sound out of everything and makes it difficult to breathe. I'd slept without getting any physical rest. My bones felt heavy, and I was too bleary to think on my toes.

At Rue Corbières, I stopped. The entire street in front of the lycée was jam-packed with students. I cursed aloud: these *grèves* were getting old fast.

But this one looked more like a halfhearted fire drill than a boycott. The students were unusually silent, huddled in groups up to the lycée front doors. I saw no outsiders—no parents or townsfolk among them—and while I recognized several profs in the mix, there were no signs, no banners, no chanting or actual protesting.

I walked up to the crowd but didn't enter. There didn't look to be any blockades up front, or even any organizers. At the other end of Rue Corbières, I could make out a clutch of policemen.

For some reason my stomach balled up. Everything became suddenly noisier, as if beneath the deadening cold my ears were picking up something they hadn't before. I backed away from the crowd and stood on the sidewalk that ran along my building's side of the street, trying to decide whether to push through to the front doors or go back up to my room and catch another half hour of sleep.

That was when I heard someone shout my name. I turned full circle but couldn't locate the culprit. Then above the crowd of students I saw a pair of hands waving, and finally his face emerged: it was Julien, the last person I'd expected to see outside Corbières at such a godforsaken hour.

He had on a silly striped knit cap pulled down over his eyebrows. As he pushed out of the crowd and crossed the street, my first thought was that he'd lost it—he'd stayed up all night and drunk himself mad, and then on a lark decided to hassle me on my way to work.

My next thought was more logical: he was a part of the strangely calm *grève*.

When he reached me he had a frenzied look in his eyes. He grabbed both my arms.

"We need to get you out of here, partner. Like right now."

"I'm not in the mood for this, man." I tried to shake free of him, but he wouldn't let go. "What's your problem?"

He started checking around us frantically, as if we were surrounded by terrorists rather than a bunch of teens.

"One of my friends at the *Journal* called me and told me—we need to get you out of here."

More glances in every direction. He started to pull me up the sidewalk toward my apartment, and for a second my words tangled up—Julien wasn't playacting.

I walked with him to my apartment door, but then he grabbed my arm again and dragged me with him across the street.

Just then two squad cars pulled up behind the crowd, some fifty yards away from us. Julien tightened his grip on my arm and yanked me into a small recess between buildings that smelled like garbage and wet laundry.

We were directly across from my *foyer* building now. I could see my room window, but couldn't remember having left the lights on. My thoughts started moving at top speed. I realized I was panting.

I checked Julien's eyes again. He looked as scared as I was.

"Tell me what the hell's going on, Julien," I said. "It's too early for games."

"No time to talk." He stuck his head out and around, glancing up the sidewalk the way we'd come. "Just forget what you know for now, and trust me on this. You're about to be blamed for something you didn't do."

I tried to step out and get a good look for myself, but he pulled me back, pinning me against the cold bricks.

"Look at me, Jeff," he said. "That's not a fucking *grève,* that's a shakedown."

"Let go of me—"

"You were walking into something bad. A cop friend I know through the paper tipped us off about a half hour ago, okay—I've got a line on things, man." He had my coat by the lapels. I shook free of him and pushed him against the opposite wall.

"You're fucking crazy, you know that? How did you know what time I go to work?"

"I was ready to wait all morning." His eyes were nervous, genuinely panicked. "In about five minutes, those kids are going to find out that their *proviseur* has been rushed to the hospital."

I stepped away from him and let my mind reel. Julien rooted though his shoulder bag and took out a huge black scarf. Then he pulled his ridiculous knit hat over my head and lassoed the scarf around my throat.

"We've got to get you to Marine's," he said. "Pronto."

He moved to the edge of the building and poked his head out, then pointed across the street to my room. I followed his arm with my eyes. Someone was moving around in there.

"You believe me now?" he said. "Come on."

$$\bullet \quad \bullet \quad \bullet$$

WE WENT WEST, zigzagging through the residential district where Marine and Julien both lived. In fifteen minutes we reached Marine's duplex apartment, at the bend of a one-way street whose name wasn't posted. As we approached the house, Julien slowed, checking behind us and taking my arm again. He led me across a dried-out strip of lawn and knocked on the front door.

When Marine finally opened up, she stood in the doorway rubbing her eyes. She had on a pair of tattered pink pajama pants and an old green T-shirt and looked as if she'd just risen from the dead. Without a word, Julien pushed in past her.

"What are you guys doing here?"

I followed them in, locking the door behind us. They entered into an immediate stare-down.

"Temporary detour, Marine," said Julien. "I swear—temporary."

"Hi, Jeff," she said to me. Then, to Julien: "Do you know what time it is? Have you guys been up all night drinking?"

"Hey, I'm sorry, Marine—" I started.

"Let me handle this, Jeff. Marine, Jeff's in trouble."

"Why in trouble? It's too early in the morning for jokes, Julien."

"*Real* big trouble, and we're not joking—this is the safest place for him."

I let my eyes move into the living room. The place looked as if a team of bandits had just fled the scene—clothes and blankets and books were scattered pell-mell across its yellow shag carpet and shabby furniture.

Now Marine looked more awake—and worried.

"I'll make coffee," she said. "Then I want to know what's going on."

"You're a gem," Julien said. "And I need your phone. Pronto."

After Marine handed him her phone and disappeared into the kitchen, I cornered Julien.

"Now tell me what the hell's going on," I demanded.

"I don't know all the ins and outs, Jeff. My friend at the paper—"

"Tell me everything your friend at the paper said, and how he knows, or I'm out of here."

"He said just what I told you, man—I told you just what he told me."

I studied his eyes. "Then how did he know what you said about Brule?"

Julien acted suddenly irritated. "I told you I work for a paper. We've got connections with the cops, and we get to hear what's gone down before it hits the news sometimes . . . Jesus, man. You're acting like this shit's *my* fault—and I just saved your ass."

Julien seemed to sense that I still wasn't buying it.

"So I didn't stay on the phone with him asking for particulars, Jeff—I went to stop you from walking into a problem."

I backed off and started thinking about what could have possibly happened to Brule. It didn't matter that Nabec knew I'd lied in giving him Brule's name. I still felt the guilt of a conspirator—I still detected Nabec's hand in this.

"But how did your friend know to call *you*?" I asked.

"We did a story on the Corbières *surveillant* boycotts last week. I told him I had a friend who worked there as an assistant. He found out that something had happened to the *proviseur* and said he heard your name in the mix, so he called me because he thought I'd like to know, Jeff."

Again our eyes locked. Either he was telling the truth or he was a really good liar. I couldn't see what he had to gain from lying— or from running to intercept me at Corbières. My mind shot to the implications: *my name was in the mix.* Somehow I was being blamed for whatever was happening.

I tried to think around that explanation to other possibilities.

"So what's the plan coming here?" I asked. "Maybe the cops just want to question me. Which is totally ridiculous—I've spoken to Brule only once in my whole life."

"We're waiting, Jeff. Where it's safe. Until I can find out what's really going on." Julien held Marine's phone up between us. "That's why I need some phone time, partner."

Julien spent almost an hour on the phone, not talking so much as listening, pacing the short hallway that ran from the living room to Marine's bedroom while I paced around in the kitchen with Marine. I drank too much coffee and started ripping through cigarettes, which was the last combination I needed. Any way I looked at it, I had to get hold of Thierry.

After a while I couldn't take waiting any longer and confronted Julien in the hallway.

"It's my turn, man. I'll give the phone right back."

Julien shook his head and covered the receiver. "Five more minutes, dude—I'm on hold. I'm trying to help you out here—five, ten minutes."

"Five minutes," I said. "Or I'm off to find a pay phone."

It was time for the late-morning news. Marine turned on the TV in the living room. But the first bits were national—nothing about Corbières or Brule. Marine kept trying to distract me by asking me this or that about what news I'd heard from back home about the Iraqi invasion, but I wasn't falling for it. When I tried to get the phone from Julien again and didn't succeed, I put on my coat and told Marine thanks for the coffee.

"Wait," she said. "Here it is."

My eyes moved unconsciously to the TV screen: shots of Lycée Corbières, and of Georges Brule being carted out on a stretcher through his private entrance.

Julien came in just in time for the reporter to say that Brule had had an adverse reaction to an unknown substance that he'd consumed voluntarily. Police were not specific, but did not deny the possibility of foul play.

Right away I had two thoughts: how many times I'd been told that Brule's win was pivotal in the upcoming national elections, and that damn vitamin powder of his. Then I started to think about what the old madame had said about Dreyfus's grim plans for me. And I remembered what Thierry had said about pinning evil deeds on outsiders.

"This is bullshit," I heard myself say.

Julien was finally off the phone. "Okay, here's what they know at the paper. Brule was definitely poisoned. Somebody tampered with some crap he mixes in with his water. And those cops are sure somehow that it was somebody working there at Corbières. This will all be on TV news soon. But here's what won't be, says my guy: they've found something in one of the assistants' lockers that looks like the same poison." Julien stopped and looked at me. "Guess whose locker."

I stood. "That's absolutely absurd. Why would I put poison in my locker after I'd used it?"

Julien's eyes grew wide. "I don't know, Jeff, but if it were me, I'd start thinking like someone who's being framed, not like Monsieur Schoolteacher anymore. Somebody has it in for you—bad—and if I were in your shoes, I wouldn't go to the cops until we figured something out."

I sat down and put my face in my hands while my thoughts spun out of control: Dreyfus, Nabec, the old madame, and all Thierry had anticipated. The word he'd used was *scapegoat*. Yet it didn't make sense. If this had been their scheme all along—to make me take the fall for an attempt on Brule's life—why had the old madame summoned me out to the cottage? If walking into Corbières that morning would have ensured my arrest, why had she warned me *not* to go?

And why would any of *them* want Georges Brule dead?

I tried to snatch the phone out of Julien's hand, but he held it away.

"I've been waiting to use that thing for like two hours," I said.

"Who you gonna call, dude?" he said.

There was no way I was going to tell Julien about Thierry—he'd want the whole story.

"That's my business."

"I've got one more call to make," he said. "Then I'm going to go see if I can round up Françoise. She might have made it into Corbières and found out something."

While he was in the hall with the phone, I listened in, but what he said made no sense. He came back out with his coat on, tossed the phone in my lap, and pointed at me like a high school basketball coach.

"Stay here, Jeff. And for Christ's sake don't tell anyone where you are. I'm gonna get you out of this."

WHEN YOU HAVE JUST ARRIVED

Marine joined me on the couch once Julien was gone. "I thought he'd never leave."

It dawned on me that this might be the first time we'd been to-gether without being either blitzed or well on our way. Even in my stunned condition, her presence was a distraction.

"Can I ask you a question?" I said. "Why is Julien going out of his way for me here?"

She shook her head and changed the TV channel. "I honestly don't understand him, Jeffrey. But this isn't the first time he has tried to play hero. Last year he drove a man he hardly knew all the way to Spain because the man was a friend of a friend at work and needed to go to a funeral. But Julien can be so dramatic, without even trying to be—he acted as if he were saving the man's life."

"He's hyperactive," I said. I suffered an unexpected twinge of amusement at the thought of Julien racing his friend's friend into another country to some church. "And one weird son of a bitch, really."

"No kidding," Marine said. "But don't tell him I told you that story. He asked me not to tell anyone when he got back. I've heard

him tell people that he's never even been to Spain. I think he
knows that he gets overly excited about things. Sometimes he's really self-conscious about it."

I took her phone into the bathroom and called Thierry. After
five or six rings the answering machine picked up, and Solène's
recorded voice said to leave a message. I called twice more, got the
machine both times, but found myself listening to the entire message, just to hear her voice.

Back in the living room, Marine handed the TV remote to me
and went into the kitchen to make waffles. I paced around until I
was sure I couldn't wait anymore—it was high time to clear out.
But beyond Thierry's place I had nowhere else to go. I could bet
that Paul and Françoise would be at school, and if the cops were
looking for me, nowhere public would do.

The more obvious option was just to make a run for it—to skip
town outright. But I had nothing but my school bag and a few
books. I didn't even have any cash on me. I thought about the thousand euros Nabec had given me after that second interview, those
two crisp bills I'd hidden under my bathroom sink. Even if going
back to my place would be dangerous as hell, that money was the
only way I could hope to last out some kind of investigation or
manhunt. And how did I know that Thierry wouldn't just turn me in
in himself?

The more I thought about it, the clearer it became that my best
move was to sneak into my apartment for some things and the
cash, and then take the most covert route to the train station. I
could hide in Paris, Bordeaux, Marseilles—any big, easy-to-blend-
in city—until the truth about Brule came to the surface. Whatever
that really was.

We ate the waffles with butter and raspberry preserves, brewed
a fresh pot of coffee, and spiked our mugs with some rum Marine
had stashed away. Then Marine announced that she was going to
take a shower. She wasn't gone a minute when I became uneasy.

My thoughts teetered between the need to run while I had the chance, and the image of Marine in the shower, water cascading over her naked body. Only then did the fugitive feeling really set in.

I took my coat into the kitchen. There was a back door that opened onto an unkempt backyard, beyond which ran a narrow alley.

I whispered a farewell to Marine and slipped into the cold.

SQUATTING ACROSS FROM my apartment in the same building recess where Julien had dragged me earlier, I blew into my hands to keep warm. The sky had the overcast look of evening, though I knew it couldn't be much past noon. The light was still on in my apartment, and my heart was pounding a new terrible rhythm in my chest. But even after hiding there for nearly an hour, I couldn't see a better option than packing a bag, grabbing my loot, and hitting the road. My guess was that if Dreyfus was the one trying to pull the curtain on me—and all the evidence I had pointed to that—he'd station some of his own guys in my apartment. Which made my task a tricky one.

Another half hour passed, and with every sidewalk passerby my confidence wavered. I started thinking about Paul, and how a few nights ago he'd wanted to recommend me to his attorney. But Paul was teaching right now, and anyway I'd feel more comfortable talking to his lawyer on a phone, from somewhere far away.

My knees were starting to ache, and my shoulders began to shiver. Every so often I could see a shadow move across my room on the second floor. My doubt redoubled; unless Dreyfus's men left altogether, I didn't stand a chance. I'd have to sneak to the train station and try to buy a ticket with my credit card, a bad idea in more ways than one. Then I'd have to find some way to hide out penniless in France.

Finally my building door opened, and two men in dark over-coats stepped onto the sidewalk across the street. I ducked down, tried to steady my breathing, peered around the edge of a Dumpster: they were heading up the street and crossing the plaza to the Marché Plus.

Up in my room the light was still on. I stayed motionless for another minute, fighting with my fear. Then I took a deep breath and bolted around to the back entrance of my building.

It was my slowest walk up those stairs to date. I reached my floor and called upon every ounce of courage I possessed to peek down the hall at my room. The door was closed. No one was in the hall, no footsteps.

My mind started ripping through the odds: Dreyfus's man sitting on my bed, lying down, smoking a cigarette, using the toilet while his cohorts were out buying sandwiches and coffees. Or else there had only been two of them. Either way, if there was someone in there, he couldn't be expecting me—he was just manning a post.

Which meant it was now or never.

I stepped down the hallway with a howling in my ears. Maddeningly, my door wasn't locked. It opened with an unusual squeak, and I leaped into the room, landing with my legs spread.

The room was empty and wrecked. I couldn't for the life of me figure what they'd been looking for. Maybe this was the kind of thing cops just did out of habit.

I opened the desk drawer where I kept my passport: gone. Then in the bathroom I fumbled under the sink for the envelope with Nabec's two five-hundred-euro bills, my heart already sinking.

But they hadn't found the money. I shoved the envelope into my backpack and darted to my closet, stuffing in whatever was readily available.

I decided on a sweatshirt and some underwear, but even that was too much—when I threw open my room door to leave, a man was standing there to greet me.

His greeting was more like a pounce. He was shorter than me, but thick and mean—he threw his arms out and charged like a linebacker.

I'd rarely been lucky in fights, except when I avoided them. But my dad had been a cop when I was a kid, and he'd taught me the basics—not that I had a chance to think those things through. What I did was a simple maneuver you can use in any scuffle, if you're quick enough. I jumped out of the guy's way, spun, and kicked him in the kidney region as he lumbered past.

The man crashed into my desk but recovered fast, spinning and reaching into his overcoat. At that point I would have shit my pants had a fresh jolt of adrenaline not surged through me.

I snatched an empty cognac bottle off the trunk beside my bed and bounced it off the guy's skull. He went down hard, with his hand still groping inside his coat.

I was out the door and halfway down the hall when the gun went off. And I was down in the alleyway beside my building before I realized that I'd been hit.

By the time I made it to the sidewalk, I knew I didn't have much walk left in me. A sharp pain was starting to pulse in my left calf. I hobbled a few steps toward the bus stop at Place Théâtre and stopped. There had been at least one other man, and I was in no shape to gamble.

I did an about-face and limped down the sidewalk in the direction of Marine's house, the nearest and safest place for me to lick my wounds. I shot a glance back and suffered a wave of relief. Just up the street, a bus was headed in my direction.

IN MARINE'S LITTLE driveway sat Julien's car, which for some reason made me uneasy. I didn't have much choice but to trust him now. On the bus there hadn't been any free seats, and I'd had to stand on my right leg like a stork, shutting out the scalding pain in my left leg and trying not to look like a wounded fugitive.

I threw open Marine's front door without knocking and locked it behind me.

Marine, Julien, and Françoise were all standing in her living room, staring at me as if I'd just set the roof on fire.

"What the fuck, Jeffrey," said Julien. "Where did you go?"

"Just a quick errand," I muttered.

Françoise came over and gave me a long hug. As I limped to Marine's couch and sat down, they all watched incredulously.

"You're not making this any easier on yourself, are you?" Françoise asked in English.

"Not for lack of trying," I said.

While Françoise tended to my wound—the bullet had actually only grazed my calf, leaving a scrape and a burn rather than a true entry wound—I told them what had gone down.

Julien brought two chairs in from the kitchen and set them across from Marine and me on the couch. He'd changed into a charcoal suit and had shaved his goatee down almost to nothing. He seemed subdued now, worlds away from his prior erratic state. Françoise sat down and got a menthol going.

"There are a few things I need to tell you, Jeffrey," she said. "I simply do not want there to be any more confusion, and I do not want you to think that I understand what exactly is happening at Corbières—or why."

I was too anxious to sit still. "Why would I think that?"

"If you remember, Jeffrey, I told you once that I divorced Marine's father. What I didn't tell you was how he went to prison a few years later, not long before he died. It was nothing similar to what you're up against, Jeffrey. He overlooked some taxes—and a few other things, which in France can get you locked away like a jewel thief. Anyway, that was how I met the man who calls himself Dreyfus."

At the mention of Dreyfus, Julien didn't budge. But he seemed to be monitoring my reaction.

"What the hell are you saying?" I asked, remembering how I'd asked Françoise about Dreyfus at the beginning of it all, after he'd approached me the first time with the job offer. "You could have told me—you could have warned me from the start."

"Now, Jeffrey," she said. "Just because I know who Dreyfus is doesn't mean I know what he has been up to, or that he might draw you into trouble. I am otherwise ignorant in all of this."

I glanced at Julien again, but for what consolation I couldn't say.

"I can't speak for what she knew, Jeff," Julien said. "But what reason does she have to lie?"

"I will give you the whole truth," said Françoise. "So that you and I can be in each other's trust. First, the man who calls himself Claude Dreyfus was my lover, before Marine's father died."

Marine stood. "I want out of this conversation."

"You expect that your mother has had no lovers?" asked Françoise.

"I'll be in my bedroom trying to think of something else."

Once Marine had left the room, Françoise gave Julien an endearing look. "Would you be so kind as to see if my lovely daughter has anything to drink in her kitchen? She becomes oddly stingy with her alcohol when I am around."

Julien obeyed. Françoise resumed in English. "Of course, the man was a prince to me while we were together. And very passionate. This was five or six years ago. When the affair ended—I knew by that point that he worked for some special branch of the National Police—he threatened me, telling me never to tell anyone who he was or what he did. And that bloody well scared me to death. And of course I knew by then that his threats had more behind them than just police precautions."

"What do you mean?" I glanced into the kitchen, thinking Julien should be hearing this.

"Julien knows this story, Jeffrey," said Françoise. "We had a conversation about M. Dreyfus not long ago. I trust Julien quite a bit, by the way—and you should too. Anyway, one evening when M. Dreyfus and I were together, I made the mistake of checking his jacket pocket for a cigarette while he was out of the room. I'd run out of menthols, you see, and in those days I didn't find regular cigarettes as repulsive as they really are."

"You're losing me, Françoise. What's your point?"

"What I found in his jacket was far more troubling than a pack of regular cigarettes. Passports, Jeffrey. French ones, very real-looking, half a dozen of them or more."

I wasn't seeing the troubling part. I sat back and got a cigarette of my own going.

"Cops come into contact with people's passports, Françoise," I said.

"Of course, Jeffrey, but these passports didn't have photos in them."

I searched Françoise's eyes. "What kind of names were in them?"

"French ones," she said. "I looked closely at a few of them. Each bore a French name but had a foreign birthplace. And I am not talking about EU countries, Jeffrey."

We said nothing for a minute.

"Since then I have always been afraid of him," added Françoise. "Very afraid, in fact, because I didn't need to be told that he was involved in rather shady affairs. When I broke it off, we didn't see each other for almost three years. Well, you can imagine my surprise when he showed up in the profs' room at Corbières with an armload of books."

"And you said nothing? You let that man keep coming to your school, teaching your kids—"

"Just wait. Eventually I went to M. Brule. But I didn't feel that I could tell him everything. So I told him only that I had over-heard M. Dreyfus speaking on the phone in the profs' room once, and that it was not the kind of conversation befitting a professor, visiting or otherwise. I suggested that perhaps it was nothing, but the seed had been planted. It was all I felt I could safely do."

Julien came back with a warm bottle of white wine and three glasses. I was hardly in a wine-drinking mood. I started thinking about my meeting with Brule in his office—so it had been Françoise who'd made him suspicious of Dreyfus.

"So what do you think Dreyfus is doing at Corbières?" I asked.

Françoise uncrossed her legs, shifting nervously in her chair. "Lord knows. But he's certainly become a frightening little man. He approached me one day in September and reminded me of my obligation to keep quiet. I spoke with him once in December—he asked me if I knew you very well and wondered where you were from in the States—but we did not speak again until this morning at the lycée."

"And you told him? You told him where I was from?"

"The whole exchange seemed harmless, really. Chitchat. He seemed only vaguely curious."

I felt very uncomfortable knowing that Dreyfus knew where I'd grown up, though I wasn't sure why. Maybe it was because it drove home the fact that he knew more about me than I knew about him.

"You said 'the man who calls himself Dreyfus.' What's his real name, then?"

She gave me an uncertain look, then glanced at Julien. "His name is Roland LeMercier, but never tell anyone that. He and a couple of detectives were in the profs' room this morning, asking a few of us if we knew of your whereabouts, Jeffrey—who had seen you last, and where. I supposed that they were suspicious because all the assistants were there—all but you."

I stood up and grimaced from the pain in my calf. "I need help getting out of town, guys."

"It won't be simple," said Julien. "You can't just march down to the train station and board a TGV to never-never land. If they name you a suspect for poisoning a goddamn *proviseur*—a guy who has one foot in the National Assembly already—they'll be on the lookout."

"There have to be other suspects," I said. "We all know Brule has enemies. Why would a foreigner, a teaching assistant from the States, try to poison him? Why would I even care?"

Françoise and Julien chuckled, but not out of amusement.

"They probably don't believe that you're just some American teaching assistant, Jeff," said Julien. "You're what—thirty?"

"Twenty-nine," I snapped.

"Whatever. You could still be over here with all sorts of other motives. There are dozens of foreign governments with interests in France. We did a story a few months ago—"

"What's that got to do with me?"

"All I'm saying is there's a lot of hype about Americans in France right now, and there are people in our government who are more than a little paranoid about CIA activity."

"But I'm not with the CIA, man. And I didn't poison anybody."

"*I* know you didn't," Julien said. "And *I* believe you, but that amounts to nothing. Tonight your face will most likely be all over the news. So you can either start trusting us now, or spend the afternoon wasting all the hope you've got left. Either way, you can't just run off on your own—even if you made it out of the country, they might find you and extradite you back here."

Now I was too spooked to step one foot out Marine's door.

"They can't possibly have cops at every station in the region," I reasoned. "And what's wrong with one of you smuggling me down to La Rochelle in the trunk of Marine's car?"

Françoise and Julien exchanged a knowing glance.

"Somehow I don't think that will happen, Jeff," he said in a low voice. "You know how she is with that precious heap-of-shit car of hers." Françoise smacked his arm and snickered.

"What about your car?" I asked. "You could drive me out of town, to Bordeaux even."

Julien shook his head. "My job, Jeff . . . if we got caught together . . ."

He didn't have to finish the thought, because I saw the implication: he wanted to help, but not at the risk of getting implicated. And I understood that—how much could I expect from any of them?

I took the phone into the bathroom and called Thierry, but got no answer. I checked the news, saw nothing new, and called Thierry again. Then I started worrying about Solène, without knowing exactly why. I decided to take a gamble, and called the Rougerie.

Bruno picked up. "Who's this?"

I hesitated. "It's your favorite American."

Long pause. "There were a couple of guys in here asking for you, my man. Guys in suits. With badges, Jeff."

I wasn't surprised, but I didn't say so. "There's a pretty young woman who may come around asking for me, too—"

Bruno laughed.

"Seriously," I said. "A younger lady. She's in trouble." I hesitated again. Dead silence on Bruno's end. "Bruno?"

"Still here."

"If she comes in, give her this number," I said, and read Marine's phone number from where it was written on the receiver. "And, Bruno . . ."

"Yep."

"Don't believe everything you hear, okay?"

There was another long pause. "I don't believe *anything* I hear, my man."

Françoise had the TV on. It was already four o'clock, one of those days when time seems to speed up just to spite you. Marine and I took seats on either side of her on the couch, but I spent the next half hour checking the window and cursing myself for slowing myself down by getting shot.

"Look, Jeff," said Françoise, pointing to the TV. "You're famous."

The news broadcast was using the photo they'd taken at the Lourange jail the night I'd been hauled in, bruised face and busted lip and all. The reporter said that Georges Brule, chief *proviseur* of the Ste-Térèse lycées, had just died in the emergency room—poisoned. The police were looking for an American teaching assistant named Jeffrey Delanne, the only employee at Corbières who had not reported to work that day.

The reporter did not say that I was a suspect, though that seemed rather obvious with my ugly mug looming there on screen.

Once I got over the initial shock, I stood and announced that I would trade what was left of my soul for a drink. Marine brought out a jug of red wine that was tangy but soothed the sting.

After a couple of glasses apiece, I knew it was time to make a move. I kept standing up and testing the status of my wounded leg. It would be fine, but running would hurt like hell.

Julien kept checking the time. Then at five sharp he stood up with a wild look in his eyes.

"Okay, Jeff, don't take this the wrong way—go to the bathroom and get out of your clothes."

I laughed and told him I hadn't heard him right. He started unbuttoning his dress shirt. "Trust me, would you? What I'm giving over is worth more than what you've got on."

I looked down at the shirt and jeans I was wearing. "You don't know that."

"All I'm saying is that if you fuck up my suit, I will personally escort your ass to the police."

I saw now in what direction his plan was headed. Françoise and Marine were both watching me, as if to say, *Don't be stupid, you don't have a choice.* And I couldn't think how to object. If posing as Julien meant getting out of town sooner rather than later, I was on board.

I went to the bathroom and stripped to my underpants. Julien handed in his pants and shirt, and I handed out mine. The suit was a nice fit. By the time I'd dressed and come out, Julien was standing in the entryway wearing my black peacoat and that silly knit hat.

"Shave your stubble into a goatee, and stay here until I call," he said. "That might be late tomorrow. Marine said she has some dye you can use for your hair." He looked me up and down, checking out his own suit. "And don't do anything I wouldn't do."

"Same to you. But why the hell are you doing this?"

Julien grinned. "Call me a sucker for foolish adventure. And this is some fucked-up shit that's happening to you. Anyway, it's the most I can do and still keep my hands clean."

He gave me a wink, slipped outside, and was gone.

Françoise left soon after. "Where will you go?" she asked me in French, then in English: "Wait—do not tell me. Drop me a line. Here is looking at you."

We gave the cheek kisses, and when she was gone I sucked down a cigarette without once taking my eyes off the blank TV. I kept seeing my face in the corner of the screen, feeling my body grow light. Not long after that, Marine sat beside me on the couch with a bottle of hair dye.

"Ready to be a blond?"

I checked her eyes. She seemed so sure of herself.

"Will it make things easier?" I asked.

"My blond friends seem to think so."

We set up a station in the kitchen, and in an hour the deed was done. Marine brought out a handheld mirror, and as we stared at my reflection, neither of us breathed. I could easily have passed as Julien's younger brother.

We started ripping through wine and cigarettes, running the

TV quietly but avoiding the local news. Then the phone rang and Marine picked it up, looking suddenly as if she'd seen a ghost.

"Who is this?" she asked. "No, you must have the wrong number."

I snatched the phone from her hand. "Solène?"

"Thank God it's you."

I looked at Marine and, seeing her perturbed expression, walked the phone into the hall.

"You okay?"

"Kind of," Solène said. "What about you?"

I hesitated. "It could be worse. Maybe. Any word from your dad?"

Long silence. Her breathing was heavy on the other end.

"You still there?" I said.

"He didn't come home last night either, Jeff. I went to Elise's, called home a few times, and in the morning she drove me back there. The front door was unlocked, and the back door was wide open. I locked those doors, Jeff. And Dad would never—"

"Just calm down," I said. "Where are you?"

"The *médiathèque*. I went to the Rougerie and asked the patron there about you—that's how I got this number. I've been here all day, I even skipped school. I'm really scared this time, Jeff. Dad always calls—always."

I realized that I was breathing loudly into the receiver. "You saw the local news?"

Long pause. "Yeah . . . what's happening, Jeff? It's not true, right?"

"No, except the part about them looking for me. You can trust me, Solène, I'm getting out of here tomorrow. I just didn't want to go without . . ." But I wasn't sure what I was trying to say.

"I won't see you again, will I?" she asked.

"I don't know. I'm in trouble."

"So am I, Jeff."

I hesitated, then said, "You know that spot under the bridge at the château? There's a bench right beside the steps. It's always in the shade of the bridge."

"I know the place."

"Find somewhere other than Elise's place to sleep tonight," I said then. "And meet me at that bench tomorrow. At noon."

I hung up without waiting for a reply. Marine cornered me in the hallway.

"Who was that?"

"A student of mine, Marine. Someone in trouble."

She snatched the phone from my hand the way I'd snatched it from hers. "I thought it was that Italian girl."

"Amelia? She's Sicilian."

"Whatever. Something's wrong with her. Patrick said she was asking him about Julien."

"I know, I know, he told me too."

"I can't believe—"

"Look, I promise you that the Sicilian girl won't be calling here," I said. "Ever."

"But you gave out my phone number."

"To Bruno, Marine. For him to give to a student of mine. She's in trouble."

Marine pointed at the phone. "You touch it again, I throw you out. Understand?"

After the local news took over every channel on Marine's TV, we tried watching a video on her crummy VHS player, a bad comedy about a go-cart race across the Sahara. Marine kept checking the job she'd done on my hair, ruffling her fingers through it to inspect the evenness of the dye. When she saw that I wasn't following the movie, she shut the thing off and got the scissors back out.

"One or two last adjustments."

We wrapped a towel around my neck and did some fine-tuning. Afterward I took a long, hot, tipsy shower, washing my bullet graze wound carefully and avoiding the mirror afterward. Then I found

Marine in the living room with the lights down low, jazz on the stereo, and our cups filled to the brim with wine.

We talked for a while about some of the Rougerie regulars in order to avoid talking about my fix, and then the conversation landed on Julien. She didn't have much to say about why they'd broken up, except that it had been a long time coming. The relationship had been on the rocks since summer. When he'd left in the fall, they'd practically called it off, though never officially. For some reason, they both rekindled it when Julien returned in December—back when I'd first met him. But things had always been falling apart, she said.

"It was something based in the past, something we had then, but not now. It didn't change with us, I guess."

While she told me all this, her looks gradually lingered longer, and not just on my hair. Then she said she wanted to practice her English with me, which the two of us had never tried before.

"How-does-one-say," she said, "*dommage* in *Anglais*?"

"'Too bad,'" I said. "Or else, 'It's a shame.'"

"It's a sham."

"A *shame*," I said, holding back a laugh. "Shame, sham. *Il y a une grande différence.*"

She smiled and lit cigarettes for us. I took one, but kept my eyes from falling into hers.

"*Alors,*" she said. "How-does-one-say, '*Tu pars quand tu viens d'arrivé*'?"

"That would be something like, 'You're leaving when you have just arrived.'"

Even before I'd translated the words into English, they hurt to hear. Of course, she was right. But that didn't mean I had to look back at her the way she was looking at me. Nor did it mean that she should move closer to me on the couch, which was exactly what she did.

Soon the irony of it was burning deep: she'd been the object of my desire for so long, and only now that I was ready to go did she seem ready to embrace me.

"You are leev-ing," she repeated in her funny English, "when you joost arrived."

My eyes finally made their way to hers. I said, "Exactly."

When she kissed me, for a long racing moment I didn't care if I spent a hundred years in exile.

I pulled her close, held her, tasted her lips until I could feel her breathing quicken, and then she moved onto my lap, straddling me. Her hands were in my hair. Fiddling with the buttons of my shirt. Her lips roamed to my neck, and in that instant I suffered a bombardment of understanding, exhilaration enveloped in letdown. Doing this with her, even if I was cold enough to go through with it, could amount to nothing as wonderful as I'd imagined in the past.

And I couldn't stop thinking about Solène.

When I pulled away, Marine moved off my lap and lay back on the couch. After a moment we exchanged a long embrace with our eyes. Then she smiled and reached for the TV remote.

The ten-o'clock news was on. The images on screen showed marches against the new conflict in Iraq: Paris, Lyon, Marseilles, Montpellier. Then came more images of Baghdad: statues being pulled down in the streets, orange flames and black clouds of smoke in the background. When the news switched to local, Marine turned up the volume.

The reporter said, "Police today answered an anonymous tip and found a federal agent dead in an abandoned cottage near Lourange this afternoon. Police believe the alleged murder is connected with the suspicious poisoning of a prominent city official and Parliament candidate at Lycée Corbières this morning, as well as with the disappearance of an American teaching assistant who is now believed to have ties to the Algerian mafia . . ."

I tuned out when my ears started ringing. I felt Marine's hand clutch mine, and we watched the images roll on and on before freezing on one that I recognized all too well. He looked exactly as I had seen him last, when he'd driven me home in his Saab—the dead agent was Solène's father, Thierry Duvin.

ANYWHERE YOU'RE WILLING TO STAY

After Marine turned off the lights and left me on her couch, I suffered several hours of what I wouldn't pretend to call sleep, imprisoned between one dark place and another. I finally dozed until I heard a pounding in the back of my skull. The pounding moved away from me yet grew louder, until it was a distinct series of knocks.

I woke up with no clue where I was—only that I wasn't dreaming. And that someone was banging on Marine's front door.

After that, everything happened in a flurry of panic.

I jolted upright. Marine was already at the window, peeking out. She squatted suddenly.

"Out the back, Jeffrey!" she whispered. "Go now!"

I was on my knees and scrambling into the kitchen, pulling on my shoes and Julien's jacket and my backpack. More pounding from the front door, angry voices calling to open up. I shot a glance into the living room at Marine. She hadn't moved, and there was a terrified look on her face. I thought I was going to be sick. Her mouth moved without making a sound: *Vas-y!*

I threw open her back door and tore across the backyard, leaped

the rickety picket fence, and sprinted down the cobblestone alleyway until I was out of breath, some dozen houses down. I ducked
behind a little utility van parked in the grass, my lungs on fire, my
hands and face numb, my wounded leg pulsing with pain. I had no
idea where I was, no sense of direction—only the knowledge that
there were cops coming, and that I'd just woken up enough dogs
to leave a handy trail for them.

The alley emptied into a street. I hesitated, took a right, and
walked until I came to a plaza whose cross-street I recognized. As
I rounded the corner I held my breath. Two bicycle cops were racing down the street toward me, their miniature handlebar lights
cutting through the thin morning fog.

A wave of nausea rose in my throat, my body stiffened—it hurt
to breathe, to put one foot in front of the other. As they drew
closer, their eyes riveted onto mine. But they weren't braking.

Time slowed to a scream as their bikes rolled past.

A HALF HOUR later, near Place Courrant, in Paul's neck of the
woods, I found a café with a back door. Paul was my best remaining bet, I'd decided, but I'd have to wait a short while if I wanted
to intercept him on his way to work. I ordered an espresso that I
didn't need, paid with a quivering hand, and took a seat in the
back with a newspaper. But I didn't give a shit for the news—I
needed to figure out who'd leaked my whereabouts, who'd betrayed me.

Bruno was the most probable. I'd called him, identified myself,
and given him a phone number that could have been traced to
Marine's. I *wanted* the rat to be Bruno—but what motive did he
have? He hated the police as much as I did.

Of course, there was Françoise, who probably feared Dreyfus
enough to succumb to him during an interrogation. There were
also Marine and Solène. But I'd marked Marine's face as she squatted in the living room: she was on my side. And as for Solène, I

didn't have it in me to suspect her. She was an orphan now—we were practically in the same boat.

Then there was Julien. He claimed to be helping out on the grounds of friendship, but we hadn't been friends for very long— or at all. We just shared mutual friends. But why would he save my ass, and then exchange clothes with me, only to turn around and betray me? Still, Julien's motives made the least sense, and so did his actions. Someone had rolled over, and the more I thought about him, the more I felt in my gut that he wasn't on the level.

On the other hand, any of them, or anyone who'd seen me at the Rougerie, might have innocently told the wrong person the wrong thing—a slip, the slightest implication that Marine and I were friends, might have done it. There were just too many variables. Which meant that I just couldn't know how the cops had found me. Not yet, anyway.

Despite the fact that I could see my own breath, I was sweating like a thoroughbred. I glanced over at the plump old woman who'd made my espresso. There were two other customers in the place: a bundled-up codger hunching over a crossword puzzle two tables over, and a slick-haired youngster in a tight jogging suit, sitting near the front door.

I kept thinking about Dreyfus, the key to all this. But it didn't make sense that he'd been at Corbières just to plot and oversee a scheme wherein I'd get framed for the attack on Georges Brule. Neither could I make any sense out of what Nabec's and the old madame's roles were. If Dreyfus and they were in league together, and if I'd been sent to Nabec only to get thrown in jail and then blamed for a crime I didn't commit, why would one tell me to keep going to Corbières while the other warned me to stay away?

Then there was Thierry's other theory—that there were Corbières students involved, however unknowingly, in some evil deed or another. What could a few high school kids possibly have to do with this? Maybe Thierry had misjudged, guessed too much, mixed up the evidence so far that he'd overshot the truth and wound up dead.

I checked the clock behind the bar. Twenty till eight. Paul would be leaving his apartment for school any minute.

In five minutes I was standing at the end of the alley that ran behind Paul's apartment building. The sun was just splintering through the clouds, but there were darker, heavier clouds to the west. As I waited at the end of his block, my knees quaked beneath the thin fabric of Julien's slacks. I peeked around the corner and down the alley, checking for Paul's station wagon and sweating ice-cold bullets. My mind started barreling through the options—if Paul didn't show, I'd have to find somewhere to hole up until my noon meeting with Solène.

Just as I was about to take off, Paul's car turned into the alley. I moved fast off the street to where he could see me.

He didn't slow right away. I could see his son, Lucien, in the passenger seat, could see Paul leaning over the steering wheel, squinting from under his bushy eyebrows. He didn't recognize me.

Just before his car reached me, I made solid eye contact through the windshield. But he didn't slow at first—he even coasted past me. Then finally he hit the brakes.

The back door handle was locked. *"C'est moi,"* I said, mouthing the words and turning my head so they could inspect my profile through the side window. Paul's lips were pursed, his eyes like steel. Lucien's window came down an inch, but I didn't hear any doors unlock.

I said, "Come on, Paul, you know I didn't do it—you *know* that."

He frowned and shook his head before releasing the back door lock.

"Thank God," I said, once I'd climbed in. "Hi, Lucien. Bad time to be me, huh?"

He said nothing, didn't even chuckle. We took a right out of the alley. Paul said, "You realize this makes me an accomplice, right? They already suspect me of helping you—they were ringing our doorbell at an ungodly hour this morning."

It dawned on me then that neither of them had a clue what I was really up against—all they had was the news, and what the police chose to tell the public. My eyes darted everywhere along the street, up and down the sidewalks on either side, expecting to see Dreyfus or one of his men emerge from the shadows.

"Where are we going?" I asked.

"Jeffrey, I can't—" Paul started to say. "I can't sacrifice everything for you, you know that."

"I know, I know. And I'm not asking you to. It all depends on who you want to believe, Paul. You know me, you've got to believe me."

I studied what I could see of his face as he drove, unsure whether I regretted trusting him, or whether I just doubted trust altogether.

After a long silence at a red light, Paul said, "You must know that your photo is all over the news, Jeffrey. Several students have even given testimony to things you've said in class—anti-French things."

I looked at Lucien. He wouldn't look back. Paul's knuckles were white on the steering wheel.

"That's bullshit, Paul. I can't prove it right now, but I know that it was Dreyfus who set me up. He's behind all this. There's something he's been involving students with at Corbières—Thierry Duvin told me that himself. I don't know how or what for, but I know it's big—and it involves international criminals, Paul. Duvin knew about it, and when he got too close, he was silenced."

Lucien actually laughed. Paul was shaking his head.

"I shouldn't be doing this," he said. "You should be meeting with my attorney, discussing the best way to turn yourself in. It's the only way, Jeffrey, you've got to listen to reason."

"Then just drop me off. I don't know what the hell I'm supposed to do, but I'm not going to wait in some prison, hoping they'll believe I've been set up, hoping they'll stumble upon the truth. Too much is against me. I've got to do something."

Paul glanced at his son, then looked at me with the disappointed eyes of a father.

"The truth?" he said. "Jeffrey, the truth is that no one can help you now but the law—you've got to fight the law with the law. The truth is that you *must* turn yourself in. I'll take you straight to my attorney's office—that's where we're headed now. He's a friend, you can tell him what you know about Dreyfus, and he'll tell you the same thing, that running only makes you look guilty."

We stopped at another light. I started ripping through alternatives, because there was no way I was going to pay a visit to Paul's attorney—that would be as good as turning myself in. The only thing I could think of, if I couldn't get out of the city pronto, was to investigate my own suspicions.

"I've been cheated by the law, Paul. I can't prove it yet, there are lots of missing pieces, but I know the police are in on it. Dreyfus works for them, and he chose me for this. I don't know why he wanted Brule dead, but I know I'm in this shit partly because I'm American."

Another brief chuckle escaped Lucien's mouth. "Oh, come on," he said.

"That's wrong, Jeffrey," said Paul. "You can't go around thinking that just because you're American you're being discriminated against. You still have a right to an attorney here in France. And you still can turn yourself in. You can't keep running—you have to stop sometime."

At the next stoplight, Paul faced me again. The look in his eyes was purely honest and terrible. But I had a plan. I opened my door and got out.

"Say good-bye to your wife for me," I said. "Tell her I'll sing the praises of her cooking around the world."

"Get back in the car, Jeff." Paul's eyes were wide and angry.

"No," I said. "You're right—I can't expect you to bring trouble on yourself for this."

"Get in, Jeffrey. I can't help you, but I can . . . Just get in." We both hesitated. "Get in, Jeff. I know a place where you can hide."

WE DROVE SOUTH to a huge public arboretum called the Jardin des Plantes, across Boulevard de Gare from the train station. I'd tooled around the park plenty in the fall, and it was an ideal spot—a ten-minute walk from the château, where Solène and I had agreed to meet, and full of private nooks and secluded areas with benches. I'd also be near the offices of the *Journal,* where Julien worked.

As we pulled past the train station, my body seized. There were more than a dozen police cars in the lot, cops congregating all over, passengers spilling out the doors. I had a hunch that the fanfare wasn't on account of the upcoming holiday.

Paul took a left and looped around the east end of the park.

"You know they are checking passports and IDs at the station, right?" he asked.

I didn't answer, didn't even give a nod. Paul pulled over and we exchanged a long, silent good-bye. His eyes had softened.

" 'Bye, Lucien," I said. "Tell everybody it wasn't me. Tell everybody that Claude Dreyfus is a fake, an undercover cop named Roland LeMercier. Don't trust him."

"Sure thing, Jeff," said Lucien sarcastically.

I climbed out. Paul rolled down his window.

"Paul," I said. "Thanks—for everything, okay? I'll write."

He took off his glasses. "The instinct to escape is not the only one worth listening to, Jeffrey. There is also the instinct to fight. Staying put, fighting where you live, fighting from your home, can be just as brave as fighting in some country halfway across the world."

"I'll remember that," I said. "But this isn't my home, Paul."

His eyes grew wide again, but in them now was the old warmth of concern.

"You're wrong, Jeffrey. Home is anywhere you're willing to stay—anywhere you're willing to make change. I believe you're innocent, and I won't tell anyone that I've seen you. But you must remember that there is also the instinct to stay and fight. You can't always run."

I couldn't have agreed more with him about fighting. I just refused to hand myself over to a bunch of riled-up, misinformed cops and hope an attorney would do it for me.

I made for the park entrance before the heat of Paul's gaze could burn any deeper.

TEN MINUTES LATER I was standing in the vast marble lobby of the *Journal* building, my heart pounding in my ears and my stomach twisting into knots. My leg hurt, but it was gradually taking backstage to my wrung-out nerves.

The front desk was unmanned, but there were three phones ringing away on it. After a maddening minute of listening to them, I decided I was losing my mind and turned to leave.

"May I help you, monsieur?"

I turned back. The woman who'd said it didn't have the secretarial look, but I knew that running for the door and back to the park would be about the guiltiest-looking thing I could do.

"Yes, in fact," I said. "I don't have an appointment but . . ." I hesitated, suddenly drawing a blank on Julien's last name. He'd told me only once, over a game of darts. "You see, I'm the brother of someone who works here, and I'm in town unexpectedly—I'd like to surprise him. I just don't know which office he's in."

The woman turned her head skeptically, then held up one finger and answered one of the phones, asking the caller to hold. She did the same with the other two, which bought me the time I needed to recall Julien's last name.

"Please forgive me," the woman said. "You were saying . . ."

"Yes, Julien Lafrene's office number, please."

The woman acted suddenly frazzled. She said something about filling in for someone else, then about the office directory, which she unearthed from a pile of papers and memos.

"Lafrene, you say?" she asked. I nodded, and she rifled through the directory. "I'm sorry. Perhaps you have the wrong newspaper, monsieur—no such person works here."

We tried a few alternate spellings, but there was nothing there. My heart sank with a crash, and for a long horrible moment I stood there motionless and dumbfounded. I was sure I didn't have the wrong newspaper.

"You're certain there's no Julien Lafrene who works here?" I asked. "Even as an assistant?"

"Absolutely, monsieur—his name would be here. Perhaps you've confused us with *Le Matin*. Now if you'll excuse—"

But I was already halfway to the door.

AT THE ENTRANCE to the Jardin des Plantes, I threw a glance down Boulevard de Gare at the hectic, cop-infested train station and felt the doom rumble in my guts. Then I slipped in and found an isolated bench, turning over the implications of Julien's lie. It was possible the woman had made a mistake. But not probable. Which meant I'd just lost an ally.

Around a quarter till noon the sun broke through the clouds, casting short, sudden shadows along the walkways. I headed toward the north end of the park, to the rose garden, which this time of year was nothing more than a collection of thorny skeletons, and suffered a memory of the first time I'd seen the garden, six months before. I'd just escaped my home country, a grand achievement at the time, and I was all wound up with rebirth; I'd felt like a new man, released from my American past, pardoned from those parts of myself I'd wanted so badly to leave behind. I realized now that all of that had been an illusion—there'd always be more borders to cross, more risks to weigh against staying put and stagnating.

This understanding, gloomy as it was, only made stronger my desire to find Solène, to take her away from this place with me. Her loss seemed yoked to mine. And I wanted that.

I left the park and crossed the château drawbridge, entering the brown castle walls, and descending the slick stone steps into the grassy moat area, where a gravel walking trail wrapped around the base of the old château, maybe fifty feet below street level. Patrick had told me once that some five hundred years ago a woman named Duchesse Anne had holed up in this château during a long siege, and by the end of it they'd hauled her out of there as dead as a post. Now I wished to God I could wash my mind of that awful history: it made the fortress walls feel like a prison. But at least there weren't any suspicious characters lurking about— just two old men on the gravel path to my left, a young couple strolling farther down, and off to my right, a blind man smoking a pipe. Near the foot of the stairs where I stood, three university-aged kids were sitting in the grass. There was another young couple sitting on the bench in the shade—the bench Solène and I had agreed on.

I went left and passed the bench, and for some reason my paranoia awoke—someone, I felt suddenly, was watching. And God only knew who that was or whose side they were on. I remembered the two kids who'd tried to tail me to Thierry's house. How had they known where to pick up my trail?

All I could think about after that was running back up those stairs into the château, where I'd have a cleaner shot at escaping to the street, if something went wrong.

Paul might change his mind and tell someone, like his attorney.

Solène might show up with cops in tow, not expecting to be followed.

She might not show at all.

I took the gravel trail around to its end, just below Boulevard de Gare, then doubled back, slowing so I could get a good look at the stairway. When the couple who'd taken over the shaded bench got up to leave, I grabbed a seat on the next bench over, which put our meeting spot between me and the stairs.

I also had a solid view of the street-level sidewalks on two sides of the château. People kept stopping and leaning against the handrail, gazing down at what I could only guess was me with a blinking neon sign over my head that said CRIMINAL.

It was two minutes after noon, and no Solène. I rubbed my hands together to warm them, and told myself that I'd wait two more minutes. Then after two more minutes I stood up and sat back down, telling myself I could wait another two minutes. Still no Solène. My nerves began to wind so tight that I thought I might burst.

I got up and made for the steps, passing a kid in a blue windbreaker who'd taken the bench the young couple had been using—the one Solène and I had agreed on. I'd almost reached the stairway when something about him struck me as familiar. There'd been a kid I'd thought I recognized in the Jardin, too, which probably only meant that my mind was playing tricks on me. I glanced back anyway, but couldn't see this one's face. He had on baggy blue jeans, gray running shoes, and an orange baseball cap. Underneath the cap, the hair was cut short and choppy; it was no one I knew.

I turned into the stairwell and almost plowed into a skinny black guy carrying an oversized shoulder bag. I apologized, stepped down and out of the man's way, and glanced back at the shorn-headed teen. He reached into his pocket and took out a cigarette. When I saw him light up, tilting his head and covering the flame with a cupped palm, I realized that it wasn't a boy at all—it was Solène, minus the long blond curls.

I couldn't doubt it now—her profile, her movements, the shape of her neck. Instantly the blood drained from my face. I hesitated and started climbing the steps without knowing why. Then halfway up I stopped, leaning against the cold bricks and trying to slow my breathing.

I couldn't just leave her. She'd come.

Just then she appeared at the foot of the stairs. She didn't recognize me at first, or at least didn't act as if she did. She lowered her head as she climbed the steps toward me, and only when she'd reached my step did she turn and look me in the eyes. Right away her face whitened. I smiled.

"Jesus Christ," she said. "I thought you were a ghost."

"Let's get to the tram stop," I whispered as we walked up. "Stay behind me a little."

We went up and over the bridge to the street-level sidewalk, and then rounded it to Boulevard de Gare. At the tram stop I still hadn't shaken the paranoia I'd felt down below the château. I glanced back. Solène stood several safe feet away and kept from making eye contact.

The eastbound tram pulled up. We got on and moved to the corner of the car.

"They think you are in Tours," she said. I grinned. Somehow I'd been wrong about Julien—his decoy had worked. "The news said you were almost apprehended there last night."

She looked around our car nervously. "Anyway, we can use Dad's Saab."

She showed me the keys. They lay glittering in her hand like priceless jewels. I checked around us. Our tram car was packed, nobody looking our way. I held her against me until the next stop, realizing that we'd cast our lots together without even needing to talk it over. I wanted to ask her if she was sure—what about college, the rest of her life?

"Dad has friends in Spain," she said, as if she'd been listening in on my thoughts. "And my brother lives there. We should go there, we'll be safe."

She reached up and touched her short, choppy hair, where all those beautiful blond curls had been. I could think of worse ways of reacting to a father's death.

"It's a cute look for you," I said. "Better than mine, anyway."

She gave me a smile that I wasn't convinced of—something was wrong.

"I'm scared," she said. "I'm not safe, Jeff."

I searched her eyes. "Why? Is someone looking for you? Would someone follow you?"

"I don't know, Jeff. Maybe, I don't know."

It wasn't the kind of reassurance I was looking for. I suffered another jolt of paranoia.

At the next stop a couple of construction workers got on and started sizing me up. We moved forward two cars. The train was packed: lunch rush hour. Someone nudged my arm and I nearly jumped. A young woman in a puffy suede coat turned to me and said: *"Pardon, monsieur."* Her look lingered, as if she recognized me.

We moved into the back corner of the next car up. I leaned and whispered to Solène without looking at her.

"Did you feel safe at the *médiathèque*?"

She hesitated. "Why?"

My knees began to shake. I took the keys from her, then stood with my back to her and started scrutinizing faces.

That was when a kid I recognized appeared in the passageway between our car and the next one up. His eyes seemed to be moving urgently from face to face.

I turned to Solène. "New plan. I want you to go back one car and get off at the next stop."

"Jeffrey—"

"Trust me," I said. "I'll get Thierry's car and meet you at the *médiathèque* at four."

I glanced back at the kid. He was about my size, big forehead and thick neck. I'd seen him lurking around the arboretum on his cell phone, just before I'd left there, and of course I'd thought nothing of it. Now he was making his way back through our car. The tram slowed for the next stop.

I turned back to Solène. "Go. Now. Four o'clock."

As she slid from behind me and into the car behind us, I moved forward toward the kid, hoping to draw his attention away from Solène.

The tram stopped. Its doors slid open, and everyone seemed to push out at once. I fought not to glance back after Solène, and instead fastened my eyes on the kid, who'd been held up by exiting passengers. Another heavy crowd pushed on before the tram doors shut, and now my hands were wet with sweat, shaking visibly.

When the tram was moving again, the kid made his way toward me, seeming to have regained his focus. Then he raised his gaze, and our eyes met. A sinister grin appeared on his face. Instantly my vision started swimming.

By the time it had steadied, I was in the next car back.

I squeezed between several rows of passengers and hurried through another bottleneck between cars—one step up, two steps over the passageway, and one step down—before glancing back. The kid wasn't there. But I was too shaken up by the look he'd given me to relax.

The tram slowed to a stop, and the doors came open. Place Manufacture, the stop I wanted, would be two after the next. I was tempted to get off ahead of time and walk it, but I second-guessed myself—part of me just wouldn't let some kid spook me into a misstep.

Now my calf was starting to throb hard. I needed to get off my feet. The tram doors had shut again. I'd moved back another car, but now we seemed to be crawling along in slow motion.

When we slowed for the next stop, I shot a glance back. The young bastard had followed me back. Now he was on his cell phone again. And looking dead at me.

I pushed through the passengers of two more cars, each like the previous: narrow plastic rooms crammed with people, strangers preoccupied with holding their ground. I was between cars when the tram came to another stop, this one more abrupt.

And the doors didn't come open. I checked outside, saw that we were held up at an intersection, and decided that I was ready for a heart attack. This wasn't just paranoia—I had a deep and dirty feeling in my gut.

When the tram started moving again I glanced back. The kid was getting closer, squeezing his way through.

He was a hefty kid for his age. I'd have to punch him hard between the eyes, maybe even break his nose—that would teach him.

The tram slowed, and at the next stop half of it emptied out. My stop was next. I raced back through another two cars, thinking there couldn't be many cars left. Now I could see back two or three cars to the rear window of the tram. There weren't many riders between here and there.

I darted through a half-empty car, over the steps, and into the next. A second later they were on me.

Three of them. As tall as me but younger. All wearing tight jeans and puffy athletic jackets—all Arabs.

As they gathered around me, my eyes shifted from their eyes to their empty opened hands.

"Excuse me," I said in French. "You must have me confused with someone else."

I made the move to push out of their circle. Nobody stopped me, so I bolted for the rear end of the car, leaping onto the passageway between cars.

And just as I was jumping into the last tram car, the tram broke speed for my stop, and I felt as if I were floating, hovering over a fraction of a second, while my eyes registered the ambush.

In the rear car were four more lycée-aged kids, standing gauntlet-style. Two on either side. Fists clenched.

I landed on my heels and spread my arms. The three Arab kids moved in behind me. I glanced around. The tram was empty except for us.

Before I could say anything, one of the Arabs lunged. I threw a big overhand right and caught him square on the jaw. He went down on one knee, but another kid came at me from the left. I dodged and elbowed his gut, but another of the boys got hold of my left arm and jerked it behind my back. I swung twice at him with my right, but couldn't reach.

Then they closed in around me. I felt a jolt of pain on the backs of my knees and fell.

And before I could take another breath, I was pinned facedown against the tram floor, groaning from the impact of boots bouncing off my body.

YES, YOU COULD CALL THAT A COCK

They stood me up, yanked my elbows together behind me, and shoved me into the corner of the tram car. All of them were breathing frantically, with wild energy in their eyes. I glanced out the tram window. We were moving past a row of old brick buildings and into a neighborhood of warehouses decorated with colorful graffiti.

I looked again at the faces huddled around me: seven of them, all lycée age, including one student from Corbières—Jean-Claude, a friend of Lucien's.

I was thoroughly confused, but I still had too much adrenaline pumping through me for that to matter. There was blood in my mouth from a kick one of them had landed on my jaw while I was down. My right cheek felt hot and swollen, and my entire skull ached. I looked at Jean-Claude.

"Mind telling these nice young men that I've missed my stop?"

Jean-Claude glanced nervously out the window. The tram was slowing.

"Of course, this stop will do just fine," I added.

"Shut up," said the Arab who'd joint-locked my arm. He said it in English.

I said: *"C'est pas gentil."*

"Fuck you, Du-lain," said Jean-Claude.

"Fuck you, you little punk—"

The tram stopped. Its doors came open and a few of the boys rushed over to block the doorways. The Arab I'd gotten smart with punched me in the gut, which doubled me over. Then the doors closed, and when we were moving again, a slim man in a gray and red tramline officer's uniform entered our car.

My heart leaped: I winked at the kid who'd punched me, and watched the officer pull a partition between our car and the next, so that we were sealed off from the rest of the train. He pushed his way between the boys up to me and took off his cap. It was Léo.

"I see," I said. "Spends the weekend in jail and figures he's a badass. Or is this something you're doing for the cops, on account of your behavior last week?"

He started to say something, but hesitated. "Keep your mouth shut, or Amad will hurt you."

He handed his cap to one of the others, who in turn handed him his signature purple scarf. He wrapped the scarf twice around his skinny neck. I couldn't help thinking how easily I could choke the life out of him, if my hands were free. I glanced sideways out the window again and saw dark clouds, more warehouses, and a few tall red brick apartment buildings jutting above them in the distance. I'd ridden west this far only once, with Solène and her friends for the soccer game.

"How far do you think you can take this?" I asked Léo. "You know the nationals are onto you, don't you?"

Léo didn't have a very good poker face.

"They can't touch me," he said, glancing out the windows as we slowed for the next stop. "But it's not personal, Jeff. I'm only—"

"Léo!" Amad interrupted. *"Il faut garder silence."*

"Tais toi," Léo shot back. *"Je connais bien ce que je fait."*

I could feel some frightening pain where I'd been kicked in the ribs. I fastened my eyes on Jean-Claude again.

"Jean-Claude," I said. "What do you guys do for Dreyfus—or should I say LeMercier—besides kick around assistants?"

Jean-Claude looked at Léo, who looked away nervously and shook his head.

"Shut up," said Amad.

"I'll knock your teeth down your throat," I said, no longer able to keep a lid on the rage. "Both of you. I swear to God."

Léo calmed Amad down.

"Jean-Claude does not know anything, Jeff," said Léo. "He's just here to help."

The tram stopped. They moved me out the doors onto the platform. Léo lingered behind.

"Léo," I called back in English. "I'll be coming for you, Léo."

They yanked my arms up so far behind my back that I bent over, nose to knees. When they let up, I stood straight and watched the tram pull off.

It was sprinkling cold rain. On the platform it was just us and one lone figure. I watched her approach, and when I recognized her, all my pain turned to loathing. It was Amelia.

She strutted up and scowled, an expression more genuine than anything I'd seen on her face since we'd met. She had on a brown corduroy jacket and a knit scarf I recognized. But for once she wasn't wearing any makeup. In the overcast light, she looked deathly pale.

"So how does a foreigner like you get into the foreigner-fucking business?" I asked.

"That's something you'll never really have the privilege of knowing, Jeffrey Delanne." Though her voice sounded cool, her right eye blinked nervously. She wore a bitter, disgusted expression. "But you should be used to not knowing by now. You've been nothing but a tool."

She rattled off something in what sounded like Arabic to one of the boys holding me. They braced me and she slapped my face so hard that I saw lightning behind my eyelids.

"Open your eyes," she said. I opened them. "That was for you."

I was too bleary to anticipate the kick between the legs. The impact forced all the air out of me and made my knees buckle.

"And that is for the other night, asshole," I heard her say.

It was the last thing I heard before something blunt struck the base of my skull. After that: oily darkness.

WHEN I CAME to, I was sitting in a folding chair with my wrists and ankles tied beneath me.

"Il se reveille," someone said. It was a young voice, from in front of me. *"Vas-y, dites-il."*

My vision cleared. I was in a dark room. I could smell sawdust and rusty metal. Above me I could hear wind and rain spattering against a thin roof. My throat was badly parched, my tongue tasted like copper, my neck and upper back were throbbing hard, and my crotch felt as if it had taken a blow from a hammer.

Soon a heavy door screeched open, and a powerful light came on, then dimmed. I spent a long time blinking in vain, but eventually my vision sharpened.

I focused on the dim yellow light in front of me, which seemed to swing and grow brighter, until I could see the lantern that it shone from and the empty space around it. Three figures stood next to where the lantern hung from a rope. I followed the rope to a dark, uneven ceiling, maybe thirty feet up, along one edge of which were long, foggy windows. I followed the rope back down. The figure in the middle, the tallest, approached me.

He was of medium height and build, and had a slight limp. He opened a folding chair and sat down where I could see him. I didn't recognize him at first—the pain at the base of my skull was making it hard to concentrate. Dark-featured, he wore bright white running shoes and a silver jogging suit, the jacket of which was zipped down to his navel. White undershirt. Thick silver necklace. Hair slicked back from a wide forehead. I thought I could smell lavender cologne, and then I realized who it was before me: Pierre, the man who'd picked me up outside the police station and had brought me to Dreyfus—the driver I'd put in a headlock.

"Welcome, M. Delanne," Pierre said in French. "It is French, this name, is it not?"

My throat was too dry for words. I ran my tongue against my teeth.

"No," I managed. "My—"

"Do you remember me?"

I studied what I could see of his face in the dim light. His mouth wasn't smiling, but his eyes seemed to be.

".Sure," I said. "One of LeMercier's lackeys."

He chuckled. "I told you, did I not, Delanne, that we'd see each other again. That's Léo standing back there, along with your good friend Amelia, who's been waiting three months, patiently, for this day. You know, don't you now, that she had the hardest role in all this—acting like she gave a shit about you, even fucking you, as a service to us? Anyway, they're here to watch and learn a thing or two. Strange, isn't it, how things tend to make sense only after the fact?"

My eyes had fully adjusted now, and my brain was moving just fast enough to register my own fear. I was confused as hell. It just didn't make any sense. What did these people want with me?

Pierre touched the knuckles of his right hand. Something bulky was fastened over them.

"My point is, Delanne," he said, "I don't know why I don't get to kill you, but I hope to find some sense in it later."

My wits were shaken, though I wasn't quite buying his act. He wouldn't kill me even if he were allowed to—not here, in front of Léo.

Pierre leaned in. "But make no mistake, Delanne, accidents happen." He chuckled for longer than was necessary and then stood. I was too thirsty for words, but I knew I had to start talking.

"Come on, Léo," I called out. "Jail's one thing, but do you really want to go to prison for a guy like this?"

"Leave him out of this," Pierre snapped. "It'll only make things worse on you."

He stepped toward me suddenly, and when I flinched he smiled. "It's a pretty simple thing I'm going to propose to you, Delanne. And I'll admit I didn't expect to have you here like this. Our mutual friend Dreyfus didn't expect it, either. But that's what makes this so . . . delightful." He stopped and stretched his arms as if he were getting ready for a workout. "So let's begin. There are two types of people, Delanne: those who are willing to tell secrets, and those who are not."

He took another step closer and squatted. Now we were within arm's reach, which put me at a severe disadvantage.

"You're one who's willing to tell secrets," he said. "I know you are, because you went to Duvin with some. A lot of good that did you. So I'm going to ask you once, and I don't want to have to ask you again . . . Where is she?"

I focused my thoughts and tried to act confused. He was talking about Solène, I was sure, but I couldn't figure why.

"Who?" I asked.

"Oh, come on," said Pierre. "You can't play dumb with me. See, I know you know. And if you don't tell me where she is, I'm going to assume that you just don't *want* to tell me. And do you know what my next assumption will be, Delanne?" He paused and took a deep breath. "It will be that pain, a little bit at a time, more and more and then gradually more, will change your mind."

A single bead of sweat ran down the center of my back. I remembered the beating I'd taken from Rafa, how strangely invigorating it had been. Pierre had no idea how much I was ready to take.

I kept my mouth shut, fixing my eyes on his.

"So I'll pretend you didn't hear me right," said Pierre. "Where is she?"

My knees suddenly quaked. I had to stall. "How about some water?"

"Things like water are earned, Delanne. I'll give you all the water you could ever want. All I'm asking you for is a location." He paused, and my thoughts went back to the first interview I'd done for Nabec, when I'd asked the man in the chair the same question. "Look, Delanne. I don't care if she's trying to mourn her father's death. I don't care that you're her teacher and that you've been fucking her. All I want to know is where she is—and I want to know *right fucking now.*"

I tried to shift around in my seat, tried to focus on peripheral things—the faint halo around the lantern, the sound of the rain outside, the smell of sawdust, the taste of blood in my mouth.

Pierre stood and walked around me. When he was back in front of me, he squatted again and took a set of keys out of his pocket, dangling them in my face. They were Thierry's car keys.

"Now, I know these aren't yours," he said, "because you don't *have* a car, do you, Delanne? So where were you headed in the suit and fresh hairdo, with a thousand euros in a backpack with some underwear?"

I shook my head. "Just trying to hide . . . until I figured out why all this is happening."

He grinned, stepped closer, and placed a hand on top of my head.

"Playing it safe, huh? See, when my boys found you in the arboretum and followed you to the château, they saw you waiting there. Why didn't she come? And where did you retrieve her dad's car keys?"

I felt a strange wave of relief. However they'd discovered me at the arboretum, somehow they hadn't seen me with Solène during our short ride together in the tram. That explained why the kid who'd chased me into the rear car had been looking around anxiously for me once Solène had gotten off—he must have boarded a different car, or maybe he'd thought that he'd lost me, and hadn't pushed his way through the crowded tram into my car until Solène was gone. I'd seen him on his cell phone as he followed me back through the car, too—that must have been how he'd signaled Léo and the other boys. So they'd outsmarted me, but hadn't found who they'd really been after.

Which meant I had to keep playing dumb.

"I don't know what you're talking about," I said. "You shouldn't trust kids so much."

It took all my courage to smile. As soon as I did—and before I could even think about how satisfying it felt—Pierre cocked back and took a big swing.

The left side of my face exploded with pain. I heard my own voice cry out. The lantern light flickered and dimmed in my vision. There was more blood in my mouth, running over my chin and down my neck. I let my head hang.

Pierre was up close now, whispering in my ear. "I won't even cut your balls off. Isn't that nice of me? We can leave that out, Delanne—if you tell me where she is."

With each breath the pain pulsed harder. But strangely my senses seemed to sharpen. He'd have to kill me, I decided.

"I was going to see her," I said. "At her house . . . where she *lives*, man."

Pierre chuckled, then walked over to Léo and Amelia. When he came back he had something long and slender in his hand. It looked like a fencing foil without any hilt.

"This is where it gets bad," he said. "But first I have a question or two for you. A little survey I like to take, out of personal curiosity." He pulled his chair closer and sat down, laying the foil across his knees. "Do you think that there is any appropriate, or *justified,* time to kill?"

I couldn't for the moment think around the thing on his lap. I was ready to kill *him,* but justification had nothing to do with it.

"Come on, Delanne," he said. "We're both thinking men. I'm curious about what an American like yourself thinks. So what do you think? When is it okay to kill somebody?"

I closed my eyes, fighting to shut out the fear.

"You want me to say 'in war,'" I muttered. "Or else 'in self-defense.'"

A big grin broke out on his face. "Ah . . . now we're getting somewhere."

He stood up and swung his switch, cutting a fast X in the air like an ill-trained Zorro. When he stepped toward me, the nerves along my spine crouched and my fingers and toes went cold.

"What about torture, Delanne?" he said. "When's that okay? In war? Your country, some suspect, seems to think so. I've got a few friends outside France, you see—military friends. Friends who've fought American troops—friends who know what real fear is, Delanne. Because they know what they're up against if they get caught by American troops. Some suspect, you see, that your people don't always play by the rules in war. But what about in self-defense?"

"All right, let's stop with the bullshit," I said. "Let's talk about you and LeMercier killing Duvin. Hear that, Léo? Solène's dad is dead because of this guy."

"I said leave him out of this, motherfucker. You don't know shit about Duvin."

"Then what do you do for LeMercier with these kids? You know I talked to Duvin, and so you've guessed that he told me a thing or two. The nationals are onto you, don't you see? They know LeMercier is a crook. And they know who you are. They're just waiting to pounce."

At that he broke eye contact, laughing in a way that wasn't very convincing. I'd touched a nerve.

"Let's get something straight," said Pierre. "My business is none of yours. And I'm not the fool that LeMercier tends to be."

I said nothing. It was clear that he was making the announcement for Amelia and Léo.

"And get this straight, Delanne: neither Duvin nor the Arab has told you the truth. The Arab would never allow himself to look bad. He wouldn't want to tell you that he's been cooperating with us to keep LeMercier from turning him in. Which it is LeMercier's right to do—he is a cop, after all. And he caught the Arab, after all. It's the most admirable thing LeMercier has done, in fact, discovering the Arab and then figuring out how to milk him and his bitch partner. Until this ridiculous business with Georges Brule. But let's not confuse one thing with another: you're not going anywhere, Delanne, until you tell me where she is. Why is that so hard to understand?"

Before I could respond, Pierre whipped the switch across my knees. It stung so bad that I growled aloud and bit my tongue. When I opened my eyes, his sweaty face was an inch from mine.

"It's your lucky day," he said. "My usual tools for this sort of thing were misplaced."

"That's funny," I managed, trying to be a good sport. "Because I *feel* lucky, you know?"

Pierre laughed. "Maybe you're missing it: when it comes to torture, you're in the worst fucking place in the world. Aside from the Chinese, we made it up—even the shit your people know comes from us, though I've been told that you guys tend to overlook certain basic principles. Like simplicity. And imagination. Take this car antenna: I pulled it off of the Saab you were planning to collect. It cost me nothing, it isn't exhausting to use, and it can be extremely effective. On the bottoms of the feet, for example. Or the face. Or the genitals. So which would you like first?"

"I don't get it," I said, hoping to stave off the inevitable. "Why is some girl so important?"

Something flashed behind his eyes. He cocked the antenna back, and assuming it was coming for my face I snapped my head to one side, bracing myself. The blow never came.

When I faced him again, he was chuckling.

"Let's call it a case of self-defense," he said. "She knows more than she's supposed to. You do too, but your testimony isn't worth a damn anymore—we took care of that."

I managed a smile. Finally I'd gotten a handle on the fear. "Sure. But I still don't know where she is. I was on my way to her dad's house to look for her."

"Come on, she's the only person who could have given you those Saab keys, my friend. So if you don't tell me where she is, I'll send you to prison disfigured. Clear enough?"

"Thierry gave me the keys," I muttered. "Before he died. And I haven't seen her since I was at Corbières. I've had other things on my mind, man. Like running from the cops."

Pierre walked around behind me. When I felt his hands on my shoulders, I jolted in my seat, my arms fighting with the ropes around my wrists. Pierre yanked my suit jacket back, reached around and tore open the front of my shirt, and then pulled back the collar. The cold air was a shock to my bare shoulders. I grew frantic.

"Léo," I called out. "See what kind of thrashing you'll get if you tell anyone that this guy killed Solène's dad?"

Right away the antenna hit: a kaleidoscope of burning colors. Hot tears burst from my eyes. I screamed, but no noise left my throat.

Pierre struck my shoulders several more times. When my ears stopped ringing, I thought I heard Léo's voice, then Amelia's voice hushing him.

I opened my eyes. The sting went deep and wide, spread across my entire back. It seemed to pulse, to burrow into my bones. Thin trickles of warm blood began running from the tops of my shoulders onto my chest. I fought to catch my breath.

Pierre leaned over me from behind. "Where is she?" he whispered.

I couldn't think, had already forgotten what I'd told him a minute ago. "I don't know," I mumbled. "Honestly . . . I don't fucking know." I wasn't even sure which language I was using.

He struck me twice more across the shoulders. I started cursing him and Amelia and Léo and all of their relatives and neighbors. He struck me several times more, but the pain just wouldn't dull— each lash dug one layer deeper, pain within pain within pain. Soon I was coughing, gasping. My vision swirled. Spit and blood dribbled from my face onto Julien's suit pants.

I raised my head. Pierre's fuzzy shape loomed before me. He was smoking, blowing it in my face. My senses revived in excruciating increments, until I felt ravenous, like a beaten animal, starved for blood—I wanted to be let loose so I could draw someone else's.

Pierre pulled his chair closer to mine, sat and leaned forward on his knees. Instantly my rage was replaced by more fear. All I could think about was that car antenna. All I wanted to know was where it was, where it would come from next, when I might expect it, and which way I might shift to minimize its scorch.

"I don't believe you, Delanne," Pierre said after a minute. "And I'm good at reading faces. Call it my one talent in the world, aside from getting people to tell me things. You see, I'm a teacher too. I don't work at a lycée, but I'm in charge of young ones. Many young ones—students, kids who want to have a future. I suppose I was born with the instinct to teach in my blood. It's more than you can say for yourself, isn't it, Delanne? You see, Dreyfus showed me your American dossier." Pierre stood and walked slowly around me. "You haven't been a teacher very long, have you?"

He crouched and unlaced my shoes, sliding them off slowly. My entire body trembled. Fear, anticipation, dread—they were more terrible than the pain itself. I would give soon, I knew, I'd tell him anything he wanted to hear, as long as he'd take that antenna away.

"In fact," Pierre said, "you haven't *ever* been a teacher, have you?"

He pulled off my socks, came around behind me again, and with surprising care tilted my chair back, until I was lying back on the cold concrete, facing the ceiling. I thought of my exposed soles. How sensitive they were to cold, heat, everything else. If my bladder had been full, I would have emptied it then and there.

"You were in a little bit of trouble when you left Arizona, too, weren't you?" said Pierre. "A young con, you, after all you claimed on your application with the French Ministry of Education. And your father a cop. A *cop*, Delanne. And not just any cop. A federal agent. What a thing to hide."

He was standing over me now, his face directly above mine. I watched him light another cigarette, then reach out slowly with it, as if he planned to drop it on my forehead.

"We're talking about a young fugitive," said Pierre. "A young fraud, coming here to France and doing what? Getting involved with people who sell secrets to terrorists. Oh, that'll sound just right for the news, won't it? A young man flees his troubles in America to come to France and be a phony. And then to take part in this horrid, awful murder. Oh, don't you worry, Delanne, everyone will hear about it. Still, I think first I'll teach you a lesson. About lying. Because I know that you know where she is."

"Please, man," I managed. "I'm telling you . . . I really don't know. Her house, a friend's house, I just don't fucking know . . . so just stop with the antenna, man . . . anything else."

He squatted beside me. "But I want you to *feel* it, Delanne—I want you to shit your fucking pants feeling it. Have you shit your pants yet?" He took in a deep, dramatic breath through his nose. "Doesn't smell like shit to me."

When he stood with the antenna, my face suffered a spasm and my heart seized. He tapped the end of the antenna on the soles of my bare feet.

"Your people have a hard time seeing certain obvious things," Pierre said. "See, if I were to stand here and tell you that I had no other choice but to do this"—he paused and gave my feet a light whack—"that would be irresponsible of me. In the purest sense. See, the crime is in claiming *not to have a choice* to do otherwise, Delanne. It's not a crime against you, or me—it's a crime against humanity, against our free will. It *diminishes* us to ignore our choice. In this sense, I don't have to strike you just now—" Another whack, this one slightly harder. "I *choose* to. In the face of several other options. Why is that so hard for some people to admit?"

"I admit it, man," I said. "I admit it, I admit it."

I couldn't think in a straight line, couldn't figure out why he was talking philosophy at a time like this. Maybe he'd seen too many movies where the bad guy gets off on sounding like Socrates before doing something savage. Maybe he was preaching to himself, or just relishing the sound of his own words. Maybe it was all just a show for Léo and Amelia.

All I knew for sure was that the anticipation of pain was killing me—all I cared about anymore was that damn car antenna.

"A thousand options," Pierre was saying. "Options *upon* options. Don't fool yourself any longer, Delanne. Your options here are obvious. All you have to do is *choose* to tell me where she is."

The next blow was the real thing. It felt like a red-hot bullwhip licking the bottoms of my feet. It made my eyeballs swell inside my head. I wailed until I was out of breath, and then I had trouble breathing: another, another, and another blow from the switch.

I might have said something about my apartment. I might have said something about Solène's dad's Saab, I wasn't sure. But I said nothing that I could remember about the *médiathèque*, which was where I was supposed to meet her—even as I wallowed in the stinging pain, somehow I kept myself from uttering that word.

I sobbed, suffered flickers of memories from deep in my past, painful moments I'd buried for one reason or another.

My mind wound its way to the second interview I'd done for Nabec, with the Texan. All the hours he must have sat in that room with his memories. It wasn't pity I felt for him now—my senses were too jumbled, too sick for that. All I could feel now was that same enormous stubbornness I'd seen in the Texan's eyes.

Only when the water hit my face did I realize that I'd passed out. My feet felt as if I'd been standing on hot coals. My chair was being lifted, a pair of hands fumbled around my waist, then undid my belt. Before I could even register what was happening, my pants and underwear had been yanked from under me, over my knees and down to my bound ankles. My vision cleared at once, and when I felt the cold air on my bare genitals, my instincts flailed, and every muscle in my body involuntarily surged. My ears filled with noise.

Pierre stood before me with his instrument, staring down at my lap.

He chuckled. "I suppose, yes—you could call that a cock."

I started mumbling incoherently. "Woke up . . . hardly slept . . . cops and ran."

"Then where are you supposed to meet her, Delanne? I know you can tell me that—I *know* you can. The pain only gets worse, my friend, and I'm not going to let you go numb—that's not going to happen. I'm not going to let you pass out, either. It's all a matter of how many testicles you want to walk out of here with."

I tried to squeeze my legs together and looked down: I was still exposed—they'd tied my legs so I couldn't close them—so he could strike me with the tip of the antenna with a well-placed swing. There was nothing to do but take it head-on.

"Know what?" I said. "Fuck you."

He shook his head, cocked back the antenna, and took careful aim before taking the swing. Fire exploded between my legs and sent a piercing burn straight to my temples. I might have passed out.

When I could see clearly again, there were shouts.

"Then get the hell out of here," I heard Pierre yell. "Amelia, gather Léo and the others."

My vision steadied, but my ears were still ringing. I could see my bare lap, a dark laceration on the inside of my left thigh, rising like a scar and pushing out a thin line of blood: he'd missed.

I looked up. I thought I could see Pierre's fuzzy shape dart off. Then the light cut out. A door screeched open and shut, and several voices called out at once, followed by hurried footsteps. A second later someone called out "Christophe!" from nearby, and I heard a voice say something in French about a car pulling up and stopping outside.

Perhaps a minute passed. The pain burned deep into my bones. Again I heard footsteps, then Pierre's hushed, tense voice.

"Untie him, then . . . take him to the office!"

More footsteps approaching. Whispers. Hands fiddling with the ropes around my arms and ankles. I wailed when they pulled my shirt over my shoulders, and suddenly I was wide awake.

Bodies were moving frantically around me in the darkness, hands fiddling with my wrists—the kids were following their orders. Someone pulled my pants up over my knees and thighs, and I howled again. When they shoved my tortured feet back into my shoes, I simply wept. But at least now my hands were free. I reached for my belt and tried to buckle it. They pulled me to my feet before I could finish the job, then they hustled me headlong into the darkness, each step an explosion of pain through my shins, up my thighs to my sore groin. I found that if I walked on my heels, which Pierre seemed to have neglected with the switch, the pain was just bearable—otherwise I might have collapsed.

After a dozen or so agonizing paces, we stopped. One of the kids pushed me against a wall and clutched my throat.

"Now you keep your mouth shut," said a young man's voice. Another screech of metal on metal, then a flashlight beam shone suddenly in front of us, and again I was rushed forward, this time along a narrow passageway, at double speed. The pain from my feet was excruciating but had already begun to abate some.

At the end of the passageway we stopped. I was held against another wall, and someone directed the flashlight at my face. Two boys had a firm hold on me from behind, one on each arm. My lacerated shoulders felt like a sunburn submerged in hot water. Gradually I got a handle on it and focused.

Two other kids stood in front of me, one with the flashlight.

"You guys can quit any time—" I started to say. Then the flashlight cut out again.

After that, everything happened fast. The kid on my left let go of me, a door beside us groaned open, and a powerful white light shone through. Someone said something about the cops. Then came the gunshot: one solitary bang, sharp and loud, followed by a high-pitched ricochet.

Feet shuffled frantically around me, the kid on my right let go of my arm, and without thinking twice I crouched and scampered back up the dark passageway away from the group, hands out in front of me like a blind man.

I was moving fast, but could see next to nothing. Yet it was as if the pain had heightened my other senses: I heard footsteps and whispers, smelled skin, breath, sweat, even from the distance I'd put between us.

Hands still out in front me, I broke into a jog until I bashed into the end of the passageway and rolled off a metal wall into an opening of some sort. I looked back the way I'd come just as a flashlight beam hit the wall I'd rolled off.

The beam grew larger—they were coming.

I moved to the left, groping along another corrugated metal wall to a corner. Then I turned with the corner and hurried along another wall, realizing I'd entered another big room, one much larger than the one I'd been tortured in. As far as I could figure, we were in some abandoned warehouse complex. I glanced back and saw the flashlight beam turn into the room I was in. Light filled the entryway, and at once I could see the ceiling fifty or sixty feet up.

I hit the deck and watched their shapes move to the right with the flashlight, in the opposite direction I'd gone. There were three of the kids, thirty or so yards off and moving away from me across the middle of the room. My heart was beating so loud that I thought it might give my position away. The adrenaline was starting to overwhelm the pain. My eyes were beginning to adjust to the darkness. I was lying in a puddle of filth.

The kids were now directly across from me, a safe distance away. But not for long.

I jumped to my feet, wincing but biting my tongue, and continued along the wall I'd been following until I reached the far corner, where the corrugated metal joined concrete. Frantically I felt along the concrete wall. Their flashlight beam started to move toward me. I found a grubby indentation in the concrete near the corner, another above it, and another going up and up—steps to a built-in ladder. A corroded handrail ran upward alongside it.

I scrambled up the ladder so fast that when there were no more steps, I almost fell.

The kids' flashlight now shone beneath me—they were angling in my direction across the giant room. Another flashlight appeared in the entryway.

"*Tu fais quoi alors?*" someone yelled from across the room. It was Léo's voice. "*Où est Delanne?*"

"*J'sais pas. Il est entré lá, je comprends pas.*"

I groped around with one hand, holding on to the handrail with the other, my body pressed hard against the oily concrete wall. But reaching farther into the corner I found no adjoining wall—it was some kind of loft space, an opening onto a platform.

I swung one leg into the opening, shuddering to think what lay waiting in that loft, then held my breath and jumped sideways, landing hard on a pile of loose boards.

"Il est là!" someone shouted. *"Là-bas, tu vois?"*

Now I was on my haunches, breathing hard, searching my pockets for a match. I found nothing—Pierre had robbed me blind.

I got to my feet again, fighting with the pain, groping in the darkness away from the opening I'd just jumped into. My nose filled with the foul smell of rotten wood. There were wet boards scattered beneath me. I could hear the distinct scratching sound of rats all around.

The loft space kept going back—it was some sort of second-story passageway. My hands were shaking all the way up to my shoulders. Then I felt a gust of fresh air blow past, and farther back I thought I could see the faintest slip of light.

I stopped when there was no more floor—the passageway simply dropped into darkness.

"Jeffrey!" called one of the boys from behind me. *"Nous avons déjà gagner, Jeffrey! Arrête!"*

I spun around and lowered myself into the darkness. Almost immediately my sweaty hands lost their grip on the overhang, and I slipped, falling a few feet onto another wooden floor.

Now off to my left I could see a distinct light. As I moved toward it, the floor shifted beneath me—I was on some kind of loading dock, I figured, a lift for lumber and such. When the boys' flashlight beams shone out from the loft space above, my heart sank to my knees. They had me trapped.

As the first of the boys came into view in the opening above the lift, I leaned, defeated, against the wall at the end.

Only it wasn't a wall.

The door swung outward, and I fell out headfirst into the last traces of daylight, flailing for the edge of the lift as my weight continued downward. I caught the edge and held on with one arm and one leg, dangling some twenty feet in the air and bracing my-self for the impact.

"Do not jump," someone said from above me. It was Léo. He was still in the tram official's suit. And he was holding a hand out to me.

"Il faut pas mourir, Jeffrey. C'est pas nécessaire."

As I hung there, time seemed to hover, and all I could think about was how right he was: it was not necessary to die. Or was it?

I let Léo help me back onto the lift. Then I glanced over his shoulder at one of his cohorts lowering himself onto the shaky el-evator platform with us.

"Wait," Léo shouted to him in French. "I've got him. Just wait up there."

I could just see Léo's expression in the failing evening light. He didn't look as if he planned to lay a hand on me. That didn't keep me from taking him by the throat.

"You little punk."

"Let go, Jeff," he managed. "It's complex. Please . . ."

I let go. But only because I could tell what was happening—he was letting *me* go.

"Tell her I'm sorry," he said then. "Tell her to go far away. And make sure she's okay."

We had a mutual concern, I realized. But I was too disgusted with him to say anything else. I looked behind me, out over the edge onto the street below.

"There must be a ladder or something," he whispered.

And there was—along the outside wall of the warehouse. A second later I was climbing down it.

Then I was on the ground, sprinting up the street on my sore feet. I didn't look back to see if any of the others were climbing down after me. And I didn't have any idea where I was headed—I just needed to find someplace to bleed in peace.

I ran blindly through the neighborhood and unexpectedly wound up on the wide Boulevard du Gare. There weren't so many cars out here, so far from the train station and *centre ville*. Tired and throbbing all over, I slowed to a walk. No one was following me, so the adrenaline started drying up fast. My thoughts grew sharp: it was probably already after four—too late to gather Solène. And there was no way to get Thierry's Saab without the keys. I cursed; my only option was to pack onto a tram back to Place Médiathèque and pretend my clothes weren't stained with blood and muck.

I was about to cross an intersection when a blue hatchback appeared in the cross street, barreling for the yellow light and horn honking.

If I'd taken another step forward, I would have been going to prison in a wheelchair.

I shouted and flipped off the driver as the car passed. Then something nearly impossible happened. As its taillights turned right toward *centre ville* and began to speed away, I realized that I'd ridden in that same car before—same dinged-up rear end, same scuffed bumper stickers.

The car stopped suddenly. Its reverse lights came on, slowly it backed up, and then I recognized the shapes of the heads in the front seat: Françoise and Marine, in that precious heap of an automobile.

TOGETHER, OR NOT AT ALL

I threw open the back door and climbed in behind Françoise without thinking twice.

Even though she didn't need to, Marine floored it and we hauled ass toward *centre ville*. With the adrenaline gone, my neck and shoulders began to throb. The soles of my feet were on fire. My face was pulsing and my right thigh felt sliced open.

Huddled down in the footwell, I couldn't see Marine's face, but I could feel her presence at the wheel; she cut the turns sharp and sped between stoplights like a getaway driver, even though there was nothing more to get away from—at least I hoped not.

I closed my eyes and imagined jumping out of the car as soon as we got closer to the media library. All I had left were impulses, actions and reactions: I'd suffered so much hell for Solène that I felt ready to murder anything that stood between us. She was the only other person in the world.

But even in my shocked condition I couldn't help being suspicious. I poked my head between the front seats.

"What the hell are you guys doing out in this part of town?"

Françoise looked at me with wide eyes. "Jesus—what happened to you?"

"No dodging—how did you end up here? I was in a fucking building just up that street getting tortured, for Christ's sake."

Marine floored the gas through a yellow light near the Bouffay district.

"You can't mean 'torture,'" Françoise said, as if there were no plausible use for the word in her language.

"I absolutely mean torture. And I want to know how you two ended up out here."

Marine slammed on the brakes, screeching to a halt at the next red light. To our right loomed the château, where I'd been followed by Pierre's little minions—where they'd almost caught Solène.

"It's simple, Jeffrey," said Françoise. "Marine called me at work and told me the cops had shown up looking for you this morning, and then—you know Lucien, Paul's boy, don't you? He's in my English class. Not a very good student—has real trouble turning in homework on time—"

"The point, Françoise."

"The point is that I overheard a conversation. Two of my students were talking in the hallway after class about the poison the police found in your locker. I heard them say they were on their way to the warehouse district. I heard your name and then heard Lucien tell them that he had seen you go into the Jardin des Plantes. Of course he told them not to tell anyone, but this is what I find curious about kids: they lack discretion, even when they think they're being quiet and secretive. So I followed a clue, that was all. Marine picked me up after school and, well . . . we weren't going to sit around at Marine's and hope you might knock on the front door."

I found a few napkins on the backseat and dabbed some of the blood off my face.

The pain had now spread all over my body and seemed to grate on my skin like a hot, dull blade. I wasn't even sure how I'd borne so much of it.

Françoise set fire to a menthol and fixed her eyes on me.

"I had heard of that bloody warehouse before, Jeffrey. It's got a bit of a reputation. There was one of those electronica parties out there last summer. Kids from Corbières were arrested."

It occurred to me then that it might have been Marine's car driving around and stopping at the warehouse that had curtailed Pierre's session with me. Not that a random car would've been enough to spook Pierre, but it was just possible that one of the kids had seen it and freaked out. It was the risk he ran by using high school kids for henchmen—they had to have been jumpy. But I also realized I couldn't recall when Léo had left the interrogation room. Maybe after he'd seen enough, he'd ducked out and spooked the others himself, raised some kind of false alarm.

"Who on earth did this to you?" asked Françoise.

"One of Dreyfus's buddies thought a car antenna would persuade me to talk."

"Holy shit, Jeff," said Marine.

"It's the same people who killed Brule and blamed me. And now he's after Solène Duvin—you know her, don't you, Françoise?"

"Yes, of course, poor girl. I had her in my class two or three years ago—an excellent student. But whatever would Roland—Dreyfus, that is—whatever would he want with a young girl?"

"Not Dreyfus—this psychopath named Pierre something or other, Dreyfus's partner. Some of these kids are involved in this Brule shit, I think. Maybe Solène knows something they don't want her to go to the police with, or else maybe they think she knows something her father knew."

We turned right onto Rue Cinquantes Otages and then took an immediate left onto Rue Chapeau Rouge, angling toward Place

Royale. Now that the streetlights were more plentiful, Françoise kept glancing back at me and wincing.

"You look terrible, just terrible."

But I was already plotting my next move. "I've got to get to the *médiathèque*—I've got to help Solène get out of town."

Marine said, "Is this the girl who called my house last night?"

I hesitated, realizing what it looked like, since we weren't sure how the cops had known to check Marine's place for me earlier that morning. But I knew Solène couldn't have been the one to turn me in to the cops—I would have bet my life on it. And anyway it wasn't any secret that Marine and I were friends. I realized then that their arrival didn't necessarily mean anyone had betrayed me— the cops might have even questioned people in the Rougerie after having questioned Bruno. They'd gone to Paul's. They'd probably even checked Patrick's apartment for me as well.

"Trust me," I said. "Solène may be in deeper shit than I'm in."

Françoise laughed. "I doubt that." She and Marine exchanged a conspiratorial glance.

"Okay, what aren't you two ladies telling me?"

"Julien called from Tours," said Marine. "We've made a plan to get you out of Ste-Térèse."

At Place Royale, Marine didn't make the turn toward Place Médiathèque—she floored it around the roundabout and sped straight for Place Graslin. Though I didn't say it, I felt uneasy about any escape Julien had helped to engineer; he'd helped me, sure, but he'd lied to me, too.

"I've got a plan of my own," I said, resisting the urge to tell them what I was really thinking.

"Someone ratted you out, my dear," said Françoise. "You can't afford that again. How do you know it wasn't this girl?"

"I don't have time to explain," I said. "But I'll bail out right now if you don't take me to the *médiathèque*. This girl's in trouble— serious trouble."

Neither of them seemed to be listening. We were still moving. I threw open my door.

"Are you bloody crazy!" Françoise shouted.

We were coming out of the roundabout, and I hesitated. Banging myself up any worse wouldn't better my chances of getting out of the city—I was lucky to be mobile. I shut the door.

"Look, her father was just murdered, probably by the same guy who tortured me. I haven't figured that out for sure. But he wanted to know where she was, and only she can tell me why."

They said nothing until we swung around Place Théâtre and came to an abrupt stop just around the corner from the Rougerie. I was still thinking about Pierre and what exactly he was using Léo and the others to do. I wondered what it had to do with Nabec, the old madame, and their intelligence brokerage. And I wondered if I had any choice but to keep following these women.

Marine turned off the car. "We're trying to help you, Jeff. Bruno says he'll hide you above the bar until after last call. This is what Julien thinks is best."

"You can't toss everything away for some fancy, my dear," added Françoise. "That would be a fine waste of everyone's energy."

I checked Françoise's eyes, then Marine's, before climbing out and limping down the street.

"Half an hour!" I called back. "It's not tossing anything away— it's collecting a friend!"

I hadn't made it far when Marine's hatchback rolled up beside me.

"Get in the car, Jeffrey," said Françoise. "No reason to make such a fuss."

IT FELL TO Françoise to head into the *médiathèque* for Solène— Marine didn't know what Solène looked like, and I looked like the living dead.

"She's cut her hair off," I told Françoise. "She'll be wearing an orange hat, hanging around up front." Marine parked among a set of cars in the middle of the lot and kept the engine running.

"This isn't smart, Jeff. Cops are looking for you all over the city. We've got a plan."

"So do I," I said. Though mine was hardly baked. Too much didn't make sense.

It was clear, at least, from what Thierry had suspected and what Pierre had implied, that Dreyfus had approached me in the beginning to associate me with Nabec, in order to frame me for Brule's murder. All the evidence pointed toward that: the photos Thierry had shown me, the anonymous tip-off to the gendarmes that last night at the cottage. They were smearing my record in order to make me a worthy suspect. It was clear, too, that while Dreyfus and Nabec and the old madame were in cahoots, not all parties were in favor of the partnership; the old madame had made plain enough that Dreyfus was blackmailing Nabec and her in exchange for his silence and his money-laundering services.

But what was Pierre's role in the partnership, and why would he have kept me from Dreyfus, if Dreyfus wanted me in police custody? Why was finding Solène more important to Pierre than Dreyfus's carefully crafted frame job? And if Dreyfus was the old madame's protection, why had she suggested that I might do something to expose Dreyfus? Surely she knew that he would only turn around and expose them.

There were plenty of questions beyond that. Why had the old madame instructed me to stay away from Corbières, which would have kept me from walking into the clever trap Dreyfus had laid for me? Why had Brule been killed in the first place? And what did Nabec care about a *proviseur* with political influence? It seemed unthinkable that Dreyfus, given his advantageous relationship with Nabec and the old madame, would take part in such a murder solely for their interests. So who was calling the shots? And what had Nabec really wanted of me, if his closest partner, the old madame, had felt the need to fetch and interview me for herself?

I had a hunch that Solène might be able to help me fill in a few blanks.

"Julien says they'll know my license plates," Marine was saying. "If they knew to come to my place. So you shouldn't even be in this car right now—"

"You don't know everything I know about this, Marine," I said. "That dead detective we saw on the news last night—he told me things that I didn't tell you, or Julien."

"And that detective's dead," she snapped. "Julien told me he has more news for you."

I sat up, but kept myself from voicing my doubts—it wouldn't do me any good to tell her how Julien had lied.

"Give me Julien's phone number," I said. "I'll call him from Timbuktu. He can fill me in on the aftermath some other time . . ." I stopped myself. More and more it looked as if I had to play along with them, including Julien, in order to have a chance. There was no reason to jeopardize that now.

After a minute she said, "Julien made it to Tours and checked into a hotel under your name. He went around using your name all over, then called the Tours police on you and described himself. He almost got arrested, Jeff. He's risking his neck for you. And it's the best thing we've got going for you right now. I don't think you're in a position to turn down his help."

"Okay, okay," I said. "What's taking her so long?"

"It's a big library."

"I know that, but what the hell's taking her so long?"

"We shouldn't be here, Jeff, we just shouldn't. It's almost five. Bruno's already opened the bar. People will be in there, people will see you coming in."

It was dark now. The rain was picking up. I imagined holing

up in a cramped attic with Solène and a bottle of Bruno's rotgut cognac. After the day I'd had, it sounded just right.

Marine was drumming the steering wheel with her thumbs. She stopped suddenly and threw the car into gear.

"Here she comes," she said. "She's alone."

I sat up and watched Françoise hurry over and get in.

"That girl is scared out of her wits," said Françoise. "I found her, but she doesn't believe you're out here."

We pulled up in front of the *médiathèque*, and before either of them could raise a stink about it, I got out and ran up the steps. When I saw Solène standing a few feet away from the big front windows, my will to help her turned to iron. She approached the glass carefully and stopped. I waved to her, motioning to the door, but she only pushed back the brim of her hat and squinted out at me. She could see me, I knew. But something was making her hesitate, and I had a hunch it was my chain-saw massacre appearance— last time she'd seen me, I'd looked much more dapper.

I followed her gaze over my shoulder to a pack of teens gathered around a concrete bench, a few of whom were checking me out. I wanted to tell them to mind their own business. But I'd already underestimated too many teenagers today.

I looked back through the glass at Solène and mouthed the words *It's okay, Solène.*

Finally she came out. I'd never seen such desperation on a girl's face, and here she was trusting me. She took my hand and we ran down the steps to Marine's car. All the way to the Rougerie, I held her while my feet and shoulders and face pulsed with pain.

"You're shaking," she said. "You okay?"

"I don't think so."

BRUNO'S WAS EMPTY. He came around the bar and looked sideways at Solène.

"My bodyguard," I said.

"We've met," Bruno said to me. "And you oughta be glad you know Julien, my man. I'm risking my tail doing this, which is something I don't do . . . Christ, what the hell happened to you? Looks like you got into a fight with a coal mine."

"You should see the coal mine," I said. Bruno smiled at me, then locked the front door and led us into the back room. He fetched some bandages and antibiotic ointment from his first-aid kit behind the bar, along with a big bottle of water and a quart of cognac—I hadn't even needed to ask.

I promised Bruno that if any American friend of mine ever visited Ste-Térèse I would send him directly to the Rougerie.

"More Americans? No, thanks."

After I'd washed my wounds in the bathroom, Bruno fumbled with his keys and opened a painted door that I'd always taken for a storage closet. Then he led the four of us up a dark, decrepit stairwell that smelled like mothballs and dead flowers. We rounded a dusty landing and went up another dozen shaky steps to a locked door. Behind it was the room where Solène and I were supposed to wait out the next eight hours.

Bruno got a lantern going and showed me how it worked.

"You start a fire in here, I won't turn you in—I'll hang you myself."

The little room was dusty and deserted except for a shabby old mattress, a pile of threadbare blankets, and a few cardboard boxes stuffed with paperbacks. There was no toilet, no sink, only an old showerhead hanging over a drain in the tiled floor of the corner. The ladies shuffled in behind us, but stopped in the doorway, peering around as you would at the mouth of a bat cave.

"Believe it or not," Bruno said, "twenty years ago this was home to me and my wife. We had electricity and water, a little heat, but that was it. Elsa was hard as nails to live up here with me, God rest her. Always had her face in the books, her. I couldn't ever bring myself to get rid of them."

Along the ceiling a few layers of wallpaper had peeled away. There were cobwebs in every nook of the room, a shuttered window covered with plastic and duct tape. Something skittered across the floor and disappeared under the mattress. Bruno ignored it.

"Back to business," he said. He pointed to a tiny chamber pot in the corner. "If you use it, bring it down with you when it's time. And for God's sake, stay quiet. I mean only whispers. I'll keep the music loud. But if you hear the volume drop suddenly and it's not one a.m. yet, it's the *flics*. All you can do after that is pray, my man."

I thanked him again. Bruno went downstairs and left a long, uncomfortable silence between the ladies and me.

Françoise was the one to break it. "This must be good-bye, Jeffrey. Once and for all."

I hugged her. "Thank you, Françoise." It seemed to say nothing and everything at once.

Marine gave me the cheek kisses.

"Don't forget us." She was looking over my shoulder at Solène, as if that depended on her.

I smiled. "That's one thing I can promise you."

There were tears in Marine's eyes. I was too sore everywhere else for that to hurt.

"We'll come back once I've had time to work on my cap-throwing skills," I said.

"Good-bye," Marine said in English. "You will find somewhere."

"And thank Julien for me, will you? For everything."

Marine smiled. "Who do you think will be coming here tonight to smuggle you out?"

Something turned over in my stomach. I told myself to hold it steady. "So long, Marine."

She shut Solène and me inside, and I bolted the door, feeling anything but safe. We sat on the floor on either side of the lantern, took a long pull apiece off the bottle of cognac, and for a while just listened to the mice scuttling about. Then, while Solène treated and bandaged my face and my lacerated shoulders, I took off my shoes and tended to my poor feet. The pain came on strong, waves of it, and not just from my scalding soles: shoulders, neck, groin— everything seemed to howl and whimper at once. Somehow it was invigorating now. It made me feel more alive than ever, more re-moved than ever from the person I'd been. Transfigured. Even though I knew that I wasn't in the clear yet. And that I'd placed myself in the hands of people I wasn't entirely sure I could trust. All I could be sure of was that even while I'd attached some part of myself to Solène, some other mad, unforgiving part of me had been liberated. I was capable of anything.

"NONE OF THEM planned for this, Jeffrey," Solène said later, once I'd told her about Léo's gang and its madman leader. "Not Léo, not any of them. What did they say they wanted?"

"You." I hesitated when she put her face in her hands. Then I handed her the bottle. "He seemed to think you had something, or knew something. The fucker mule-whipped me with a car an-tenna, Solène. Now's the time for you to tell me why this guy's hunting you."

"Léo introduced me to those people, Jeffrey, but he's not a bad kid. He is just passionate, a bit bullheaded. And a little naïve sometimes."

I told Solène that Léo had stood nearby and watched, but that in the end he'd helped me escape. Neither of us said anything for a while. The music downstairs grew louder, the sound of voices and laughter rising steadily with it.

We exchanged a long, hard gaze. She handed me back the bottle.

"I was with them," she said finally, switching to French. "I was part of the group. Léo got me into it last year, and I only went every so often. But that man's name is not Pierre. It's Christophe. He's the reason I stopped going to the meetings."

She explained how Christophe had organized a young activist group back when people had started talking about the removal of *surveillants* from regional lycées a year ago. I tried hard to keep my cool.

"It was just fund-raising at first," said Solène. "For campaigns and community events. We made flyers, gathered pledges for campaign donations, little things. Then in the autumn M. Dreyfus began asking certain students at Corbières if they would like to be more involved in the community, with part-time nonprofit work and such. It was when the unemployment rate here became very high, you see. It's very important in France to do community service, for the résumé."

"I don't think you can call what these kids did to me out there community service."

"It changed, Jeffrey. Last summer, when I first met Christophe, we were working with university students, handing out propaganda, getting petitions and pledges signed. And at first Christophe was a fun guy. He was likable, very charismatic and passionate, and we trusted him. I guess his grandfather was a famous gendarme general, and he worked as an officer with the National Police. Sometimes, yes, he gave us more serious tasks, like counting up the donations for the month. Just a few of us at a time. Not often. And we felt special, you know?"

"Was it a lot of cash?"

"I only got to do that once—Christophe never liked me very much. The time I did it, I remember thinking, *Holy shit, this is so much.* Thousands and thousands in donations. It felt nice to be trusted like that, with something big and successful like that. And it was for a good cause."

I tried to concentrate around the swelling pain from my shoulders and feet, to process the implications of all that cash Pierre had had them count up. It seemed unlikely that a group of high-schoolers, no matter its size, could raise so much cash from fund-raising.

"But you *had* to know that this Christophe guy was trouble," I said. "Didn't anyone suspect that he was up to something else?"

Solène sighed. "Not at first. You met my dad—he would have been immediately skeptical of anything I did to be politically active. He would have made me think I was involved in some big conspiracy, he would have made me quit. Sure, maybe I had some doubts about Christophe. But he told us all these things. How we were part of a nationwide project, you see, how it's hard to see the big picture when you're a critical part of it. It sounds stupid now. But at that time it was—okay, I knew there were other things that were not . . . quite right. I don't know how to explain. It was a strange thrill. Not to do bad, but to do curious, private things for someone, a fascinating individual, you know?"

I would've been a hypocrite to blame her for that.

She told me that back in the fall Christophe had started having those who were old enough to drive deliver packages to different places across the city, sometimes even out of town, as far as Lourange or St-Nazaire. Sometimes they'd pick up boxes of flyers from print stores and deliver them to so-and-so's place—always a friend of one local assemblyman or another. Other times they'd sit in a room at the university and make phone calls for donation pledges. As for the fund-raising events themselves, they were usually pathetic get-togethers, boring as hell. Others were bigger affairs where Solène and her friends were introduced to supposed bigwigs.

Christophe's interactions with those kids who remained grew gradually more intense. He had them skip classes, made huge promises, told them continually about the people he knew all over the country, higher-ups in universities, government offices, *grandes écoles.*

"Léo's been accepted at La Sorbonne," said Solène. "He hasn't even taken the *bac* yet."

I had a good laugh over that one. "He'd last one semester."

Solène shrugged. "Christophe pays Léo a salary. Some others get paid too. All of them will go to excellent universities, and some have internships scheduled years in the future. They have contracts. A future. I had trouble believing it in the beginning. Until he got me a letter of recommendation from an assemblyman he knows, a left-wing politician, of course."

I studied her face—she wasn't bullshitting—then I lifted the glass from the lantern flame and lit two of Solène's cigarettes, handing one to her. A troubling connection had started to crystallize in my mind.

"Did he ever have anyone deliver money?" I asked. "You know, from the fund-raising events, after he'd had them count up the cash?"

Solène shrugged. "Maybe. I never drove. I rarely went to these things after December, Jeffrey. When I did, I went to be with my friends—you met Melanie. She was heavily into it."

"Tell me about when he had you count money—did he have you document the amounts?"

"Yes. Of course. That's the law—you have to document money amounts for nonprofit things like this. In France, anyway. We even gave our signatures with the amounts."

I stood. "Those sneaky sons of bitches." If what the old madame had said about Dreyfus hiding money for them was true, it was a safe bet that Pierre, aka Christophe, who'd admitted to being Dreyfus's partner, was using "fund-raising" to launder cash. This must have been Dreyfus's alternate role there, to draft politically eager kids, kids without a future, without much to lose, into the so-called fund-raising business—and then to let Pierre guide them farther down the rabbit hole. That must have been what Thierry had figured out. I was ready to bank on it.

What still didn't fit, what still made no sense, was the plot to kill Brule. Had he been a threat to Christophe's and Dreyfus's laundering? Maybe Brule had been onto something beyond the suspicions Françoise had planted by going to him earlier that year.

The few missing pieces, I decided, were still larger than the ones that had fallen into place—these assemblymen whose influence Pierre had procured for his little helpers, for one. There was also the matter of what the old madame had said about Dreyfus: if he was so useful in the money-laundering scheme, and if, as a federal agent wise to their secret-selling business, he held so much over their heads, why would they be eager to expose him? And why would they need my help?

"Tell me about these assemblymen," I said. "Were they men like Brule?"

"No, no, Jeffrey. Christophe wouldn't have had anything to do with politicians like Brule—he's too much of a liberal. His connections are progressives, liberals, the sort who support decentralization, yet do not support those crazy antiterrorism bills and anti-immigration legislation, like Brule's party does. But I only met one or two assemblymen, I can't even remember their names. There were others from his same party, Léo said. They hated men like Brule. Men like Brule pose a threat to our government, Jeffrey. Some believe that Brule's party has ties to the UK and the U.S., but who knows? Pass that cognac?"

I passed it over, but was thoroughly lost in thought. It was a stretch, I knew, but if Pierre and Dreyfus were in league with political parties who wanted Brule out of the picture, then I was looking straight down the barrel at a motive.

Not that it really mattered. All I really wanted to know was how I could either prove my innocence or flee the country, and the only mysteries that truly bothered me anymore were why I personally had to be the fall guy. And why Thierry had to die.

Solène took her cap off and ran her fingers through her short hair. The cut made her look a lot younger, almost too young to be nursing a liquor bottle.

I asked her about Amelia. She didn't recognize the name, but said there had been a few other girls working for Christophe. When he held the first meeting of the new year, Solène said, there weren't more than fifteen kids left, and Solène and Melanie were two of three girls. There was Léo, two or three loudmouthed boys from Corbières, a close-knit Arab threesome from Dubois, and an older girl who worked as Christophe's secretary—a short, round-faced young lady with big green eyes and a sly smile. Everyone knew she was Christophe's lover, though he rarely spoke of such things. At that meeting Christophe seemed to have shed all of his fun-loving self for a hyper, obsessive one.

"After that," Solène said, "a few others, including Léo, were invited to private meetings that I wasn't invited to. Christophe would call me every so often, but more and more he contacted me through Léo. Melanie and Léo would go to these private meetings and afterwards wouldn't say a word about what went on at them."

I couldn't hold back any longer. "You should have said something to your father about this motherfucker—this was exactly the sort of thing he was looking to find out—" But I stopped short and didn't push the issue. Couldn't. I knew what it was like to have a cop for a father, the rigid rules that accompany growing up, every morning and every night, for what seems like an eternity. To your friends you're the offspring of a lawman, a tough brand to live up to, and then over time you learn how to prove that the brand doesn't matter, that you're willing to go just as far as the next kid to be independent, to shake free of those constraints. You learn that like everyone else you have the capacity to be bad.

"Remember, these were my friends," Solène was saying. "When things got scary with Christophe, I felt like I had to keep an eye out for them. Like it was my job to act if something went wrong."

There was also the matter of Melanie, she said. When Solène

found out that she'd been sleeping with Christophe, and that he'd slapped her around once or twice, Solène knew there was no way she could break ties with his group until Melanie was safe. Then in late February two things happened at once: Melanie confessed to Solène that something shady was going to happen at Corbières—something that had her badly shaken up—and Christophe threw a blowout party in a warehouse in the Manufacture. There was a big university contingent at the party, but also lots of businessmen and other older characters in the mix. Solène hadn't wanted to go. Melanie dragged her along anyway.

They weren't at the party an hour when Melanie disappeared. Solène got worried and explored several passageways and rooms around the warehouse, thoroughly spooked. Then she accidentally walked in on Christophe and Melanie in an office space just beyond the bathrooms. Melanie was crying. There were stacks of euros spilling out of a giant suitcase, and Melanie seemed to be protesting against something Christophe had asked of her. "I won't," she was saying. "Have somebody else do it." When Christophe turned and saw Solène in the doorway, he barked at her to go find Léo. Solène told Christophe to go find Léo himself, and a second later she was standing face-to-face with Christophe's green-eyed secretary, who threatened her, yelling at her to remember whom she was talking to. Solène stumbled back up the hallway to the party. She didn't see Léo or Melanie again that night.

But that wasn't what scared her shitless. What she couldn't get over were the pistols she'd seen lying on the desk—and the stacks of spanking-new French passports sitting right next to them.

Guns and passports—as if laundering dirty money weren't enough. And of course the green-eyed secretary was Amelia.

It wasn't tough to put together the rest. After I'd been singled out as the scapegoat, Amelia had entered, perhaps to keep an eye on me, perhaps to make sure I didn't go anywhere or do anything that didn't jibe with the plan. I thought back to that day in December when we'd met. She hadn't been the needy one—she'd played on my needs. It had been a frame months in the making.

"I talked to Melanie on the phone the day after the party," Solène said then. "She swore that everything was fine. She said I'd misunderstood what was happening, that I'd just walked into the room at a bad moment. After that, for the last few weeks, I've been invited to meetings and given tasks, but Christophe has kept me at a distance—he *hates* me now.

"I missed the meeting last week on purpose. That's probably why he wants to find me. He probably thinks I'll go to the cops. It's this stuff with Brule, Jeffrey—he must have killed Brule for his friends, the assemblymen he knows. I know Brule wasn't very popular with those people. And Christophe hated Brule. They killed him and they think they can pin the murder on you."

Hearing her say it was like hearing that jail cell slam shut behind me all over again. Dreyfus had put me in touch with Nabec in order to bolster the image of me as an American fraud—the kind of guy who might even be willing to do a contract murder for some outlaw Algerians.

Of course, I had no proof. But I knew Solène had nailed part of Dreyfus's motive: the hit was most likely political, for their assemblymen friends on high, planned as far back as December. All they'd needed was a suitable scapegoat. They'd found out a bit of my past, my not-so-stainless record back home, my father's work with certain agencies, my fudging on the job application with the French Ministry of Ed. All minor, circumstantial stuff. But enough, perhaps, for a French court of law. Tying me to Nabec and terrorist suspicions only sealed the deal.

But why, then, had Nabec proceeded with me the way he had? Why the unnecessary conversations and offers, why the pains to persuade and tempt me with money and slippery rationales? Why all this talk of trust and loyalty, the intense moments of identification with each other—why relate to me on the basis of our shared inability to belong anywhere in the world? If Nabec and Dreyfus had only wanted to have me photographed getting out of Nabec's fancy car, and then to have me arrested out at Nabec's suspicious hideaway, everything else seemed too time-consuming, too malicious—even for a cold, black-hearted son of a bitch like Nabec.

Even as the pain throbbed across my body, I could envision with striking clarity the genuineness of Nabec's gaze. There had been something else going on. It had been more than just a game.

I was watching the lantern light play against the ceiling, leaping and fluttering like something mad. The truth only half mattered, I realized. Nothing it could do could contain my thirst for payback. Sure, my suffering paled next to Solène's—I hadn't paid half what she'd paid. And sure, part of me was drawing closer to her, finding ground for the first time in that larger realm of compassion and empathy. But I was still torn between running and vengeance. Some control mechanism inside had broken loose, and now not even the truth could keep me from losing it. I only hoped Solène could.

WE WOUND UP sorting through the boxes of paperbacks. Most of the books wouldn't open without their brittle jackets cracking. We figured it didn't matter; clearly Bruno only cared for their presence. There were mysteries, romances, adventure stories, and spy novels. English and American authors were mixed in with French: Melville, Gide, Verne, le Carré. But we gravitated toward the few travel books in the mix, particularly those with maps in them. We talked about places we could run off to—Solène was ready to go anywhere—and I started worrying about crossing borders without a passport, without any cash, and finding a place where the French couldn't easily extradite. She pointed to San Sebastian in northern Spain. Her mother had fallen in love with Basque country, she said. It was a tough place to fit in, an even tougher place to be found.

"If we need to hide," she said, "it should be there, in San

Sebastian. At first, anyway. Mom believed the Basque came from another time. Their language too. There's nothing comparable."

In the shifting lantern light, the contours of Solène's youthful face glowed like an angel's.

I said, "We'll go together, or not at all."

She kissed me, and I let her. Afterward I held her close.

"This place feels haunted," she said.

She was right, though I said nothing. Soon she was dozing in my arms.

For a long time I sat and listened to the call and response of music and voices below us, thinking of all the hours I'd burned downstairs, absorbed in the pursuit of another language. With all this death and corruption around us now, I couldn't see what any of it was worth.

When the music grew quiet below us, I remembered what Bruno had said about the cops, and grew stiff. Solène jolted awake. On her watch it said a quarter after one—closing time.

We cut the light and sat there in the quiet darkness, unsure where we would be in an hour, or in an hour after that. It was enormously liberating. With each moment I felt my pain and outrage turn into grit.

Soon there were noises on the stairs. We got to our feet and moved to the corner behind the door. But whoever had come up was hesitating.

I put my ear to the door.

"Hey, Jeffrey," whispered a voice from the other side.

I waited a long time before answering. "Who is it?"

"Open the goddamn door, Jeff."

I knew the voice, but it wasn't Bruno's. I squeezed Solène's hand, pulled back the bolt, and turned the knob. Before me stood my sketchy impersonator.

"Get out of my suit," said Julien. "I'm sick of wearing your pants."

FAR MORE PERMANENT
THAN PRISON

Back in my old clothes, I felt nothing like my former self. Julien was all bent out of shape about his suit, which had dried, but was discolored with dirt and sweat and blood.

"What the hell did you do? Have a picnic in a goddamn mine shaft?"

I showed him the swollen cuts on my face, the deep bruise on my neck, and the lacerations on my shoulders. I showed him where I'd gotten shot running out of my own apartment.

"You should see what they did to my feet," I said.

"You could at least have asked them to take off the jacket first."

Downstairs it reeked of spilled beer and something mysteriously sour. Solène and I took seats at a sticky table in the back room while Julien and Bruno went up to the bar and argued in whispers. Finally Bruno tossed his keys on the bar and came over. He looked me in the eyes and tipped his faded fisherman's cap.

"Stay out of jail, my man," he said. "You owe me that, at least."

"Stay in business," I said, grinning back at him. "You owe us all that."

Julien locked the front door after Bruno, went behind the bar, and grabbed three glasses and a bottle of scotch.

"Bruno owes *me* more than anybody else," he said. "And more than he's willing to let on."

Julien had the usual wild look in his eyes, though now it made things seem more uneasy than ever.

"So do I," I said, trying to keep from sounding doubtful. Still I had to sound cautious. "Why are you risking your ass like this, Julien?"

He checked his watch. "It wasn't much of a risk. If the cops had jumped me in Tours and then checked my ID, they would've known they had the wrong guy, Jeff. I was meaning to get out of town for a bit anyway. They haven't been giving me much time off at the paper."

I looked hard at him, but it wasn't the time to settle up with his lie—not yet. I had to calculate what he was up to, and if he was still my best shot at getting out of town.

"You find out anything more from the people you work with at the *Journal*?"

His eyes shot to mine and away. "Nope. No more than you'd hear on the TV anyway." He checked his watch again. "We've got to leave here for the train station in literally five minutes."

I took a big drink of scotch, which went down like tap water. Solène set fire to two cigarettes and handed one to me. I couldn't think what angle to take. It was irritating me.

"Yesterday you said trains were a bad idea, man."

Julien's eyes fastened onto mine. "I'm not going to get you caught, partner. The decoy I made in Tours turned things around. I was at the Ste-Térèse station an hour ago, and there's only one cop out front, plus the station security idiots. One cop—they think you've left town and gone east."

"You said yesterday they'd—"

"I'm saying now that it was too risky before, but it's not anymore. You can take a direct to a big station, say, Bordeaux, buy connection tickets at a machine, and be on another train in ten minutes. It's the best thing you've got going. That's God's honest truth, Jeff. I'm not gonna get you caught by the fucking cops."

"You said they'd check passports on trains leaving the city, man, and I don't have one."

"I was just talking precautions, buddy—precautions were different yesterday. They won't do that on a domestic train, a train that terminates in France. This way you could transfer in Bordeaux to a local train, get off near the border, and hitch over— that's what I'd do." He stopped and checked my eyes. "Worry about a passport later. They find out you didn't do this shit, then you get a passport at your embassy in Spain. Right now you just have to get out of town by train. The last train leaves for Bordeaux at two, and it's almost one-forty."

There was something veiled in the way he was talking. It made me hot all over, and I started thinking about how I'd go about knocking him out if he tried to put one over on us. But what motive would he have for that? I wondered if there was some kind of reward on my head. I wondered if they even did that in this part of the world.

Julien shot a glance at Solène. "Would you give us a minute?"

He waited until she closed the door to the bathroom. "Get over the border as fast as you can." He looked at the bathroom door and lowered his voice. "And don't fart around in Bordeaux—that will be the best time for you to dump *her*, by the way. Take a local to Biarritz and from there thumb over."

He stood, looked down at the shirt I'd soiled for him, and cursed.

"Buy tickets from the machines in the station lobby. That way, when the conductor comes by to check tickets, he won't look too closely at you, and won't ask for a passport." He did a lap around the foosball table, then looked hard at me again. "I'm serious—lose her, buddy. I'm talking sincere, sound advice. I mean, I hate to sound paranoid. But if I was in your shoes, I wouldn't trust anybody."

Look who's talking, I thought. Then I had an idea: "Why Spain, then? You've been there?"

He took his eyes from mine. "Sure, lots of times."

"Pleasure?"

"Nah, business stuff, with the paper, you know."

It wasn't just his tone that said he was lying. And it wasn't just the new lie—which I could put together from what Marine had said the other night about his Spanish excursion—that told me he was putting on an act. He was trying too hard to persuade me to do things his way.

I was sure now that Julien was more involved than he was pretending to be. More involved in everything. I couldn't say how, I just knew it. He wouldn't deliver me to the cops—he'd had all night to do that. There was some other strange motive there. But though I saw now that I couldn't trust him, I realized that I also couldn't afford not to; the risks on all other sides outweighed this one.

"Tell me why I should trust you," I said. "Why are you all of a sudden my best friend?"

He gave me a genuinely hurt look. "You really expect me to answer that, Jeff?"

"No," I said, crushing out my cigarette. "Forget it. But she's with me. And anyway I've got a hunch she's going to end up being a big help."

He poured us another scotch while standing. "I'm not going to argue with you, partner."

When Solène came back, Julien eyed her suspiciously, then checked his watch.

"Okay, it's go time. It'll cost you fifty or so apiece to get to

Bordeaux, another twenty or so to get to Biarritz . . . This is when you tell me that you have a little cash."

I shook my head. "Punks took my money. I had a thousand fucking euros in my bag—"

Before I could finish, Solène tossed a roll of euros on the table.

"That's two grand," she said. "I've got more in my savings account."

I gave Julien my best poker face. "I won't say I told you so."

OUTSIDE IT WAS raining so hard that the streets looked covered with motor oil. From where we were, it would be less than ten minutes across *centre ville* to the train station. Solène and I strapped ourselves into the backseat of Julien's banged-up Civic, and Julien revved the engine so loud that I thought fire might burst from under the dash.

"Idle's a bit low," he said.

He slammed it in gear and we peeled into the street. All the way down to Rue Celeste he held the speed limit, but then he blew the first stop sign doing a sideways skid, mumbling praise to himself before pulling a last-second gangster turn at the next right toward Place Médiathèque.

Solène's expression didn't show much faith. I knew of nothing to convince her otherwise, just as I knew of no way to say, *Don't worry, I'll take care of him,* that he wouldn't hear, or spy in his rearview mirror.

At the red light of Boulevard du Gare, we stopped. Left would take us to the train station, right would go to the highway. Julien checked his left-side mirror. The light went green, and stomping the gas he jerked the wheel right.

My thoughts scattered. Solène's hand clenched my knee. I'd had enough.

"Okay, Julien," I said. "Tell us what's on your mind—where are we really going?"

Julien got in the left lane, then floored it and started mumbling to himself.

"To the station," he said finally. "Really. Someone's following us."

I looked back and saw a single pair of headlights in the rain. We raced for almost a mile and took the first entrance ramp, direction St-Nazaire—west.

I could feel the nerves tightening in my arms and hands, but my fingers remained steady. Who was it? Pierre? Nabec? Dreyfus? Wouldn't the police just throw on some lights and a siren?

"Come on, Julien. You said something about a time crunch."

Julien brought the Civic up to 130 km per hour, then took his foot off the gas. While we coasted, I glanced out the back window: same pair of lights, same distance behind us.

Julien suddenly gripped the wheel tight. I grabbed Solène's hand and squeezed just as Julien stomped the brakes and yanked the wheel to the left. Then we were skidding sideways, cutting through an emergency turnaround.

Three-quarters of the way through the turn, Julien stomped the gas again, and we fishtailed, peeling off in the direction we'd come, back toward Ste-Térèse proper.

I shot another glance back and watched the other car slow but continue east. A moment later, Julien's grin consumed the entire rearview mirror.

"*Pas pour les amateurs,*" he announced. "*T'as vu? Pas de tout pour les amateurs!*"

After we'd exited the highway, Julien said something in German. Solène's eyes grew wide with fear. I mouthed the words *It's okay* to her in English, though I knew I couldn't be sure of anything anymore.

In four short jig-jogs we were pulling into a walled-in parking lot. I felt every muscle in my body sigh with relief. It was the backside of the train station.

Julien pointed across the lot at a ramp that ran inside. "Back entrance."

Solène threw open her door, but hesitated.

"What's really going on here, man?"

"A two-a.m. to Bordeaux," he said. "Just like I said. Go under and follow the signs to where it says 'Ticketing.' Buy tickets from the machine. There probably won't be anyone at the ticket booths this late anyway. Go direct to Bordeaux, at Bordeaux go local to Biarritz. Have a good story ready about where you're going and why. Now get out of here before I get in trouble."

Solène had already climbed out. I opened my door and suffered a twinge of disorientation. I felt torn between reckoning with Julien and just letting him be. My instincts told me that none of that mattered anymore.

I started to get out, but Julien reached back and grabbed my knee. "Just wait a second." He reached into his jacket.

"What the hell's your problem?" I said.

Julien slid a small revolver out of his pocket and tried to hand it to me.

"*Hell* no," I said. "I've got enough jail time coming as it is."

Julien smiled. "Come on, think. Cops aren't the only ones after you. Whoever cooked this up might have bigger plans—plans far more permanent than prison, Jeff."

I glanced out the windshield at Solène. She pointed at her watch. My thoughts were whipping past in no readable order beyond *why is this happening?*

I gestured to Solène to wait, and gazed down at the gun. Tempted now to take it in my hands. If only to feel its cold weight.

"How would I get over the border with it?"

"You'll stick it in your pants like a can of beer, how else? You'll be hitching anyway, or whatever. It's not like they'll run you through any fucking metal detector at the Franco-Spanish border. Just don't show it to that girl. Now take it—it's untraceable, and you can just toss it when you're sure you don't need it."

I didn't need it now, but I took it and gripped the handle anyway. It was warm, much heavier than I would have thought. It lay in my palm like a toy gone bad.

Julien took it back and released the cylinder. I noticed that he was wearing driving gloves, which seemed just like him. But I didn't know this guy, I realized—I had never known him.

"Thirty-eight Special," he said. "Five shots. A little too much recoil for my taste. Look."

He loaded a cartridge into one of the chambers, closed the cylinder, and aimed the gun at the floor between us.

That was when it clicked. That was when my mind finally made the leap.

If both Dreyfus and the cops wanted me arrested, someone at odds with both parties was giving me an escape route. And the only other party I knew of in this mess was Nabec and his partner, the old madame. All my evidence suddenly pointed in that direction—what the madame had said about not going to school, how Julien had mysteriously intercepted me the morning before at Corbières, and the way he had found out what so few could know.

He had to be working for Nabec. But why? What did Nabec and the old madame care if I escaped Dreyfus's hands? How did my escape serve their purposes?

Julien and I were looking down the barrel of the gun.

"Keep it like this," he said, lining the cartridge up two chambers to the right of the breech. "That way your first shot won't fire—like a safety. But believe me, the second one will."

Even if I was wrong, I realized, I was in better shape with the gun than without.

"I'm not even going to touch the trigger," I said, shoving it into my coat pocket with the other three bullets. A wonderful sense of control washed over me.

"Hold it tight when you pull the trigger," he said.

"Good-bye, Julien." I got out.

"Angle the barrel down a hair," he called after me. "Squeeze with the finger, not with the hand."

"I'm not stupid, you know."

He reached out the door to shake my hand. I didn't take it, but instead I gave in to the urge that had been gnawing at me all night.

"I'm onto you, Julien."

I leveled my eyes on him. His expression went blank.

"What are you talking about?"

"I went to the *Journal*. They've never heard of you. I don't know what you're up to, but—"

"You must have gone to the wrong place, Jeff. I work at a different—"

I shut the passenger door in his face before he could finish. Solène and I ran across the lot.

IT TOOK US a few tries to find a functioning ticket machine, and by that time my nerves were grinding hard. Maybe a dozen other passengers were lurking about, a few bums posted up by the glass front doors. But I couldn't bear to lay eyes on anyone, couldn't get the machine's buttons to do what they claimed to do.

Now I was about to lose my cool, so I surrendered the ticket-buying task to Solène. She hit Reset and scrolled down the battered screen to BORDEAUX. The fine print under the city said, CONNECTION ESPAGNE.

She hesitated, looking me in the eyes. "Is this where we're going, Jeffrey?"

I tried to nix Julien's corresponding advice from my mind, and checked the big clock beside the train schedule board: five minutes before two. No trains leaving for anywhere else until 3:00 a.m. I'd be damned if I'd hang around the station another hour, I decided. From Bordeaux we could take whatever route we wanted—and from there we could run for it on our own terms.

When I spotted a station security guard exiting the nearest platform and heading our way, I punched the button for Bordeaux, then pressed two.

We fed Solène's cash into the machine, and when the tickets ejected below, all my bodily pain seemed to dissipate.

We ran for the stairs, rushed down, and headed for the sign that read QUAI 3.

Once we made it to our platform, a flood of relief ran through me. We slowed, counting down the cars to ours.

Then came an exquisite wave of euphoria. I hadn't been more eager to leave a place since I'd left home.

We boarded a few cars down from our own. Even as it happened, I felt the moment brand itself on my memory, for life: a sensation so longed for that it was strange to realize. Finally it was happening. Finally I was free.

That was when I saw him.

Several cars down, across the platform: Nabec, standing with a suitcase in one hand and a briefcase in the other. He was staring straight at me.

For a horrible instant my mind refused to recognize it.

I only had a minute. But I'd settle for the minute-long version. Because here stood the man whose business was knowing the truth. And all I wanted was to ask him why he'd made it all so excruciating, only to set me free—that, and to tell him I'd figured out that Julien was his man.

On either side of him, passengers from his train filed past. Nabec brought one hand up in an awkward sort of salute. Then I heard a voice from the intercom of the train I was supposed to be boarding: *"Mesdames et messieurs, bienvenu, vous êtes . . ."*

I turned and looked back up at Solène. She was already in the train, watching me with a troubled expression. I handed her the tickets.

"We should board separately," I said. "Just in case. Meet me in the rear smoking car in ten minutes, okay? I'll make sure all's good."

"Okay," she said. "Ten minutes, rear smoking car." She disappeared into the train car.

I turned back to face Nabec. But he was nowhere in sight.

Instantly my face grew hot. I took a few steps toward where he'd been standing, then stopped. I knew I hadn't imagined him—he must have slipped down the stairs to the underpass. But what did it matter now?

I turned back to board my train. Before I could, two of Nabec's goons were on me.

One was faster than the other. His hands latched onto my left arm. I jerked away, twisting free, and swung the same elbow back, connecting with his jaw. The other one went for my neck. I ducked and came around with a hook that caught him square in the kidney. He grunted, but stepped back and landed a lightning-quick jab between my eyes.

My eyesight skittered, I felt a sharp pinch on my wrist, and my arm got yanked behind me.

I was on my knees when my vision cleared. They stood me up and pinned my elbows behind my back. All over my body the pain awoke. My hearing and vision instantly muddled. I heard a train whistle blow, but now we were rushing through the underpass, up a steep flight of stairs, down a shallow ramp—out the way Solène and I had come in.

• • •

OUTSIDE, THE RAIN had thinned. Across the parking lot near the rear entrance I could see a dark sedan. My whole body seemed to convulse. Nabec had never imagined letting me go. It was only another part of his sadistic game.

When we were almost to the sedan, I heard the two-o'clock trains pushing off. I didn't turn to watch. Instead I fixed my gaze on the car. It was not a Mercedes.

I looked at the man on my right. He had an overgrown flattop and a gray mustache. His cheek was red where I'd elbowed him.

"We still pals?" I said nervously. He looked away, which was big of him.

They opened the back door for me. I peered in at the rear seat, where there was a bulky shape sitting in the dark. Immediately his presence took hold of me. I was more afraid than any time I'd been brought to him before—more afraid than all those times put together.

I took a deep breath and climbed in. But before the door could close beside me, as soon as I saw the silhouette of a frizzy Afro, I went rigid from head to toe.

The man in the backseat was Claude Dreyfus.

ON WHOM A MURDER
MIGHT BEST HANG

Dreyfus said nothing until we'd pulled out of the lot.

"Don't act so shocked, Delanne. I did not arrive where I am today without knowing some things about the anticipation of one's enemy."

"Is that what you call killing Brule?" I asked in English. "Anticipation?"

Dreyfus chuckled and lit a cigarette. "Let us make this easier for us. We have a half-hour drive. I could have you placed in the trunk."

I held my tongue as we drove from the city, fighting to tear my mind away from Solène, to keep from looking over at the despicable man sitting beside me. Only when the city lights began to fade behind us did my outrage give way to courage.

"So where are we going, Roland?"

He looked perturbed, but managed an unconvincing smile. "I see you've done some detective work of your own. Not that it will do you much good where you are going."

"So it's off to jail, is it?"

Dreyfus hesitated. "We shall see about that. But, perhaps,

yes—perhaps we are going to the jailhouse with Jeffrey Delanne. One cannot be sure what the Arab will fancy. But then he will have to run his fancies by me, as usual."

This time I chuckled along with him, though my heart was full of malice. It gave me a twisted thrill to suspect more than he thought I did.

"That's been the agreement all along, hasn't it?" I asked. "At least since you found out about the Arab's little intelligence brokerage, right?"

Dreyfus took a drag off his cigarette, but wouldn't look at me. "Bravo, Delanne. You've uncovered another meaningless morsel of truth." But his voice betrayed him. His eyes seemed to be watching the reactions of the men in the front seat, who, I realized now, looked very little like Nabec's goons—they were feds.

"What's the matter?" I said in French. "Don't they know about your little agreement with Nabec, money laundering and all that?"

"Shut up," Dreyfus said flatly. "Or I'll take you to see Christophe again before delivering you to the gendarmes. They're looking for you all over, you know, Delanne. Did you really believe that your silly disguise would work?"

We pulled off the highway onto a smaller road, and entered the same woods I'd been dragged into so many times already. My heart grew heavy and my stomach went sour. It was inevitable, I realized, that I'd wind up out here again.

"And do not fool yourself," Dreyfus said after a minute. "My men know what they are taught to know. What they overhear from fools in one language or another does not affect their obedience. I could have them execute you right here on this highway, if I wished—that would be quite a favor to the Arab, would it not? My advice is that you hold your tongue when he arrives."

I tried my best to return his smug smile, but what he'd said about Nabec shook genuine fear into my bones. I remembered what the old madame had said about Nabec having no intention of killing me. But what was that promise worth? Then for a moment I focused on the image of Nabec standing on that platform, gazing back at me. It made little sense. If we were going to meet him, why hadn't he ridden with me himself? And why had they needed Julien to deliver me the way he had?

My hands trembled in my lap. I imagined Solène sitting in the smoking car on that train to Bordeaux, hands trembling too, hoping I hadn't betrayed her, wondering every half minute whether I would suddenly appear in the aisle—or if Christophe would, in my place.

We pulled to the side of the road and parked the Peugeot. I closed my eyes and told myself over and over that it didn't make sense for Dreyfus to kill me, if he wanted me to take the fall for his own crime. But my spooked nerves weren't buying it.

After a moment I could feel Dreyfus's eyes on me. "Scared, Delanne? Understandable. I happen to know that a business like the Arab's does not run smoothly with loose ends left to dangle. Of course, your testimony is by now essentially worthless, and anyway with men like him, testimonies are only a fraction of the legal battle—*finding* the Arab would be difficult enough for the courts, you see. But that does not mean he would be at ease with you in jail."

I decided I had nothing to lose anymore by calling Dreyfus out.

"That's why I was arrested that night," I said. "To make me a better scapegoat for murder."

Dreyfus couldn't help letting the side of his mouth curl into a smile. "Sure, Delanne."

"And the photos that Duvin got hold of—all taken care of by your men and furnished anonymously to the gendarmes."

"Sure, whatever you wish to think, Delanne. It hardly matters."

"But those men Nabec had me interrogate, they were killed afterward, which doesn't—"

"The Arab's business with those men was his own. And if they died, they deserved it."

He sighed and checked his watch. Then he began fiddling with his collar, as if he were worried it was crooked, or that his tie needed adjusting. I remembered what Françoise had said about Dreyfus's vanity.

"I must say," I said, "as much as it hurts to be screwed like this, I've got to hand it to you—Nabec and his partner seemed to me to be a pretty big catch."

Dreyfus faced me and raised one eyebrow. "You met his partner, did you?"

"Only briefly," I said. "She didn't strike me as someone who'd like being blackmailed, though—or as someone who'd trust a fed with her money."

Dreyfus seemed to be restraining himself, remaining poised for the arrival of Nabec.

"Let's just say that they've made good use of my services and leave it at that," he said. But it was as if he needed to express the full extent of his power—he just couldn't leave it at that. "Truth is, they've grown accustomed to our agreement. People like the Arab know well enough about the costs of running a business. They know that I am an asset to them."

His smugness was making me sick.

"And those kids you're using to launder their money with Christophe," I said. "You're an asset to them too, right?"

Dreyfus glared at me for a second before letting his expression turn phony again. "Yes, in fact. They are given futures, Delanne."

"And handguns, right?" I shot back, thinking about what Solène had seen at Christophe's warehouse party and about the story Françoise had told about finding photo-less passports in Dreyfus's jacket.

"And what about the fake passports, Roland? Who gets those? Harmless Arab friends of yours and Nabec's?"

Dreyfus looked at me wild-eyed.

"You're not going to succeed in ruffling me," he muttered between his teeth. "Because it doesn't matter what you've found out—no one shall ever believe you."

He reached up to loosen his tie with an unsteady hand. I thought, *What the hell.*

"The Arab scares you too, doesn't he, Roland? It's understandable—he is very intimidating, and you never know what 'fancy' will take him next."

Dreyfus huffed. *"T'es idiot."*

"Am I that stupid?" I asked, switching back to French along with him. "Tell me this: How much did those assemblymen pay you to bump off Georges Brules?"

Dreyfus grabbed me by the lapels of my coat. "Now I've had quite enough of your tongue."

"Come on, no one will believe me—why not enlighten me? You've already ruined my life—why not fill in the gaps? Was it about Brule's political party—about keeping a guy like Brule from getting into the national assembly and upsetting the balance everyone's so worried about?"

"Don't be a fool," Dreyfus said, letting go of me. "They'll never keep the balance from being upset." He glanced out the window. "Where the fuck is that goddamn Arab?"

But I wasn't going to drop it so easily. "It was personal, then? I'll bet that was it—it got personal and you wanted him dead. But that doesn't sound very Frenchman-like of you, Roland."

Now Dreyfus looked mad enough to blow. "What the hell do you know about what's French and what isn't, you shit?"

"Oh, come on," I said. I wasn't playing anymore, either. "Do you honestly think that just because people like me come over here and don't start talking and acting like you guys do, we don't see through your puffed-up bullshit? Brule stepped on somebody's toes back when he was working for the National Police in Paris, didn't he?"

"The man was a fucking Boy Scout," Dreyfus spat. "And they wouldn't have him in their assembly, simple as that—not if he didn't have a past, or something to hide, like they've all got." He paused, and a sour look appeared on his face. "You think the people who make the laws actually make one another *follow* the laws, De-lanne? You think a straight-shooter like Brule would have fit nicely with the rest of them? In Paris? This kind of shit happens all the time. Now stop being so naïve and shut the hell up."

I sat there in silence for a moment and felt my heartbeat grow louder in my ears. What I said next just spilled out of my mouth.

"All for a bunch of phony passports."

"You don't know when to stop, do you?" Dreyfus snapped.

But he wasn't done yet. He had a lot on his mind, and he was frustrated at having been made to wait for Nabec with the last guy in the world that he wanted to talk to. He turned on me again.

"Do you imagine for one second that these politicians, these cocksuckers in Paris, are the only ones in the world taking money from people who fancy themselves terrorists and need a country to live in? If this is what you think, if this is what you've been raised to think, then you're just as stupid as every other American I've ever met, Delanne—stupider."

It was getting harder and harder to hold myself down.

"Brule was a hard-liner on immigration," I said. "He would have fucked it all up."

"You and Duvin were perfect for each other, you know that?" he said. "He had his head up his ass too."

At the mention of Thierry, my blood reached the boiling point. It was bad enough that my life had been ruined because a crew of assemblymen didn't want an incorruptible addition to their Parliament. That Thierry had had to die was just too much.

Before I could make a move at him, a pair of headlights glowed in the glass behind us, and I was struck by an unexpected wave of nausea. I looked back. A black Mercedes sedan pulled past our Peugeot and parked in front of us.

Not a moment later, Nabec's long black Bentley pulled up and parked behind us, sealing our car in between itself and the Mercedes. Dreyfus gave orders to his men in the front seat. They got out. Through the windshield I saw Rafa step out of the Mercedes. I could hardly hear around the beating of my own heart.

"Nabec's assistant," I said.

Dreyfus forced a chuckle. "Oh, don't worry—the Arab himself is in one of those fine automobiles. The young man seems to be waving for us to step out."

Dreyfus opened his door, and as I climbed out of the Peugeot behind him, time slowed. It was sleeting now. Two of Nabec's shorn goons stood on guard beside the Bentley. Dreyfus's men stood on either side of Dreyfus and me in the road. Rafa stepped up. He nodded hello, and gestured gracefully back to the Bentley.

"Le Monsieur will join you shortly," he told Dreyfus in French.

Dreyfus took my arm and walked me over to the Bentley. The car was empty, not even a driver up front. When we shut ourselves in, the dim golden dome light above us stayed on. Dreyfus took the seat that faced me, his back to the front of the car.

I could hear the breath passing through me as if I were underwater. I could smell the residue of Nabec's cigar smoke. It made me think of what he'd said about private loyalties. Why, after all that, had he betrayed me to some spineless, crooked fed?

I knew the answer: business. As Dreyfus had said, it wasn't personal. He just happened to have Nabec's business by the balls.

Dreyfus checked his watch and gave me another smug smile. "Hurts, does it not?"

As he laughed, my restraint began to waver.

"Sure, sure," I said. "You win, LeMercier. Your plan unfolded beautifully, and you can't blame me for being mad, so come on—why me? Out of all the criminals you no doubt come into contact with—why me?"

Dreyfus looked at me incredulously, then grinned, reaching up and pinching his throat, a gesture I remembered from the very first, when he'd approached me with his offer.

"All we had to do was sit down and decide on whom a murder might best hang," said Dreyfus. "And you happened to be right there. Of course, all we had to do after that was investigate your past—but surely you see how it all worked."

When he laughed this time, I imagined myself choking the life out of him, right there in Nabec's Bentley.

"And you made it easy, Delanne," he added. "You walked right into it. But to be honest, you had a hunger in your eyes. Something I saw the first time I met you at Corbières. You practically announced yourself as a worthy candidate."

He checked his watch again. Then he put his hands to the window, trying to see out through the tinted glass.

"But how the hell—"

"Enough of these pointless questions, Delanne. I'm finished explaining to you things you shall never understand."

But though his words sounded smooth, his voice still betrayed him. I'd noticed that his right knee had started bobbing ever so slightly. He hadn't planned on waiting this long. There was sweat on his forehead and on his fat, poorly shaven jowls, the vaguest trace of uncertainty in his eyes. I reached into my coat pocket for a cigarette. Dreyfus didn't budge, but kept trying to see what was happening outside.

I fired up and realized that my heart would beat out of control if I didn't do something. And now. My ringing ears were killing me, and I didn't care who joined us now—Nabec or Satan himself.

But Dreyfus and I were still alone.

I checked the window beside me, but couldn't see very well through the tinted glass. I felt some courage muster inside and then faced him again, gazing not at his eyes but at his throat.

At once my vision steadied, and the ringing in my ears stopped. Finally I could see past my own rage to Nabec's plot. Finally I understood why we'd been left alone for so long—how carefully I'd been maneuvered to this place. In this car. With this man. Gun in my coat.

I reached into my pocket with one hand and with the other held my cigarette in the air between us. When Dreyfus opened his mouth to speak again, I flicked the glowing butt straight at his face.

It didn't land in his open mouth like I'd hoped—it hit him smack on the forehead, then fell in his lap and rolled down between his legs. He jerked back in his seat, swatting at the thing as it smoldered under his crotch.

By then I had Julien's revolver trained between his eyes. He looked up and froze.

"Now just what do you think you're doing?" he asked, still digging halfheartedly for the cigarette between his legs.

I aimed the gun at his throat and squeezed the trigger. The hammer clicked: dry fire—the same way it had been loaded. Dreyfus flinched like someone who'd just received a hundred volts.

I grinned and kept the barrel aimed at his throat. Then I remembered something Julien had said: *Aim for the throat.* I recognized it now: the old madame had said the same thing out at her cottage. This must have been their ultimate plan for me—to dispose of Dreyfus. Literally. To play the assassin and rid their world of his parasitic presence.

He got the cigarette butt out from under himself onto the floor and stomped it out.

"It's not even loaded," he said. His voice was almost a whisper. "Now give it over, Delanne. The joke is up."

I said, "Next one's the real thing, Roland."

His little eyes twisted up in his face. "Now look—you can't kill a cop."

"You did. You killed Duvin."

"That's different, Delanne. I'm a cop. And not just any cop. You can't kill a cop like me."

But I wasn't thinking about their world anymore—I was thinking about my own. Because I was finished being a pawn in someone else's game. I could choose for myself.

In that instant I realized that I didn't need to let Dreyfus live to determine my own role. I could kill him for Brule, for Thierry, for Solène, for every other life he might ruin to serve his own greedy ends—I could murder the son of a bitch for myself.

And I didn't care anymore if that made me an outlaw. After all I'd been through, those hang-ups were long gone.

Slowly Dreyfus reached for the revolver. "Hand it over slowly," he said. "Carefully."

When I squeezed the trigger again, my ears went deaf.

Dreyfus blinked, once and hard. At first he looked more startled than shot. Then a thick stream of blood erupted just below his chin. As he raised a hand to meet it, a constipated expression appeared on his face. He fell sideways on the leather bench.

After that I was out of the Bentley, pointing the gun at Nabec's two goons and Rafa, pointing the gun back and forth between Dreyfus's men. I moved away from them into the middle of the road, screaming at them all not to move.

It was snowing now, in tiny flecks—the first I'd seen in France. Every man but me had his hands up. It took a long, howling instant or two for me to realize what they were making obvious: they weren't trying to stop me. They didn't even seem remotely interested in that.

Rafa opened the driver's-side front door of the Mercedes and stepped away from it.

"*T'attends quoi, alors?*" he said. "*Vas-y!*"

He was gesturing into the driver's seat—telling me to move, to get the hell out.

I aimed the gun at Rafa's throat. He smiled. "*C'est la seule balle, Jeffrey.*"

One bullet. Somehow he knew it just as well as I did.

I took a step toward the open front door of the Mercedes. The car was empty, the engine running. Still I hesitated, until one of the goons stepped toward me, keeping his hands where I could see them. On his right hand, two fingers had been taped together.

"Drop the gun, Delanne," he said in English. "Drop it and take the goddamn car already."

At once, hearing his accent, I recognized the man, though I was too charged up to be stunned. It was the Texan, the second guy I'd interrogated—the man I'd beaten up for Nabec.

I looked down at the gun in my hand. I'd almost forgotten it was there. It fell and hit the concrete, flipped over, clicked.

I leaped behind the wheel of the Mercedes, then slammed the door shut and shoved the gearshift into drive.

I didn't bother to check the rearview until I'd put a dozen miles between me and them. Nor did I take my foot off the gas until my mind had snapped back into place.

Here's what it assured me: I was still alive.

THE GUY YOU MIGHT HAVE
WOUND UP BEING

After I'd driven pell-mell through those strange woods between Ste-Térèse and Lourange—after I'd put at least an hour between that fucked-up place and me—the adrenaline drained. I pulled down a forested dirt road, turned off the engine, and fell asleep with my head on the steering wheel.

In a dream I saw Solène riding on that train to Bordeaux. Alone. I saw her standing on a beach in front of the ocean, sunlight ripping through the clouds behind her. Alone. Then I dreamed that I was driving again, nodding off and snapping awake, yanking the car back onto the road. I kept taking my foot off the gas, stomping the brakes while that Mercedes charged forward. Until I couldn't manage the turns. Until I sailed inch by inch off the highway into darkness.

THEN SOMEONE WAS knocking on the car window. I jolted awake and found myself still sitting in the driver's seat of the Mercedes, clutching the wheel like a man headed over a cliff.

The sun had come out, but it was still freezing cold. There were evergreen trees all around, so many evergreens, all of them covered with the thinnest layer of snow. When I saw the man who'd done the knocking, a leather-faced old codger in a sweatshirt and jogging hat, I fumbled with the switches on the armrest until I figured out how to lower the window.

"What do you want?" I asked him in French.

"You can't sleep here, monsieur."

Our eyes locked. "I'm already gone."

I had the car in gear before the old man could say anything else.

It took me another hour to find the *autoroute* loop around Ste-Térèse. I pulled to the side of the entrance ramp and threw the car into park, realizing almost instantly that I was making the decision to act without weighing the risks. It wasn't that I didn't have a choice. I just didn't care for my options.

I took the loop to where the signs said DIRECTION BORDEAUX, and drove south through the morning in numb silence.

Later I would remember those hours as the most lonesome of my life. I can't say that I was driven by fear. My thoughts were fastened on Solène and that southbound train—she had been abandoned, yet again. And all I could do about it, besides hope, was drive fast.

IT WAS IN Biarritz, just before the Spanish border, that my frantic impulses faded away and pure paranoia kicked in. I arrived just after noon and the sun was blazing: clear, powder-blue sky, a dark and endless ocean in the distance. I realized that I was worn out and pulled into the parking lot of a run-down hotel—I needed to sleep just a bit, to be on my toes before crossing. But then part of me wanted to get it over with, to barrel across that border once and for all.

I don't know what made me finally notice the envelope sticking out from under my seat, but I tore it open in a daze.

Inside was a stack of weathered, small-numbered, nonsequential euros—five thousand in all. I counted through them, numb to the possibilities they held. There was also a French passport, whose photo wasn't mine but looked exactly like me, and a French driver's license, both bearing the name Benjamin Cove. No middle name. Birthplace: San Luis Obispo, California, where I'd never even set foot. I was a naturalized French citizen, the passport said. In the same name were a valid registration for the Mercedes and an insurance card. And a letter:

Partner,

Here's the big question: How do you kill an undercover cop who's become a giant pain in the ass? We're not talking about any undercover cop here, we're talking about a well-protected fed, a man doing dirty work for national assemblymen who help harbor terrorists—a man whose mouth might have done a lot of damage to a smooth-running business.

Here's the big answer: You get someone else to do it, and you let that someone else take the blame.

That's where you came in.

But first imagine you're me, and you get back from three months in Germany (yes, working as a translator, which you know a little about) and some newcomer, who happens to be an American, is frequenting your bar and moving in on your girl. Then imagine your employer—and I'm not talking about some newspaper here—tells you that her associates need somebody on the outside to perform a not-so-desirable task. Who you gonna recommend? A Frenchman? A Brit? A Spaniard? Yes, J, I pointed you out to the Arab and my boss (the lovely little lady with the gold rings), who had Dreyfus approach you at Corbières with what for him was a double-veiled proposition.

But the whole truth is that the Arab simply loved you. He's the one who wanted you to make it through this in one piece. Sure, he could only hope to lead you to a moment of confrontation with Dreyfus—and to groom you for it, using you first to interview a man who'd actually come to us to sell us the intelligence you retrieved (which resold for a moderate price), then testing you with one of our own guys. Rest assured, the first guy you interviewed was a real traitor to his people; the second was only there to see what you'd do, and whether you'd lie to us. So Dreyfus needed a man to pin a messy murder on, and the Arab needed a man to kill Dreyfus.

Worked out pretty well, really.

This is what he wants me to say: he saw it in you, man, saw it in you and knew that you could pull the trigger. And, yeah, when I met you in December, I chose you because I saw it in you myself.

Why did it have to be done? Well, I guess since you're reading this you've earned the right to know: Dreyfus might have turned us in at any point. So we decided to appease his assemblymen's wishes for Brule, and then to make the whole thing backfire on him—and in that order, so that we could implicate him in Brule's death and spoil whatever evidence he might have planned to bring against us. Who's going to believe the findings of a dead renegade undercover? You can put the rest together: why I kept you from the cops that morning, played decoy for you, gave you a gun, brought you to Dreyfus's men at the train station.

The meeting with Rafa, as you've probably put together already, was set up to lead the cops to you—we knew Rafa was being watched. I should tell you, too, that you'll still be implicated in Brule's death, along with Dreyfus. This way nobody will be surprised that you killed your partner in crime, the renegade cop. Pretty clever, huh? You've got to hand it to that Arab. He also wants me to say that the beating was Rafa's idea, and he approved it on principle—you lied to him—and on the condition that Rafa took it easy. But look, you've got a kick-ass car. And a fresh passport. It could be so much worse, partner. So just cross the border.

I'm awful at good-byes, just awful! How's this: Destroy this letter, but don't forget me. Think of it this way: I'm the guy you might have wound up being, so count yourself lucky. Good luck, and don't do anything I wouldn't do.

—J

After reading it over a few times, I sat back and felt my blood simmer. Even though I'd already deciphered that Julien had been playing a hand in Nabec's and the old madame's game, there was no reason to be proud: I'd still drawn cards from a rigged deck, and played them according to the dealer's design. In a way, though, it didn't matter. What the dealer couldn't see was that I'd played the last card for myself, and no one else.

And Julien was right. I'd been lucky. At least I was still breathing.

At least I was sitting here in a swanky car with a fresh set of papers and a ticket to ride, ready to quit one country for another. At least I had more on my mind than just running from my soggy past, which up till that point had been the story of my life.

And now I had a mission: I'd find Solène even if it killed me.

BEFORE PULLING BACK on the *autoroute* south from Biarritz, I took out my new passport and memorized the information on it—birth date, issue date, passport number, and date of expiration. I found it strangely fitting that these meaningless numbers, and not anything I'd said or done, would in the end serve as my salvation.

As I drove south my thoughts returned to Solène, and how I'd go about finding her. Soon I saw a highway sign that read ESPAGNE 1 KM—though of course the place was only a means to an end.

I made for the border and nobody stopped me. It was much easier than you'd think, in a sleek Mercedes sedan.

There was very little mystery swimming around in my head after that. I could see far enough down the highway.

ACKNOWLEDGMENTS

Thanks to so many, but especially to Matthew Flaming, Lindsay McClelland, and E. A. Durden for the invaluable direction and fuel. Thanks also to Brian Morton, Melissa Hammerle, and the New York Times Foundation for the funding and support; to my benevolent friends in New Orleans, Asheville, and New York, who offered their spare bedrooms, kitchen tables, basements, and fire escapes to the completion of this novel: James Armstrong, Melissa Ritchie, Emily Sims, Uriah Cain, Katie Hill, and Dan Warren; to Chris Parris-Lamb, at The Gernert Company, for his sharp eye and outstanding vision; and to Julian Pavia, at Crown, for his superb guidance and know-how. Thanks to Floyd, of course, for his legacy of stories and to Pamela for her insistence on the pen. But most of all, thanks to my wife, Ellen, for her enormous faith, patience, and inspiration.